TOO BIG TO DIE

This Large Print Book carries the
Seal of Approval of N.A.V.H.

AN ODELIA GREY MYSTERY

TOO BIG TO DIE

SUE ANN JAFFARIAN

THORNDIKE PRESS
A part of Gale, a Cengage Company

Farmington Hills, Mich • San Francisco • New York • Waterville, Maine
Meriden, Conn • Mason, Ohio • Chicago

Copyright © 2017 by Sue Ann Jaffarian.
Thorndike Press, a part of Gale, a Cengage Company.

LIBRARY OF CONGRESS CIP DATA ON FILE.
CATALOGUING IN PUBLICATION FOR THIS BOOK
IS AVAILABLE FROM THE LIBRARY OF CONGRESS

ISBN-13: 978-1-4328-4618-3 (hardcover)

Published in 2018 by arrangement with Midnight Ink, an imprint of Llewellyn Publications Woodbury, MN 55125-2989 USA

Printed in the United States of America
1 2 3 4 5 6 7 22 21 20 19 18

To Midnight Ink, the publisher who saw something worthwhile in both Odelia and me and packaged us up and presented us to the world. Thank you.

ONE

He'd won the duck in a poker game. That's what my husband had claimed two nights ago as he proudly presented me with the yellow fuzzball.

"Greg Stevens," I'd told him sternly as I watched our dog and cat eye the newcomer with interest, "what in the world are we going to do with this little guy?"

"Keep him as a pet. What else?" He rolled his wheelchair over to me and held out the creature. "He even comes with some food."

The duckling was so tiny and sweet, I couldn't help but take it. I brought the little animal up to my face and rubbed its softness against my cheek while it emitted tiny squeaky quacks. Its downy coat was like velvet against my skin. I giggled when its small beak nibbled the end of my nose.

"Cute ducklings grow into large, annoying, and noisy ducks," I reminded him as I continued cuddling the small bundle that fit

7

into the palm of my hand like a fragile egg. "Best served with orange sauce."

As if afraid I'd cook the little bugger up right that minute, Greg snatched him out of my hand and cuddled him against his chest. "Don't listen to the mean lady," he cooed to the duckling. "She'll do no such thing."

"Maybe not," I told him, laughing, "but Muffin is eyeing that duck like it's prey. Our cat may be small, but she's still a cat, and cats hunt. Remember what she did to that lizard last week? Until that little guy is bigger, it's going to be duck-hunting season around here."

Greg looked from the duckling down at our cat. Muffin was on the small side and a loving, cuddly animal with a soft purr and large, curious eyes, but she was also a bruiser when it came to doing feline things like hunting and protecting her territory. Even Wainwright, our eighty-pound golden retriever, knew better than to mess with her when she was in jungle cat mode.

Greg cut his eyes to me. They were sad with the realization that I was right. "So what do you suggest we do?" he asked. "Cage Dumpster until he's big enough to go a few rounds in the ring with Muffin?"

"Dumpster?"

"That's what I named him," Greg explained. "Matt said he found him near a Dumpster a few days ago in a box. No idea where he came from. He brought him to the poker game for show and tell."

"And somehow little Dumpster ended up as part of the pot?" I asked with suspicion. "Matt must not have been having a good night."

Greg laughed. "Actually, he had a very good night. But his wife told him to take the duck to the game and find him a home. He wasn't to bring him back." Greg looked a little sheepish. I knew that look. It was the look he got whenever I proved him wrong on something. "Dumpster can be a bit noisy," he finally admitted.

"Yeah," I said, eyeing Greg. "I can tell. He hasn't shut up since he got here. As he gets older, those cute little chirps are going to become louder, more insistent quacks."

I took a seat and watched Greg cuddle the little bundle of yellow fluff. It pulled at my heart. If we didn't nip this in the bud right now, we'd both be convinced that Dumpster should become a part of our family. Greg and I both love animals, but cats and dogs were different than ducks. We live near the beach in an urban area with homes crammed together. As Dumpster got bigger and noisier, our neighbors might not be too happy about living next to Old MacDonald's farm.

"I think we should shut this little guy up in the guest bathroom for now," I said, sad myself. "Maybe in the tub with some food and a big pan of water. It will give him some good room to move around and still confine him, at least until we can find a home for him. We can move Muffin's litter box out of there for a few days."

"Of course you're right, sweetheart," Greg said with a deep sigh. "I'll make some calls. I know a guy who lives on a nice piece of property near San Diego. He's a client and he has a few kids. Maybe I can talk him into taking Dumpster. If not, there's a guy on one of the basketball teams that lives in Hemet. He might take him. I think he has lots of animals." He paused, then said, "How about your mother? She loves animals." His voice was full of hope, and I could tell he really wanted to keep Dumpster in the family. My mother lives in a retirement community not far from us. "Her place allows one pet under twenty pounds. Dumpster shouldn't get that large."

"Ha!" I said with amusement, thinking about my septuagenarian mother with a duck. I'm sure she'd like the idea just to be different. Knowing her, she'd probably even manage to leash-train it. "I think that pet policy only refers to things like cats and dogs, and fish, providing they stay in their tank. Remember last year when one of her neighbors brought in a big snake and it got loose? The whole place was in a tizzy. I'm surprised none of those old folks keeled over from fright." I laughed. "Seaside barely allows *us* on their property, Greg, and even then we can't bring Wainwright." I paused. "What about your parents?"

Greg fixed me with a one-eyed stare. It was his *get real* look. Greg's parents, Ron and Renee, are lovely people but fairly proper. Renee Stevens runs a tight ship at her house. They were the opposite of my quirky nonconformist mother, even though they all got along surprisingly well and had become friends over the years. "Seriously, can you see my parents with a duck?" he asked.

"Only on a plate in a fine French restaurant," I said with my own laugh. "Not to mention they travel a lot." I gave it more thought. "How about one of those sanctuary farms?" I suggested. "I know there's at least one here in Southern California."

"Don't they mostly take in abused animals and animals from factory farms?" Greg asked.

"I believe so," I said. "But we could give them a call. I hardly think they'd turn down such a cutie as this." I smiled at Dumpster, who answered with a tiny quack to prove my point. "Especially if Dumpster came with a nice donation."

The next morning I called the sanctuary farm while Greg called his client and the basketball guy in Hemet. Both the farm and the fellow in Hemet said yes. We decided to go with Tip Willis, the guy from Hemet who played on one of the other wheelchair basketball teams, because he said his kids had been wanting a couple of ducks. The only hitch was that they were going out of town for a big family reunion and couldn't take Dumpster for about a week or so. He asked if we could hang on to the little guy until then.

Winner. Winner. Duckling Dinner.

My only concern was that we'd get too attached to Dumpster to let him go when the time came. But we'd cross that emotional pond when we got to it.

Two

June in California, especially for those of us who live near the ocean, can be on the cool side. It's something people living in other parts of the country don't quite understand. They think California is sunny and in the low 80s all year long; not true. We can get quite chilly in winter — not Arctic cold like some places, but definitely cold enough for jackets. In late May and June a marine layer comes in, blanketing most of the coastline in SoCal and keeping high temperatures at bay. It can even be gloomy and damp. This annual weather event is called "June gloom" and sometimes extends into early July. This year the gloom broke shortly after the Fourth of July. It had managed to dull the viewing of coastal firework displays, but it kept us cool during a barbecue at our home with friends. Now, just a few days later, temps were soaring like a rocket to the moon and weather reports were saying the heat wave could last for at least five days, maybe a whole week.

Greg and I were running errands the Saturday after the Fourth. We started early, with breakfast at a favorite place almost next to where Greg gets the van serviced in Long Beach, the next city over from Seal Beach, where we live. We left the van in their capable hands and walked/rolled over to grab some eggs. From there it was to a home-repair place for some hardware stuff for a few small repairs around the house. After that we were off to get food for our animals and a bit of wood shavings to make Dumpster more comfortable in the tub. Following the pet store, Greg and I would finish our rounds at the grocery store, then it would be home to unpack everything and cool off. The rest of the weekend we planned to stay home, cool and comfy.

Dumpster had been with us a few days and was quickly devouring the food Matt had passed along to Greg. I'd gone online to see what to feed the little quacker and had learned a lot of interesting things, but I also learned that most urban pet stores didn't carry what we needed. They carried a lot of pet food that *contained* duck, but nothing *for* ducks. I ended up ordering Dumpster's food from a farm supply company with fast shipping. We wanted to get a good supply to give to Tip and his family, kind of like a duck dowry. I also supplemented his pellets with treats of grapes. One thing for sure, Dumpster was stealing our hearts. A couple of times we brought him out to the living room for supervised visits with the rest of the family. The little duckling was quite sociable with Wainwright, who nudged him around with his nose and licked the duckling's head. Dumpster wanted to make friends with Muffin, but that budding relationship was brought to a halt whenever Muffin decided to bat Dumpster around like a catnip toy.

Greg pulled the van into a handicapped spot in front of the grocery store. "Well, sweetheart, this is our last stop. I can almost taste the cold beer waiting for me at home."

"Waiting for *us*," I corrected. We were both sticky with sweat from popping in and out of the van on each errand. Each time we went from a cool van to an air-conditioned store, but the short distance between each was brutal. I could feel perspiration dripping down the curve of my back. It was days like this I wished we had a pool. Our best friends, Seth and Zee Washington, have a pool, but currently their back yard was being relandscaped. The Washingtons usually hosted the Fourth of July barbecue for both of our families and friends, but this year we'd had to move it to our place, which was more cramped but was a fun time anyway.

We climbed out of the van and were almost to the door of the grocery store when the sound of barking stopped us. We hadn't brought Wainwright with us. We never took Wainwright on errands when it was hot out because it meant he'd have to spend too much time in the van. It was dangerous to the animal, and in heat like this it didn't take long for a dog to get heat stroke. The same went for kids, but at least children could be taken inside the store with you. Except for the pet store, Wainwright would have had to sit in the van like a roast in an oven.

Greg stopped his wheelchair and looked around the parking lot, trying to pinpoint the location of the barking. It wasn't robust, more like a high-pitched long whimper. Then it would stop; a few seconds later it started up again. It sounded like a small dog. It didn't take Greg long to zero in on the source of the sound. With a mighty push on his wheels, he headed back across the asphalt separating the parking lot from the store and down the aisle where we'd parked, following the uneven plaintive cries. He finally honed in on a white Mercedes sedan parked just three stalls down from our van. Inside the car a Jack Russell terrier was alternating between panting and whining and was clearly in distress. A single window, the driver's window, was lowered only about an inch for ventilation, which in this heat wasn't helping much.

The parking stall on the driver's side was empty. Greg wheeled up and tried the doors on that side of the vehicle while I went to the other side of the car and did the same. All held fast. Shifting my sunglasses to the top of my head, I cupped my hands around my eyes and peered into the car, taking stock of the situation. "I don't see any water in there for him, Greg."

"Did you lock your dog inside, pal?" asked a burly Latino man with perspiration beading on his bald head and colorful tattoos running up and down his arms.

"It's not our car," I explained as I kept trying to get a door open. The man tried to help by giving solid yanks on all the doors himself, but none would budge — not even when he raised one foot against the side of the car and tried to leverage with his considerable strength and weight. He tried the trunk, also with no results.

"That's inhumane," a woman with two children said as she passed by.

"Sweetheart," Greg called to me as he started to roll toward our van, "call the police. Tell them what's going on."

"Police or fire station?" I asked. "I'll bet the fire department could rescue the little guy faster."

"Police," he clarified. "Report vehicle vandalism in progress."

I was on the phone explaining the problem to the emergency operator, still not sure where vandalism came into the picture, when Greg returned with the crowbar from our van laid across his legs. Now "vandalism" became as crystal clear as the cloudless blue sky above.

Greg was wearing a baseball cap against the bright sun. It was dark blue, with *Ocean Breeze Graphics* stitched across the front in white. Ocean Breeze Graphics was Greg's graphics and printing company. Along with his partner, Boomer, they owned three shops in three different states — the Denver shop was called Mountain Breeze and the Phoenix shop was Desert Breeze. The hats had been bought when Greg took on the sponsorship of a local Little League team the year before. Each of the shops had supported a team in their community with their own hats. As Greg approached, I took note that he'd turned the cap around, bill side pointing to the rear. He always did that when he was about to get serious about his actions, usually in sports.

"You want me to help, pal?" the burly man asked Greg, holding out a hand for the crowbar.

Greg shook his head and flashed him a grin. "Nah, I got this, and with pleasure. But if you would, go to a back window and distract the dog so he doesn't get hurt from any glass." The man did as Greg asked, coaxing the little animal into the back seat and talking to him through the glass of the rear passenger's-side window. With the dog occupied, Greg took his position at the driver's window. I understood why he chose that window. With it lowered, even a little, it would give easier to blows.

A few other people had stopped to watch. As Greg raised the crowbar like a bat, he warned the growing crowd, "Stand back, folks, and be ready for the car alarm to go off."

With one mighty swing, Greg landed a heavy blow to the window. My husband is very strong in his upper body and works out religiously several days a week to stay that way, in addition to playing wheelchair basketball. He may not have use of his legs, but even in his late forties his upper body is muscled and ripped. Without a shirt, he's beefcake calendar material.

The window didn't break but cracked, with spiderweb fissures branching out from the spot where the blow had landed. A cheer went up from the crowd urging Greg on. Phones were everywhere, recording and snapping photos. No alarm sounded. I went back to the call I was on, changing my story from animal endangerment to vehicle vandalism in progress.

Greg wiped a hand over his sweaty forehead. Raising the crowbar again, he took another big swing. The crowd cheered. More shatter patterns. The safety glass held but started to cave in. The dog inside was going berserk, circling and barking with what little energy it had left. Greg raised the crowbar again. I could see the underarm sweat stains on his T-shirt spreading like spilt water trickling across a tablecloth. Another spread around the neckline of his shirt. "Keep trying to keep the dog back," he called to me and the guy helping.

We went back to calling to the animal, but the dog was overexcited, confused, and getting more dehydrated by the second. It took him a little bit to be persuaded to our end of the vehicle. When Greg thought the animal was out of the way, he landed a third brutal blow to the window. This time a large hole was created and Greg was able to use the end of the crowbar to punch out glass to make a bigger hole. Still no alarm. I found it odd that the car was locked but had no alarm set, especially on such an expensive car. On both Greg's van and my car, the alarm was set when we locked it with the fob, and we never left it unlocked.

"Hold on, little fella," Greg cooed to the dog, trying to calm it down. He tried to reach through the window, but his low profile wouldn't give him the length he needed. The man who'd been helping came around and reached through to unlock the door. As soon as the door opened, the dog headed for it. Greg picked up the animal and cradled him in his lap. While the crowd went crazy with excitement, I trotted to our van and returned with a bottle of fresh water and one of Wainwright's portable water dishes we always kept with us. I filled the dish and held it out to the dog, who was still in Greg's lap. The little animal drank in a frenzy. Again the crowd cheered. I handed the water bottle to Greg, who knocked back a couple of thirsty gulps.

Greg checked the dog's tags. "According

to these, his name's Maurice."

"That's kind of a wimpy name for a cool little dog like that," said the big guy.

"I'm Greg Stevens, by the way," Greg informed him. "Thanks for your help." The two men shook hands. Greg indicated me. "And this is my wife, Odelia." I shook the man's hand. His meaty paw was strong and damp with sweat and his skin calloused. This was a man who did physical work every day and probably outside. He was as brown as a pecan shell, and his round face was lined around his dark eyes. His thick moustache was glossy black.

He hesitated, then said to us, "My name's Burt. Burt Sandoval."

Greg turned to me. "Sweetheart, can you jot down the other info on the dog tags or reach into my pouch to get my glasses so I can read it?"

"I have a better idea," I told him. "Hold out the tags." Greg did so and I snapped a photo with my phone of both sides of the name tag and the license tag, which hung from a blue collar studded with rhinestones. There was a phone number engraved on the flip side of the one bearing the dog's name.

"Should we call this number, honey?" I asked Greg. "Maybe the owner doesn't realize how close Maurice came to biting the big one."

Before Greg could answer me, a shriek came from the edge of the crowd closest to the store. "That's *my car*!"

A woman in black short-shorts and a pink tank top wobbled her way to the front on ridiculously high-heeled sandals. She had long streaked blond hair and large designer sunglasses perched on her nose. *Bling* was splashed across her huge and obviously fake boobs in rhinestones. She leveled a long manicured nail lacquered in bubble-gum pink at Burt. On her wrist dangled a gaggle of thin gold bracelets. Draped on her other arm was a very expensive handbag. She looked mildly familiar to me.

"You. Did *you* do this?" Her accusation fell from full lips smeared with hot pink lipstick. Her face was heavily made up. Upon closer examination, I upgraded her age from twentysomething to mid-forties. She was of a breed so common in Orange County — a middle-aged woman trying to convince people she was younger and not pulling it off very well, no matter how much money she spent doing it. The idea that I knew the woman nagged at me like a hang-nail.

"No, he didn't," Greg said, still clutching the dog. "*I* did. I saved your dog's life."

Greg had poured some water from the bottle into his hand and had rubbed it over the dog's head and paws to cool it down faster. The animal looked exhausted from its ordeal, but better, and made no movement to greet its owner. "It's in the upper 90s today. What were you thinking, leaving a dog locked in a car?" Greg lectured. "And without any water."

"And what business is that of yours?" the woman yelled back at him.

Greg snarled at her, "Cruelty to animals is *everyone's* business." A big cheer went up from the crowd, along with boos in the woman's direction.

Burt Sandoval stepped forward. "We're with him on this, lady." Another cheer erupted.

The woman considered Burt several seconds, studying him up and down, then swept him aside like a bad queen dismissing a servant. She moved closer to Greg, realizing he was the brains of the rescue operation. She made no movement to get her dog but instead pointed her lethal fingernail in his face. "I want your name. My husband's going to sue your sorry crippled ass, that's for sure." Another chorus of boos went up from the small crowd.

I started to protest her attitude toward my husband, but Greg shot me a look, reminding me that he could fight his own battles — something I well understood, but my loyalty and love for him made me want to tackle her to the hot pavement.

The woman was underestimating my hubby, something a lot of people do to folks in wheelchairs. I've never known Greg to back down from a fight when he knew he was in the right. He edged his wheelchair closer to her. "Bring it, lady," he challenged. "And while your husband's at it, you can lawyer up to fight animal cruelty charges."

"I'm calling the police," the woman countered. She pulled a cell phone from her bag. The case of the cell phone was as covered in rhinestones as the dog's collar and her boobies, although the wedding ring I noticed on her left hand did not look like rhinestones. The main diamond was huge and the setting heavy with smaller diamonds surrounding it. If I did attack her, that ring could be used as a serious weapon to fend me off.

"Don't bother," I told her. "I called them. They're on their way."

"You called the police?" she asked, surprised.

"A crime was in progress," I told her.

"Animal cruelty, like my husband said. In California it's a crime punishable by a hefty fine and/or jail time."

The crowd murmured their agreement and several chanted, "Lock her up! Lock her up!"

"It's a much more serious violation than your broken car window," I continued.

The woman turned her attention to me and took a step in my direction. "Do you have any idea who I am, you fat bitch? Who my husband is?" she asked in a low, menacing voice. "I'm Marla Kingston. I'm married to Kelton Kingston. Ring a bell?"

Immediately four words filled my skull: *Shit on a stick!*

THREE

The crowd went quiet, shocked into a stupor by the mere mention of the name of one of the most powerful and feared businessmen in all of Orange County, possibly in all of Southern California and even beyond. Kelton Kingston was admired for his business acumen and hated for his ruthless treatment of both business adversaries and employees. He gobbled up companies, liquidated them, and tossed people out of work as if they were used tissues. He destroyed lives and the environment as thoughtlessly and as thoroughly as a fire-storm.

Then it hit me why Marla Kingston seemed so familiar. Before marrying Kelton Kingston several years ago, she'd been Marla Sinclair, one of the women featured on a reality show showcasing wealthy Orange County divorcées. Her last season on the tasteless wallow in unconscionable high-end spending and low-end values had tracked her courtship and eventual marriage to Kingston, who was a couple of decades her senior.

A buzz went through the crowd as they recognized her and her husband's name. "OMG," I heard a woman say, "that's Marla Sinclair Kingston!"

If I had any sense, I'd write the woman a hefty check for her broken window, grab Greg, and drive off. But I had zero sense and zero tolerance for people like Kelton Kingston and his wife. He was the kind of man who, when he showed up on TV in interviews, prompted Greg and I to shout expletives at the screen; our middle fingers got a workout in the same direction.

It's really a good thing we don't have impressionable kids.

Kelton Kingston is also a client of Templin and Tobin, the law firm at which I'm employed as a paralegal, although Kingston only deals with the firm's main office in Los Angeles, not us peons toiling away at the small Orange County outpost. I glanced down at Greg. He was staring at Marla with even more contempt now that he knew her connection to Kelton Kingston. Greg didn't know that he was a client of my firm. For confidentiality reasons, I don't talk about our clients, not even to my husband. I quickly weighed whether this was a conversation I should have with him once we got home.

I put my hands on my bulky hips and studied the woman in front of me, righteous indignation strong-arming my natural instinct to flee. This overdone, overblown woman was that horror show's wife, or at least his fourth or fifth wife, depending on which tabloid you glanced at while standing in line at the supermarket. I think there was a scandal about whether or not Kingston was legally married to number three.

Like a boxer meeting her opponent in the center of the ring, I took a step in Marla's direction. Mrs. Kingston-number-whatever was about five foot nine and probably tipped the scales at 115 pounds tops, although I'd bet her driver's license listed 102. I stand five foot one at best and tip the scales at about 220 pounds — never mind what my driver's license says about my weight, except that I'll admit it's a lie.

"And do you know who *my* husband is?" I countered. Instead of waiting for an answer, I pointed at Greg. "That man. That wonderful, smart, caring man who saved your poor dog's life." A cheer went up from the crowd. "And I'll take him over a Kelton

Kingston any day." Another cheer.

She sneered at me and squared her shoulders. It really did look like we might come to blows in the parking lot, and from the way the crowd was hovering, they were probably hoping we would. Scorching heat or not, they were willing to stick around for a good show.

"Odelia," I heard Greg say in the way of a low warning.

"Odelia," Marla Kingston repeated with a bigger sneer, making my name sound like a joke. She was about to say something more when a short siren blast broke the tension, making most of us jump. The crowd parted like the Red Sea as a patrol car nosed forward.

"Good," Marla said. "Now we'll get somewhere." She pulled on her shirt bottom, making sure the fabric was tight over her boobs, as two Long Beach patrol cops climbed out of their vehicle.

"What's going on here?" the cop who'd been driving asked. He was African American, tall and lean, and middle aged. The name tag over his right shirt pocket said *J. Baker.* The other cop was young, white, and a half foot shorter. He was farther away and I couldn't read his name tag. Both were wearing mirrored sunglasses.

Before the question was fully voiced, a sea of hands and arms gestured toward Marla and us, and the crowd started addressing the police like a hive of angry bees. After about thirty seconds of the loud babble, Officer Baker raised his right hand, palm out. "Enough." He didn't raise his voice. The firm authority of it made his point. The crowd didn't go silent, but the buzz lessened to a low hum. "You," he said, pointing at me, "tell me what happened here."

Marla stepped forward. "They broke into my car."

Baker slowly turned his head in Marla's direction. He stared at her in silence, and even though no one could see his eyes, the crowd quieted, and so did Marla. Baker turned back to me and gestured for me to answer.

"My husband and I were on our way into the grocery store when we heard a dog whining. Then we saw this little guy," I explained, gesturing to the dog now asleep in Greg's lap, his brush with death long forgotten. "He was panting and suffering in the heat, so my husband rescued him."

"That's the truth, Officer," a man in the crowd confirmed, defying Baker's orders. "Several of us were here when it happened." Marla shot him a withering look and he

31

melted back into the crowd.

She pointed at Greg. "He broke my car window and tried to steal my dog. He said Maurice was in danger," she snapped in a high voice as she pointed to the shattered car window, "but I don't believe it. They were looking to snatch the dog for ransom, considering who my husband is. Everyone knows I'm devoted to Maurice." She gestured toward the crowd. "They all saw it. They were all probably in on it. Some sort of stunt to get fifteen minutes of fame on YouTube and make a few bucks." She curled her lip and turned her head slowly, making sure everyone got the benefit of her vile accusation. I saw a few phones lower, but not many. Most continued filming, happy to catch not only a scene, but a low-level celebrity for their amusement. "I'm Marla Kingston, wife of Kelton Kingston."

At that announcement, Baker lowered his sunglasses a few inches down his long nose and peered over the top of them at her. From where I was standing, he didn't look impressed by her revelation. He turned his head in my direction. "And you are?"

"Odelia Grey," I answered, "and this is my husband, Greg Stevens." I put a hand on Greg's shoulder. "Does it really look like we're running away with her damn dog? We brought it water. We didn't drive off with it. I'm the one who called 911."

Now Baker stared at me over the top of his lowered glasses. Then he stared at Greg, and then back at me. "*You're* Odelia Grey?"

Uh-oh.

The crowd went as silent as a mass grave and tilted forward, understanding from Baker's tone that Marla Kingston might not be the only newsmaker in their midst.

"ID, please," Baker ordered before I could answer. "All of you." And just to make sure we understood, he pointedly looked at Greg and me, then at Marla Kingston.

"You know who I am," Marla protested while I pulled my ID out of my purse and Greg produced his from his wallet. I took Greg's from him and handed them both to Baker while the officer and Marla had a stare-down. Seconds later, Marla Kingston rooted around in her purse and pulled out her wallet. She made a big deal out of it, heaving big bored sighs between each deliberate movement until Baker had all three of our IDs in hand.

After looking over the IDs, Baker turned to his partner and waved him over. Now I could read his name tag — *M. Patterson*. Baker whispered something in the younger cop's ear, who in turn stared at me. "Seriously?" he asked. "That's her?"

I felt my face grow hot under the scrutiny, and it had nothing to do with the stifling heat of the day.

"Check them out," Baker ordered Patterson, "then take a few statements." As the crowd heard this, several slowly peeled away, disbursing in several directions, returning to their business, most unwilling to be stuck answering police questions. Had this been a murder, I knew the police would never let them go. But this was hardly a murder, and the handful of gawkers that remained seemed determined to get juicy gossip even if it meant being held up with annoying questions.

While we waited on our IDs being checked, Baker asked Greg to explain how and why our crowbar was put to use. When Marla tried to interrupt she was halted with another steely look from Baker, who had taken off his sunglasses and hooked them in his shirt's neckline. Greg recited everything accurately, from the moment we parked the van, right up until the moment Marla Kingston had shown up screaming.

"That's not true," Marla snapped once Greg was done. "They were trying to steal Maurice."

"Oh, *puleeeze,*" I said with exaggerated

sarcasm, one of my better talents. "Not only can everyone here confirm Greg's story, but most got video of it." I swept my hand in the direction of the now smaller crowd. As soon as I did, phones started disappearing.

"You," Baker barked in the direction of a young guy wearing bright blue sunglasses. He was in his late teens or early twenties, wearing saggy board shorts covered with a tropical print and a faded green T-shirt. Under his arm was a skateboard. "Let me see your phone."

"You ain't taking my phone, man," the kid shot back. "I know my rights." He jutted out his chin, from which a tuft of fine light hair sprouted like that on a billy goat. Other than that puff of hair, his skin was smooth as a baby's and golden from the sun. The hair on his head was sun-bleached to a very pale yellow.

Baker sighed deeply, then said, "I just want to see the video. Did you get it?"

"Yeah, man, I did," the kid replied, still clutching his phone in a death grip. "The dude in the chair is telling you the truth. He smashed the bitch's ride to save the mutt."

I could see that Baker was weighing his options carefully, like any seasoned veteran. He obviously wanted to get to the bottom of things but didn't want to cause an incident. Police were treading carefully these days with all the negative publicity, some warranted, some not. Baker addressed the crowd. "Anyone get the video who is willing to let me watch it? I won't take your phone."

A murmur went up from the crowd, but no one came forward. Instead, the small crowd started to move backwards until Patterson stopped them. "Folks, we just want to see the video, that's all," assured the younger cop. "As soon as we do, we can resolve this and all go on our way."

To emphasize Patterson's words, Baker held out his hand, palm up, to the kid. "No one is leaving here without us seeing that video." When the kid didn't move, Baker added. "We can wait all day in this heat if we have to, folks." Suddenly, several phones appeared and were thrust in the direction of Officer Baker, but Baker took none of them. Instead, he continued looking at the kid with the skateboard, hand outstretched, waiting. "No, I want his." He paused. "What's your name, son?"

After a pause of his own, the kid replied, "Charlie." When Baker stared harder at him, the kid said, "Charles Benjamin Cowart. You happy now?"

"Take off the shades, Charlie," Baker

ordered, "and let's see some ID." Reluctantly, Charlie removed his sunglasses, hooking them in the neckline of his shirt as Baker had done to his own. He produced his ID and handed it to Baker, who checked it over, then handed it back.

"Oh, come on," snarled Marla. She glanced down at her watch, then glared at Baker. "I have places to go. People are waiting for me." As much as I hated to agree with her, I wanted to end this standoff and get home to a cold beer and air conditioning. I was melting like soft serve ice cream and could feel the skin on my arms starting to collect a sunburn.

"Well, Charles Benjamin Cowart," Baker said to the kid. "What's it to be? Standing here in the hot sun or letting me see your phone?"

With great reluctance, Charlie queued up the video and gave the phone to Baker. The cop watched it, and those of us close to him could hear the audio. Charlie must have been on the scene early because the video started about the time Burt Sandoval asked if we needed help and continued until the cops showed up. I couldn't see the phone screen, but from the sound he'd caught it all, including the smashing of the window and Marla Kingston arriving on the scene in full diva screech mode.

When it was over, Baker said to Charlie, "You're a regular Steven Spielberg."

Charlie snorted with disdain. "I'd rather be Quentin Tarantino."

"I just bet you would," Baker replied. "We'll need a copy of this." He reached into his breast pocket and produced a card. "If you want to hang on to that phone, email the video to the address on this card." When the kid hesitated, the cop added with unquestionable authority. "Now."

Charlie took the phone back and punched the screen while studying the business card. A minute later, Baker reached into a pocket and pulled out a cell phone. He checked the display, then said to Charlie, "Thanks. You have anything else you want to add?"

Charlie shook his head. "I was passing through when it went down. Just heading into the store to grab something to drink."

Patterson approached. "The IDs check out, but there are quite a few outstanding tickets on Mrs. Kingston. Parking and moving violations. At least a dozen." I could have sworn I saw a tiny smile peek out from behind Baker's closed lips at the news.

Baker glanced at Charlie. "Give my partner your contact information, and you can go."

With Charlie turned over to Patterson, Baker scanned the remaining dozen people. "Where's the guy who helped you?" he asked us.

Greg and I looked over the crowd, then shrugged, almost in unison. "Looks like he took off," Greg said. "But he said his name was Burt Sandoval."

"And how do you know this Sandoval guy?" Baker asked.

"We don't," I replied. "He offered to help us get the dog out of the car."

"You mean steal my dog, don't you?" sneered Marla as she stood adjusting her stance from foot to foot. Either she had to go potty or her ladder-height shoes weren't comfortable or maybe she was worried about those outstanding tickets. I was also pleased to see that, like the rest of us, she was sweating like a pig in the heat; her heavy makeup was not holding up well.

Baker turned to her. "From the video, I'd say they weren't stealing anything, but they did save your dog's life." He pointed at the dog, who was still asleep in Greg's lap, totally unaware of the brouhaha his predicament had caused.

Patterson returned and whispered something to Baker. This time the smile didn't play coy but spread across Baker's face in a thin line of off-white teeth. Baker whispered something back. Patterson got out a small wallet-size portfolio that I recognized as a ticket book. Not that I'd received that many tickets, but enough to know. Patterson got busy scribbling on the pad. I held my breath, sure Greg and I would be cited for something. I saw phones come out again and knew there would be more videos.

"Mrs. Kingston, you'd better find another way home," Baker advised. "A tow truck is on the way to impound your vehicle until you pay those tickets. You can get the location of the impound lot from the driver."

"You can't do that!" Marla screeched.

"We can and we did," Baker said calmly.

Patterson ripped a slim piece of paper from his pad and handed it to Marla, along with her ID. She snatched it as if it was hot from a grill. "That's a violation for endangering an animal," Patterson explained. "You can pay it at the same time you pay those tickets."

Marla waved the ticket in Patterson's face. "I'm not paying this or those bogus tickets. *They're* the ones who vandalized my car. Do your job and lock them up or my husband will have your badges."

"Mrs. Kingston," Baker said calmly. "You should be thanking these people. That ticket will cost you $100. Had the animal been injured, it could have cost you $500 and time in county jail. Now I suggest you put a leash on that dog and remove anything you want from your vehicle before the tow truck gets here."

"And what about them?" Marla waved the hand holding the ticket in our direction. "Arrest them."

"They've done nothing wrong in the eyes of the law," Patterson explained. "They rescued an animal in danger."

"And it's all on video," Baker added. "If you want to file a personal complaint against them for vandalism, you can do so when you pay the fines."

"This is an outrage!" Marla screeched. She turned to the crowd to make her case. "You all saw this. You see how I'm being treated. My rights are being violated."

More of the crowd broke off, some heading for the store, others for their cars. No one stepped up to defend the former reality star's honor.

Patterson handed back our IDs. Like the rest of us, sweat was dripping down the side of his face. "Give me your phone numbers, and then you can go as soon as you give the dog back to its owner."

"And you two," Baker snapped in our

direction, "stay out of trouble. We know all about you."

No problem there.

Greg was reluctant to hand Maurice back to Marla when she reached for the animal. The dog didn't seem too eager to go either. I could tell Greg wanted to give Marla a tongue lashing but was restraining himself. As soon as the dog was handed over, we stored Wainwright's dish back in our van and went on with our grocery shopping. Just before we entered the store, I turned back and saw that the tow truck had arrived. I'm sure if Baker and Patterson had not hung around, the driver of the truck would have been assaulted by Marla Kingston. Waves of anger were coming off her to rival those coming off the blacktop.

FOUR

I was putting away our groceries when Mom called to say she was on her way over. I'd barely put away a loaf of bread when the doorbell rang. Greg was in the living room playing with Muffin. We'd picked up a new stick aerial toy to help get her mind off of hunting Dumpster. She was loving it, attacking the feather on the end like a lion picking off an antelope. Wainwright was supervising, his head following the up-and-down and side-to-side swing of the stick. As soon as he heard the doorbell, he got to his feet, letting loose with the bark he reserved for friends and family. The old dog moved slower these days, but his enthusiasm was still intact.

"I'll get it," I told Greg as I passed by him. "It's my mother."

I nudged the dog aside and opened the door. Sure enough, my mother, Grace Littlejohn, was on the landing, looking cool and collected in a summer denim skirt and floral print blouse. On her feet were hot pink sneakers. Mom was of average height, slim, and on the brink of turning eighty. She was also still pretty spry. Wainwright's tail wagged happily as she opened the screen door and quickly came inside. I just as quickly shut the front door so we would not lose the cool air being kicked out by our AC. Before greeting me, Mom bent down and said hello to Wainwright. The grand-doggy and grand-kitty always came first.

"Were you parked in front of our house when you called?" I asked her.

"Maybe," she replied without looking at me.

Finished greeting the dog and cat, Mom stood straight, her big purse hooked over her right arm. Her eyes shifted between Greg and me with disapproval. "How come you two always have the most fun without me?" she snapped. Before I could tick off several reasons, she added, "I swear, you do it on purpose."

"What are you talking about, Grace?" Greg asked her.

"That smashed car window," Mom replied with her usual impatience. "The dog rescue. At the grocery store. You knew you were be-ing videoed, didn't you?"

In a flash of memory, I recalled all the phones held aloft during the rescue of Maurice, and it wasn't just Charlie Cowart's. "Yes, Mom, we did," I answered. "But that happened less than two hours ago. How do you know about it already?"

"Already?" Greg parroted with surprise. "Where?"

"It's on YouTube," Mom explained. She put her purse down on the coffee table and pulled out her iPad. My mother was an ace with her iPad. She even had her own blog called An Old Broad's Perspective, which was surprisingly popular, and not just with the AARP crowd. Sometimes I wished she'd just sit and knit or get addicted to playing bridge.

"There are a couple, but this one is the best. It's even gone viral!" She made the announcement like we'd just won Powerball.

In no time, my mother was showing us a video of what had gone down in the parking lot of the grocery store. It began just as Greg raised the crowbar and took his first swing. There was a lot of background chatter and cheering. The video zoomed in on Greg's face, then pulled back as he took another crack at the window. There was another close-up at the final swing. The taker of the video seemed to be standing several yards back because the wider shots got the entire car, including Burt and me near the back trying to entice Maurice away from the front. Then the camera scanned the crowd briefly, showing its enthusiastic support and several others also taking photos and videos. In the front of the crowd was Charlie Cowart taking his own video, the one the police watched. The clip then went back to the action and recorded Burt helping Greg open the door to the car to free the dog. A loud cheer went up from the crowd when the animal was safe in Greg's arms, and another went up when I produced the doggie water dish.

Mom paused the video and tapped the screen. Specifically, she tapped the image of me bending over to present the water to the dehydrated animal. "Not your best side," she said without ceremony. "That outfit makes you look like one of those black-and-white cookies."

I looked down at what I was wearing. I still had on the same outfit, a white boxy camp shirt and black capris. I thought I looked passable, considering it was Saturday and a thousand degrees outside.

"You know the ones," my annoying mother continued. "Round cookies with half white icing, half chocolate."

"I know what a black-and-white cookie is, Mom," I said, barely keeping the snarkiness out of my voice.

I glanced at Greg. He was looking anywhere but at me and Mom, but there was a trace of a suppressed smile on his face. "What do you think, honey?" I said to him. He wasn't getting off that easy.

He shrugged and still didn't look at me. I was positive that if he did, he would break into laughter. He knew how my mother got under my skin, especially her barbs about my weight. "I think you look nice, sweetheart." Finally, he glanced up and tossed me a wink. "You always look nice."

I shot my mother a smug smile.

"He has to say that if he wants to keep getting nookie," she said, delivering the line with her usual deadpan zing.

"Give up, sweetheart," Greg said to me with a little pat on my ample behind, which only underlined my mother's comment. "You can't win this, although I do think black-and-white cookies are delicious." I smacked his hand away.

"Is that why you came over, Mom," I asked in a tense voice, "to insult me and whine about you not being in the video?"

She shrugged. "Insults comes naturally.

It's a gift." She pointed at the iPad. "But I sure wish I had been there. I'd love to see Marla Kingston in person. I'll bet she's had a lot of nips and tucks over the years." She started the video again, and the three of us watched it until shortly after the cops showed up.

"Who took this video, Grace?" Greg asked when it was over. "Can you tell?"

"It's someone called the Human Stain," Mom answered.

"Like the Philip Roth novel?" he asked.

"Yes," Mom responded with a nod. "At least that's the name of her YouTube channel. Her real name is Holly. She goes all over Southern California filming people and stuff she finds interesting or newsworthy. Sometimes she travels too. Sometimes it's fun stuff and sometimes it's serious, but it's always interesting.

I moved the iPad closer to me. With a few taps I was at the profile page for the Human Stain. There was a headshot of a young woman with long straight dark hair. Her face was mostly obscured by the back of a large cell phone turned sideways so that all you could see was her mouth and forehead. The profile read: *Female voyeur located in Southern California. People fascinate me from afar, not so much up close. Name's Holly, as in the poisonous plant.* I read the profile out loud.

"That's kind of cynical," Greg noted. "I'll bet she's pretty young."

"Young or not," Mom said, "she's been doing this for a couple of years and has well over twenty thousand subscribers."

"That's pretty impressive," I agreed. I got up and headed for the kitchen. "Mom, Greg and I were about to have a cold beer. What can I get you?" My mother and my half brother Clark were both recovering alcoholics with many years of sobriety behind them, so I knew she wasn't going for the beer. She usually went for hot coffee. "I even have some freshly brewed iced coffee in the fridge."

Mom and Greg both had their heads bent toward the iPad, watching a replay of the video. Mom glanced up. "Iced coffee sounds good, Odelia. It's hotter than Satan's ass out there today."

Was Satan's ass hot? I pictured the Devil posing naked for a cheesecake calendar. He looked strangely like Ryan Gosling. I shook my head hard to clear the image.

When I returned with the two beers and a tall glass of iced coffee, Mom was gone. A few minutes later she emerged from the hallway that led to the guest bathroom.

"Do you know there's a duck in your tub?" Mom asked calmly as she took her place back on the sofa. "Cute little bugger."

"I won him in a poker game," Greg said without taking his eyes off of the iPad. Mom didn't ask anything else about Dumpster and Greg didn't offer. It was as if winning a duckling in a card game happened every day.

As I put my mother's beverage down on a coaster on the coffee table, Mom glanced up with a smirk. "Better be careful, Greg, or Odelia might get jealous."

"What are you talking about?" I asked. I stood next to Greg and looked at the screen over his shoulder. Instinctively, he put an arm around my waist and drew me close. Just as naturally, one of my arms went around his shoulders.

"Just watch," Mom said as she replayed the video, stopping it shortly after Greg took his first swing at the window. At this point the camera had zoomed in on Greg's face, beaded sweat and all. It hung there nearly a full minute, then went wide as he took another swing with the crowbar.

"So?" I asked. "We saw this before."

"Hold your horses," Mom said. She started the video again for a bit, then paused it again. "And here." Once again the camera zoomed in on Greg's face. It was the last swing. The video zoomed in again soon after, showing Greg's head bent down slightly as he comforted the dog. The camera stayed on Greg and the dog a pretty long time, then again went wide and took in more of the activity, including the part where Marla Kingston came screaming onto the scene. "And again here," Mom noted as she paused the video again. Once again the camera zoomed in on Greg. This time the camera caught him dressing Marla down over her treatment of the animal.

"I think this Holly person has a little crush on your man," Mom said before taking a drink of her iced coffee.

Greg and I both laughed, then I said with another chuckle, "Greg's pretty cute, Mom. Why shouldn't she?" I squeezed Greg's shoulders. My hubs was good looking, with slightly wavy brown hair and a neatly trimmed Van Dyke beard. The thin strands of gray now showing in each only added to his rakish good looks. To top it off, he possessed a killer smile that radiated a hint of mischief. In spite of the wheelchair, many a time I saw female heads turn to watch him with appreciation when we were out in public.

"I'm just saying," Mom continued, "that

51

she seems rather taken with him. You don't see her zooming in on anyone else, do you? Not even that Marla monster, and she's famous."

"Grace," Greg said after shaking his head, "I'm sure some of the others involved got close-ups too. Maybe she edited them out." He paused, then tacked on for good measure, "Then again, I was kind of the superhero of the day."

"Superhero?" I asked. I rolled my eyes at him, but only in jest. Greg Stevens was *my* superhero and had been almost from the day we'd met. He laughed and gave my bottom another friendly pat.

I could tell my mother wasn't buying it. "I'm just saying that I've looked at a lot of the videos from today that have posted already, and none of them have close-ups of anyone."

"Well," I said, "she can have all the close-ups she wants. I have the real thing." I bent down and kissed the top of Greg's head.

While we sipped our beverages, Mom showed us several of the other videos on YouTube. It was shocking how fast these had been posted and even more shocking how many views they'd already received. Greg's heroics had indeed gone viral. The videos had popped up online faster than weeds in a neglected lawn.

Once we'd seen several, I moved away from the iPad and stretched. "Mom, do you want to stick around for an early dinner? Greg is grilling salmon." It was sometime between lunch and dinner, but we'd not had any lunch because of our large breakfast and all the hullabaloo. "We'll probably start the grill in about an hour."

"Nah, but thanks," Mom said as she stuffed her iPad back into her bag. "I have to finish packing for my trip." She looked up at me. "You didn't forget I was leaving town tomorrow, did you? I need you to water my plants while I'm gone since Art will be on the trip too."

Seaside, the 55+ community where Mom owned a condo, isn't far from us. We live in Seal Beach, and Seaside is in Long Beach, almost spitting distance from where we'd had our encounter with Marla Kingston today. Several of the residents of Seaside, including Mom's good friend Art Franklin and his lady friend, had signed up for a one-week trip to Branson, Missouri, an entertainment mecca, particularly for older adults. The trip wasn't sponsored by Seaside but by a travel group specializing in trips for seniors.

"No, Mom, I didn't forget," I told her

with attitude. Actually, I had forgotten she was leaving tomorrow. For some reason I thought her trip started next weekend, but I wasn't going to admit it. "I'll make sure your plants survive."

"Do you need a lift to the airport, Grace?" Greg asked.

"Nah," she told him with a wave of her hand. "Since so many of us from Seaside are going, they're shuttling us to the airport together."

After saying goodbye to us and our animals, Mom started for the door. "You two stay out of trouble while I'm gone," she admonished, wagging a finger between Greg and me.

"It's not like we plan this stuff, Mom," I told her as I walked her to the front door and gave her a kiss on her cheek.

"Yeah, Grace," Greg added. "Trouble hits Odelia like a tornado, striking with little to no warning."

I watched as Mom climbed into her car and drove off, then I turned on my husband, hands on my hips. "Really, Greg? Trouble hits me *like a tornado*? I don't recall the crowbar being in *my* hands today." I wasn't angry, just trying to make a point.

"You forgot about your mother's trip,

didn't you?" he said, trying to deflect the issue.

"So did you," I accused.

"Guilty." He rolled over to me and flashed that bad boy smile of his. "Now — about that nookie. We have time to kill before I fire up the grill for dinner."

FIVE

When I got to work on Monday, there was a brand-new crowbar on my desk with a red ribbon tied around it and no note. I was pretty sure who'd left it there. It had Mike Steele's sarcasm slathered all over it. By evening several of the amateur videos had made their way to the local news channels.

We'd received several calls at home for interviews Saturday night and Sunday, but Greg had declined them all, only giving the comment over the phone that he'd seen an animal in trouble and had done what any good citizen would do in order to save it. I pointed out that giving an interview on camera might actually be good for his business, but he wasn't hearing of it. But even without Greg's cooperation, one of the reporters had seen Greg's cap, done their research, and given it a good plug on the 6 p.m. news. Friends and family also called on Sunday about Greg's heroics. The one call that really annoyed me was from Detective Andrea Fehring of the Long Beach Police Department.

Andrea Fehring is a friend of sorts. I mean, she is a friend and has been a guest in our home, and my mother swears Clark has a crush on her. But she's also a police detective that we've crossed paths with several times in a crime-related capacity — not that we committed the crime, but Greg and I always seem to be witnesses or be attached in some sick way to these crimes. Well, mostly it's me, but sometimes Greg's hands get dirty too.

"Can't you two have a normal Saturday?" Fehring had asked as soon as I picked up the call. I'd seen her name on the display but knew if I didn't answer, she'd keep calling. Mike Steele was like that too. He'd call and call and call until you either picked up or called him back.

"We *were* having a normal Saturday," I told her. She'd called while Greg and I were relaxing on Sunday evening on the patio after it had cooled down a bit. I'd just returned from taking Wainwright on a walk down to the beach and back. When Greg raised a questioning eyebrow in my direction, I mouthed *it's Fehring* at him.

He grinned and whispered back, "What

took her so long?"

For some reason, Fehring keeps an eye out for any questionable activity involving Greg and me. Mom says it's because of Clark. I think it's because of her friendship with Dev Frye, a former Newport Beach detective who is also our friend. Greg and I both believe when Dev retired and moved to Portland, he made Fehring pinkie-swear to keep an eye on us.

"We were just running errands Saturday," I told Fehring. "I suppose those two officers squealed to you about us."

"They didn't have to," Fehring said. "I was out of town until today and caught it on the local news."

"So are you calling to lecture us?" I asked.

There was a pause, then she said, "No, I'm calling to say good work — both of you. That poor animal could have easily died."

The kudos caught me by surprise. Fehring didn't hand them out often or easily. "Thanks, Andrea, and hey," I said with spunky cheer, "at least there were no dead bodies." Greg gave me a thumbs-up and went back to reading his book.

"It's early yet," Fehring quipped. It was the exact comment Clark had made when he'd called Saturday night after talking to Mom.

When Greg left for work this morning, I warned him that reporters might come by the shop, but he assured me that he and Wainwright could handle them. I'd looked down at our trusty elderly canine with his graying muzzle and smiled. The dog wagged his tail in response. Wainwright was as harmless as little Dumpster, but he was thoroughly trained to protect Greg and had even protected me at times. He had that magical doggie sense of who was a threat and who wasn't.

I work three days a week as a paralegal at Templin and Tobin, better known as T&T. Usually my days in the office are Monday, Wednesday, and Thursday. Sometimes, if we have a heavy workload or a big project, I'll come in more often. The Orange County office isn't nearly as busy as the LA office, which is why I can enjoy such great flexible hours, but it's also a big concern. For quite a while there have been rumors of T&T closing the small Orange County satellite office. It's only been open a few years and is a big expense. It was opened to better serve the clients in Orange County and northern San Diego County, and to entice new clients from those areas. Often attorneys from Los Angeles come down for meetings held here, and Steele heads a lot of projects for those more southern clients who don't want to brave the traffic to Century City, the section of LA where the main office is located. Steele is the manager of the OC office and the only resident partner. When he came to T&T from his prior firm, where we had also worked together, he brought in a lot of new business for T&T, and I've always suspected that's one of the reasons why they kept the office open.

I've asked him about the rumors several times, encouraged by other employees and even the associates since I have a closer relationship to Steele than most in the office. As I expected, he didn't give any indication that the rumors were true or false, but I didn't expect him to say much. Steele can be a real ass, though he's also very loyal to the worker bees under him. But he's also a partner of the firm, and as such he has an obligation to the other partners not to be a gabby goose. When pressed, all he'll say, or rather bark, is, "If you're so damn worried, maybe you should all get back to work and earn your keep."

Greg and I have discussed what I might do if T&T closes this office. We only have a few attorneys in Orange County and most are young. T&T would probably offer them spots in LA, as they would Steele. It was the staff that might suffer. I was pretty sure Steele would want to take his secretary, Jill Bernelli, with him. I'd hired her after he'd gone through a string of secretaries. She'd followed him to T&T when he changed firms, but would Jill want to make the ugly commute to Los Angeles? I doubted it. T&T has a couple of paralegals in LA. I'd met them all and had worked closely with one of them, as well as with some of the LA-based attorneys, but that didn't mean they needed me there, not to mention I would not like that commute either. In the end, Greg and I adopted a wait-and-see attitude. My husband was sure I could find another job quickly, but I wasn't so optimistic. I'd gotten used to working part-time and I was in my mid-fifties — not a good age to be looking for work in a snug economy.

Being mid-summer, the office was even slower than usual, which gave me a good chance to catch up on some clean-up work, such as boxing up old files for storage, reorganizing my computer files and desk, and even doing a little dusting that the regular cleaning crew missed. That was my plan today, and I'd come dressed a little more casually than usual. Not jeans casual but business casual, because you never knew when a client might pop in or someone from the LA office might decide to pay us a visit.

My first order of business was to consider the crowbar. It was slim and sleek and jet black, with not a scratch on it, unlike the well-used one in our van. The curved end was forked, like the tongue of a snake. The large ribbon was glossy red and full. The crowbar looked dressed to go to a party. I picked it up. It was heavier than it looked and solid in my hands, and it could do a lot of damage to a window, desk, door, or even a skull. With none of that in mind, I left my office in search of Steele. When I approached his office, I saw the door was closed.

"Now what has he done?" asked a familiar voice behind me. I turned and focused on Jill. She was sitting in front of her computer, a mug of coffee in one hand. Jill was a no-nonsense type with a slender build and close-cropped brown hair. She never wore any makeup, and even though she was in her fifties, she was cute in a pixyish tomboy way. She was married to Sally Kipman, one of my high-school classmates.

I stopped short at her question, then looked down at the crowbar. I was gripping it with two hands, one over and one under, like I was about to head into a nasty fight.

The bow had slipped, the bulk of it hanging beneath the crowbar like an ugly growth.

I laughed and relaxed my grip, letting the crowbar casually hang to one side. "Nothing, but I think Steele left this on my desk. I wanted to thank him for it."

Jill cleared her throat. "Actually, that is from Sally and me. Didn't you see the card?"

"There was no card," I told her.

"Damn," she said, slightly annoyed. "It must have fallen off. It was taped on but was small. It just said *keep on swinging.*"

I laughed as I walked closer to her desk. "Thanks — I think." I looked down at the lethal weapon in my hand. "And here I was giving all the credit to Steele. Sorry about that."

Jill laughed herself. "That's why we had a note. I told Sally if we didn't include one, you'd immediately think Steele left it."

Jolene McHugh came around the corner. A senior associate with the firm, Jolene had also worked with us at our last firm. Jill did secretarial work for her, as well as for Steele and occasionally for me. She was holding a small white card in an outstretched hand. She seemed unsure which of us to hand it to. "One of you must have dropped this. I found it in the hallway near reception."

"That's the card," exclaimed Jill happily. "It was meant for Greg and Odelia."

Jolene handed it to me. "So I gathered from the note on it." She indicated the crowbar. "Does this have anything to do with the local news last night?"

"No," I lied. "Why do you ask?"

"Yeah, right," Jolene said with a grin. She pushed a lank of her bright-red hair back with a hand. "My husband and I caught Greg's heroism on the late news." She paused, a look of concern on her face. "But did it have to be Marla Kingston's car?"

"Trust me," I answered, "we didn't know that at the time, although I doubt it would have made any difference to Greg." I looked up and down the hall, making sure no one was listening. "You don't think that will come back to bite us on the butt, do you?"

Jolene shrugged. "Hard to say. Depends on whether or not Kelton Kingston realizes who you work for, or . . . ," she trailed off.

"Or what?" I asked.

Jill took a deep breath and answered before Jolene. "Or if his wife convinces him to file a lawsuit, he may go to T&T to get it rolling. We are his lawyers, after all."

"But if the firm takes that on, wouldn't it be a conflict of interest on their side?" I asked, worried about the consequences.

Jolene gave it some quick thought. "I seriously doubt the firm would take on a suit against one of its own employees. In fact, I'm sure of it."

"But if Kingston finds out you work for T&T," Jill added, "he may simply insist they fire you."

"Can they do that legally?" I asked, my head swinging back and forth between them like a pendulum. Immediately there was a *clunk* inside me as my gears shifted from worry to anger. Just as quickly, I had a mental argument with myself, telling my anger to cool its jets. Nothing had happened yet, so I shouldn't get my undies in a bunch.

I turned to Jill and pointed at Steele's office. "I should talk to Steele. Is he in?"

She nodded. "He was in early this morning. He's been on and off the phone since."

"Do you know who he's talking to right now?" I asked.

She put her coffee down and stared at the phone, specifically at the light that indicated Steele's line was in use. "About an hour ago he got a call from Joe Templin." She looked up, her brows knitted into a pair of slim woolly socks across her brow. "They've been on the same call since." She paused, then tacked on, "And just before you came by, Steele was yelling."

My gut lurched. Joe Templin was the Templin of Templin & Tobin, one of the two founding partners. I'd gotten to know Simon Tobin a bit and liked and respected him very much, but Joseph Carlisle Templin was another kettle of fish. I'd only met him twice, and both times the hair on my neck stood on end. That was enough to convince me to stay out of his way. He had a reputation of being cold and calculating, rolling over opponents and sometimes staff with ferocity. Simon Tobin, on the other hand, was urbane and gracious, with a calm demeanor. Friends since high school, they'd started the firm a few years after law school and built it into a powerful, well-respected entity. How the two of them had managed to stay partners for nearly four decades was anyone's guess.

I looked at my two coworkers. Jill's brows had relaxed, but her jaw was set like chiseled stone. Jolene's skin was fair with clumps of freckles. When she got mad or upset, her skin turned milk white. Right now she looked like she should be quarantined for a bad case of measles. "Should I wait until he's off the phone and talk to him?" I asked, looking for guidance from either of them, "or go home and eat a pint of Ben & Jerry's?"

Before either of them could say anything, loud yelling came from Steele's office. It was Steele's voice. Then we heard another loud voice respond, but it wasn't as loud. We all heard my name mentioned. The three of us stared at each other, eyes wide, mouths shut, as if burglarizing a house and the owner came home mid-burgle.

"Who's in there with him?" Jolene asked, breaking the silence.

Jill shook her head. "No one. He must be on speaker."

Turning, I started back down the hall, the crowbar feeling like a hundred-pound anchor in my hands.

"If Steele asks, are you going back to your office?" Jill asked. I turned to look at the two women. Jill was now on her feet, standing next to the younger and much taller Jolene.

I shook my head. "I'm going home. Tell Steele whatever you'd like." I took a deep breath as I fought back tears. "No, tell him I went home sick. It won't be a lie." I got a few more steps, then turned. "No, I'll be in my office," I said, changing my mind. "My mother didn't raise no cowards."

"That phone call might not have anything to do with what happened with Kingston's wife, Odelia," Jolene said with encouragement. "Maybe your name was mentioned because Templin wants you to work on something. You know Steele isn't good about sharing." I wanted to grab the lifeline of hope she was holding out, but I didn't believe it. One look in Jolene's blue eyes and Jill's brown pair, and I could tell neither of them did either.

I spent the next hour or so doing what I'd planned on doing today. After getting a cup of coffee, I got to work sorting through old files and boxing many for storage. I was ankle-deep in a sea of expanding files and closing binders when Steele showed up at my office door. His sleeves were rolled up and his tie loosened, his face gaunt like he'd been dragged a few miles behind a messenger bike. Usually Steele is impeccably dressed and groomed. It was clear he'd not had a good morning.

"I need to talk to you, Grey." He voice was clipped and tired, all his usual sarcasm stripped away. He stepped inside and closed the door. He gestured toward my desk chair. "Take a seat."

Stepping over the files on my floor, I plopped down in my chair as I was told. "This is mostly the Hampstead matter," I told him, gesturing to the mess on the floor, trying to keep things business as usual. "I

68

thought it was time to send it to storage."

He didn't answer or even glance at the scattered files. Instead, he took a seat in the visitor's chair on the other side of my desk. His eyes landed on the crowbar. It was on the edge of my desk, the once-happy red bow now looking disheveled and sad, broadcasting the dread in my gut. Steele's mouth, tightly closed, fought to hold back a smile as he ran a long finger along the cold black finish of the tool. Then he picked up the crowbar with one hand and placed it on the floor next to him, out of my reach.

"Really, Steele?" I asked, going from worried to annoyed. "Maybe you should also confiscate my scissors and letter opener while you're at it."

Six

I didn't want to go home. No one would be there but Muffin and Dumpster. And in the mood I was in, I'd probably pick them both up to hug them for comfort and smother them between my big boobs. Mom was out of town, but even if she wasn't, she's not exactly the consoling type. I could have swung by Zee's home but mentally crossed off that option, even though she's my best friend in the entire world. There was only one person who could comfort me when I was this devastated.

Ocean Breeze Graphics was humming with its usual busy activity when I opened the glass-doored entrance and stepped inside. I'd parked in the small lot in front of the strip mall housing the shop and sat in my car a full five minutes before I could no longer ignore the heat that filled the vehicle once the engine and AC had been switched off. I hadn't called first, although I probably should have. I hated bothering Greg at work when he was super busy, but this concerned him too.

As soon as I entered the shop, cool air hit me, bringing me out of my stupor. I was relieved to see that only Chris Fowler, Greg's manager, was there. Greg has three employees — Chris, Aziz Hajjar, and Lupe Juarez. I didn't see Lupe or Aziz anywhere. It took Chris a minute before he saw me, but once he did, he came right over and unlatched the gate in the counter that divided the private work area from the customer area with its self-serve copy machines, rental computer stations, and a few chairs for those waiting for jobs to be finished. There was even a flat screen TV hung from the ceiling for waiting customers to watch. It was always tuned to CNN with the volume set low. The main counter was split into a high counter and a low counter, the lower counter to accommodate Greg's wheelchair when he was taking care of customers. He also did a lot of work for people in wheelchairs, as that community liked to give business to its own. Currently there was only one customer in the place — a middle-aged Asian man checking out his phone while he waited on one of the plastic chairs.

"Mr. Fujita," Chris said to him on his way to greet me. "Your job will be done in five minutes." The man nodded at Chris before going back to his phone.

Chris greeted me with a big smile of slightly crooked teeth. "Hi, Odelia," he said, shutting and latching the gate behind me. "Greg's in his office."

"Where are Lupe and Aziz?" I asked, more in the way of small talk to calm my nerves. As soon as I spoke, Wainwright trotted out from Greg's office in the back, his tail wagging, a big doggie smile on his face. Wainwright might be moving slower these days, but his ears were still keen. Greg's office had a large window in one wall so he could keep an eye on the shop. He'd turned to see what had attracted Wainwright. When he saw me, he gave me a big smile and a wave.

"Aziz is out making a delivery, and Lupe's on vacation," Chris told me as I bent down to greet Wainwright and rub him behind his ears. "She went to Mexico to see her grandmother. She's not very well."

"I'm very sorry to hear that," I said with genuine concern as I straightened up.

Lupe had been working for Greg for almost two years. She was a young single mother. Even though Lupe had little education, Greg had taken a chance on her and

72

was helping her get her GED and her citizenship. She'd turned out to be a very hard worker. Greg had a keen eye for good employees and often gave chances to people that others would not. It seldom turned sour for him. His business partner, Boomer, had come to him unable to find a decent job because of all his piercings and tattoos. He was super smart, and while he worked at Ocean Breeze he had finished college with honors. It had been his idea to expand, and it had been a sound one. Greg rewarded him with a buy-in to the company. After marrying, Boomer moved to Colorado to set up Mountain Breeze Graphics. Aziz had lost his previous job when all the hysteria over Muslims raised its ugly head. Chris knew him and his family and vouched for him. He'd also turned out to be a very good employee.

"Is there anything Greg and I can do for Lupe?" I asked Chris. Even Chris had been a risky hire. He'd shown up looking for a part-time job as a skinny, pimply-faced high-school dropout with almost no self-esteem. He had dropped out of high school because of bullying. As with Lupe, Greg had helped him get his GED. From there he went on to community college. He ran the shop in Greg's absence and was almost as good as Greg with graphic work. Along the way, Chris had filled out nicely and had gained confidence in himself.

Chris flashed another smile. "You know how the boss is; he's already helping." I smiled back. My husband was a superhero, with or without a crowbar. After a couple of years of rebellion following the injury that had put him in a wheelchair as a young teen, and many second chances, Greg had straightened his life around and felt the need to pay it forward by doing the same for others. But before you think he's some sort of saint, let me be the first to tell you that he's not. Greg has a bad temper, but only when pushed to the brink. He seldom backs down from a physical altercation. And he has a very bad habit of leaving dirty laundry on the floor and hair in the sink. He's also not that great at poker and loses more than he wins at his twice-monthly poker game with his pals.

With Wainwright in tow, I made my way to Greg's office. He used to have a large wooden traditional desk that took up a lot of room in the middle and wasn't the easiest for him to get around. Several years ago he'd put money into customizing his office. Now there were wheelchair-height counters on all three of the windowless sides, with a nice-size floating extension that jutted out in the middle of the room. His computer sat on the extension, along with our wedding picture and a photo of us with our pets, including our cat Seamus, who had crossed the rainbow bridge a couple of years earlier. The counters were just deep enough to accommodate lateral file cabinets underneath, and the file cabinets were spaced apart so that Greg could access them from the side instead of them being set flush against each other. Each of those spaces was wide enough for Greg to slip into with his wheelchair and use the counter above as more workspace. Lighting was set up to cover all work areas. Greg was using one of those spaces now as he pored over some designs.

"Sweetheart," Greg said, "hang on a minute. I'm almost done with this project." True to his word, a minute later he turned and greeted me properly. "What a nice surprise — and great timing. Guess who called me about an hour ago?"

Holding back my tears and anxiety, I shrugged.

"Burt Sandoval," he announced. "You know, the guy who helped with Maurice on Saturday."

My surprise shoved my misery aside for a

moment. "What did he want?"

"I have no idea. He just called and said he needed to talk to me." Greg moved closer, studying my face. "Are you okay, Odelia?"

I'd been leaning against his doorjamb. Wainwright had returned to the bed Greg kept in the corner for him. At the question I melted, sliding down the edge of the door frame to the floor into a soppy puddle. The tears had been there all along, just barely held back during the drive from my office to Ocean Breeze. Wainwright immediately left his bed and came to me, nudging my chin and giving me doggie kisses. Animals always seem to know when you're upset.

"Sweetheart," Greg said, his voice concerned, "what's the matter?"

"I . . . I," I began, then stopped to take several deep breaths. Like a scared cat hiding under the table, my words didn't want to come out. Once they were out, they were real. I took another deep breath. But the truth was, whether they were whispered or shouted from the top of the highest building in Orange County, what had happened was real. I gave Wainwright a big hug around his thick neck and told him to go back to his bed. I could tell he wanted to stay with me, but his solid training won out. He returned to his big round soft cushion, from where he kept a careful eye on me.

"I . . . I," I tried again. "I was fired!" The three words shot out, quick and harsh like small, sharp slaps.

Greg's mouth dropped open. A few seconds later, he rolled over to his door to quickly close it and give us privacy. I got to my feet so he could. "You were fired?" he asked.

I nodded, then shook my head side to side. I took one of the visitor chairs in Greg's office. Greg rolled over to the other side of his desk to retrieve a box of tissues. He handed it to me. I pulled out a couple and mopped up my face. I noticed my makeup was coming off with my waterworks. Great. Now I'd look like a sobbing zombie.

"Were you fired or not?" asked Greg. He'd moved to the side of my chair and held a comforting hand to my back. I felt the warmth through my blouse and immediately started calming down.

"Kind of, sort of," I sniffed. I grabbed a few more tissues and began blotting around my eyes, especially under them, where I was sure my melting mascara was pooling. *Waterproof, my fat ass.*

"A little more clarification, please," Greg prodded.

77

I left my chair. Greg has a tiny fridge in his office. It's installed under one of the counters behind his desk. There's a larger one in the small breakroom for his employees, but he liked to keep water and snacks closer to him. Before I answered, I grabbed a bottle of water from the fridge, twisted the top off, and gulped down a good third of its contents. I still hadn't told him about Kelton Kingston's connection with T&T. Now there was no way to avoid it.

"It has to do with Marla Kingston," I told him once I came up for air. I leaned against the counter, clutching the water to me like a lifeline. The bottle was cold and wet against my blouse. I didn't care if it left a wet spot. It felt good. I took another slurp from the bottle while Greg watched me, fidgeting as he waited for more information. "Kelton Kingston is a client of the firm. A big client who brings in lots of income."

"You never told me that," Greg said, his face showing surprise.

"I don't talk about our clients. You know that," I replied.

"Yeah, I know, but you should have told me this over the weekend, considering what happened."

"I thought it would just blow over," I

sniffed. "Instead, it's blown up — in my face." I took another drink of water.

"Okay," Greg said. "Tell me what happened. Tell me everything." Greg was on full alert.

"According to Steele," I reported, "Kelton Kingston called his good buddy Joe Templin yesterday afternoon at home demanding that the firm sue the people who broke into his wife's car and humiliated her. Templin said they couldn't handle the lawsuit because I was an employee of the firm and it would be a conflict of interest. Steele said Templin claimed he tried to calm Kingston down and offered some sort of settlement, like maybe we would pay for the broken window and provide a public apology."

"Like hell!" Greg spit out. "We did nothing wrong. I'm not apologizing to the Kingstons and neither are you — not even to save your job. And what right does Templin have to even make such a suggestion without speaking to you first — or did he?" From his corner, Wainwright went on alert.

Holding my right hand palm down, I patted the air, pushing it down as if into a box, gesturing for Greg to calm down. If he calmed down, the dog would also relax. "No, he didn't," I continued, "but let me finish." I took another deep breath. "Apparently, Kingston wasn't satisfied with that offer either."

"So what does the ass want?" Greg asked. His hands were on the wheels of his wheelchair, inching it back and forth as if he was preparing to push off for a race. Greg did that when he was agitated, like he was getting ready to launch himself at an opponent.

"In a nutshell," I answered, "he wants my head. He told Templin that unless the firm fires me, he will pull all of his business from it."

"That's preposterous!" Upon hearing the anger in Greg's voice, Wainwright made a move to get up, but Greg commanded him to lay back down again. Greg stopped fidgeting with his wheelchair and zeroed his eyes in on mine. "I was the one who broke that window, not you. The firm can't take your job away for that." He ran a hand through his hair — another nervous gesture. "What does Steele have to say about this? I can't believe he'd go for it."

I pictured Steele coming into my office, his face flushed, shoulders tense, to tell me what was going on. At first I had thought he was angry with me and I was ready to defend myself, but in short order it became clear he was angry with the firm, specifically with Joe Templin. "He's not happy with this at all," I told Greg. "In fact, he and Templin got into a knock-down, drag-out fight over it on the phone this morning."

Before I could say another word, Greg grabbed his cell phone from the desk and dialed. My money was on either Seth Washington for legal advice or Steele. Greg put it on speaker, and after just two rings the call was answered. It was door number two.

"I've been expecting your call, Greg," Steele said in a weary voice.

"Mike," Greg barked into the phone, "what is this bullshit about Odelia losing her job? *I'm* the one who broke that window, or are you the only one on the planet who hasn't seen the videos of it?"

"Calm down, Greg," Steele said, "before you pop a wheelie. And Odelia wasn't fired. We put her on administrative leave until we can get this sorted out and Kingston calmed down."

Greg glanced at me. "You didn't tell me that."

"You didn't give me a chance," I countered.

"We're hoping," Steele said, "that Kingston's anger will dissipate quickly and he'll move on to some other poor schmuck to terrorize. Maybe there's an orphanage he can burn down."

Poor schmuck? But this wasn't the time to quibble.

"And if he doesn't drop this stupidity?" Greg asked. "If he persists? What then?"

"We'll address that then," Steele answered. He paused. "Look, guys, Simon Tobin really likes Odelia, and she's done him a few personal favors. He's out of the country right now, but we've spoken to him. I know he'll go to bat for her. He doesn't care for Kingston one bit and has a lot of sway over Templin."

"You know, Mike," Greg said, "I'm not a lawyer, but I am an employer, and I'm not so sure the firm can treat Odelia like this. Maybe we should get some legal advice to be on the safe side."

A big sigh, thick as a plank, came from the phone. "As I told Odelia, the firm decided to put her on administrative leave, *with pay,* until they sort this out. The firm's board is going to review this and make a decision. In spite of the work Kingston brings to the firm, he's not well liked. Only Joe Templin seems to tolerate him."

"Birds of a feather," Greg snapped.

"Look," Steele said, "I'm in a tight spot here. I'm your friend, but I'm also a partner and have a duty to the firm. But, believe me, when Kingston first told Templin that he wanted you two sued, Templin immediately said he couldn't do it. Templin is not happy about this either. We just need to be patient and wait out Kingston's tantrum. He's nothing but a big baby. This thing with the dog showed his wife in a bad light, and all the videos on the net and TV didn't help. His pride is hurt, along with hers. They aren't people who take being humiliated lightly."

"We were in the right, Steele, and you know it," I said, adding to the discussion. "The cops on the scene knew it and the crowd knew it. So will a court unless Kingston pays off people."

"I really don't think it's going to come to that, Grey," Steele said. "So just relax for the next week or so, get your nails done, redecorate your house, have a spa day with Zee. It will all work out in the end."

Greg and I stared at each other in silence. We both trusted Steele but didn't trust the firm. Not that I thought my employer was dishonest; I didn't. But when faced with losing a major part of their income, I wasn't sure loyalty to an employee who'd only been with them a few years would rise to the top. My old firm had burned me even after decades of service. I could see that Greg was thinking the same. Behind his blue eyes the gears were working, grinding out our possibilities and our chances.

"Steele," Greg finally said into the phone, his voice tight as strings on a violin, "I know we can trust you to do the right thing, but I'm not so sure about the firm. We'll sit tight for now, but know that if Odelia's job or reputation is damaged in any way, we'll be lawyering up."

When the call ended, I took my seat on the other side of the desk next to Greg. He took my hand, a small gesture that made me feel better. We sat in silence a few minutes, mulling over the conversation with Steele. Finally, Greg said, "You know, sweetheart, we'd be fine financially if you didn't work there."

It was the conversation we'd had before when the rumor of T&T closing their Orange County office first raised its head. "I know," I answered, turning my face toward him. "But I like working, and I like my job."

"You'd find another or maybe even something else. You're really good at computer research. Maybe you could work as a contractor doing that, like that woman who used to do it for you and Steele." Greg squeezed my hand. "I'll bet even Steele and the firm would throw work your way."

It was another conversation we'd had that if I did lose my job, I could grab some freelance jobs doing research like Barbara Marracino. She and her husband Larry had done research for attorneys and other professionals, including for Steele. Larry had done field work as an investigator while Barbara did the computer work from their home. After Larry died, it became solely a computer research business. When Barbara retired, she'd given me her secret stash of investigative websites, which had proven very handy in several situations, both for the firm and for me personally. I was sure I could do it, but I really did enjoy going into the office and working with people directly. I wasn't sure I wanted to be stuck at home working by myself. I was about to say that to Greg when we heard two short, loud pops. Wainwright scrambled to his feet and started barking. If the door hadn't been shut, the animal would have dashed out.

Greg's head snapped toward the front of the shop. "Was that gunfire?"

We both turned to look out the window to the open work area of the shop. Chris had ducked behind the counter. Mr. Fujita was nowhere in sight. Everything seemed to stop, as if someone had hit a pause button. Seconds later something crashed into the shop's front door, and a man stumbled into the shop and dropped to the floor. Chris poked his head over the counter. "Greg!" he shouted as he got to his feet. "Quick!" Chris hopped over the gate, not bothering to unlatch it, forgetting his own safety.

Greg yanked open his office door and propelled himself quickly to the front with me on his heels. Wainwright got there ahead of us. Had he not been a senior canine, I'm sure he would have scaled the gate like Chris. We opened the gate and the three of us spilled into the customer area, Wainwright growling and barking. Greg quieted the dog and ordered him to his bed. Wainwright did as he was told but clearly wasn't happy about it. It was his job to protect Greg, and Greg was interfering with his job.

I looked down at the floor. Chris was crouched next to a large man clutching his gut. It was Burt Sandoval, and he was in bad shape.

Greg stabbed at the face of his cell phone, calling 911. A second later he was explaining the situation and requesting an ambulance, reciting the shop's address into the phone with clear-headed precision.

"We're getting help," Chris told Burt. "Hang in there."

In response, Burt moaned. It was then I

86

saw the blood. It was seeping out from under Burt's hand. He was wearing a black T-shirt, and the color of the shirt was doing its best to hide the growing stain spreading across Burt's ample middle. Chris saw it too and looked up at me, his small brown eyes wide as dinner plates in horror. I knelt down on the floor next to Burt.

"Burt," I said. "What happened? Can you tell me?" I was growing alarmed at his ashen skin and the way his eyes kept trying to roll up into his head. I softly touched the hand grabbing the wound site. Burt yelped, but the pain made him more alert.

"The ambulance is on its way," Greg announced. "We need to put something clean against the wound to stop the bleeding." We all looked around, but clean bandages weren't at hand. "Chris," Greg said, "run and get a new roll of paper towels." Chris took off toward the back of the shop. "Get a couple," Greg called out after him. "And shut my office door. I don't want Wainwright out here again. There will be too many people."

Chris shut Greg's door before dashing for the back. He returned quickly, ripping the wrapper off of a roll of paper towels as he ran, another roll tucked under one arm. He started to unroll several sheets, but Greg stopped him. "No, just use it whole," he instructed Chris. "Press it against the wound to stop the bleeding. Sheets will absorb too quickly and get soggy."

Chris knelt down next to Burt. We worked as a team. I gently raised Burt's hand off the wound. He cried out and grabbed for me with his free hand. I managed to get the bloody hand up enough for Chris to insert the thick, round roll of towels against the wound and gently press to stop the bleeding. We heard a siren approaching.

"Chris," Greg said, "go out and flag the ambulance down so they don't waste time looking for us. And try to push those people back." Still holding Burt's bloody hand, I pressed down gently on the towels while Chris darted out of the shop to greet the ambulance.

Outside, a couple of people from the other businesses in the strip mall were staring through the windows into the shop, watching us, buzzing low and excitedly. I heard more sirens. Gunshots weren't common in this area. It wasn't a big crowd, just a handful, but as with Maurice's rescue, I saw a couple of cell phones being held out to capture this horrific moment on video. Two times in three days. We were on our way to becoming YouTube stars, but it was not in a good way.

"Help is here, Burt," Greg said to the injured man. "Hang on."

Burt nodded feebly, then the hand in mine went slack.

SEVEN

Burt Sandoval didn't die on the threshold of Ocean Breeze Graphics. His life ended soon after arriving at the hospital, in spite of the efforts of the paramedics and ER staff. We were told he'd received not one but two gunshots to the gut, which matched the number of shots we had heard. It wasn't difficult for the Huntington Beach Police to locate Burt's vehicle. He'd parked his late-model silver pickup truck in front of Ocean Breeze. It was the only vehicle with its driver's door hanging open — the only vehicle with a blood trail leading from it to the shop's front door. From the blood, it looked like Burt had been shot just as he got out, then stumbled into the shop for help.

We were all grilled by detectives. So were the other shop owners and the few customers of those establishments who'd hung around to watch the excitement.

"You're the guy who saved the dog, aren't you?" the detective who talked to Greg and me asked after he'd gotten our names and other basic information, along with our report of the shooting. He'd identified himself as Detective Conrad Chapman. His partner was talking to Chris in the lunchroom. Chapman was short and wiry with pasty skin and pale red hair. He was what would be called a strawberry blond. His suit was slightly disheveled. We didn't catch his partner's name, but he was Latino, taller, and just as wrinkled. The heat wave was still beating Southern California into the pavement, and it was not weather to be out and about in while wearing a coat and tie.

"Yeah," Greg answered, "that was us."

"And you didn't see the shooting, right?" the detective asked, not for the first time.

"No," I answered. "Like we've already said, we were in here but only heard the shots."

We were back in Greg's office. Chapman and I sat in two chairs near Greg's desk. Wainwright was curled up asleep on his bed, tuckered out by all the excitement. When the police arrived, he'd nearly gone hoarse from barking until Greg calmed him down. The poor dog knew something bad was afoot. Chapman had pulled his chair up close to the desk to facilitate taking notes. We'd been going over everything in detail with him for about thirty minutes already. Greg wheeled to his mini fridge and pulled out two bottles of water. He placed one in front of Chapman, who nodded his thanks and stopped to twist the cap off and take a drink. Greg held the other out to me. "You want a cold one, sweetheart?"

I shook my head. I was clutching the water I'd opened earlier. "This is fine."

Greg twisted the top off the water he was holding and took his own thirsty drink. "Yes, we were in here when we heard it," he explained after he'd swallowed. "And we looked up just in time to see Chris — that's my manager — take a dive behind the counter." Greg and I knew the drill. The cops would ask the same questions over and over, interwoven with new queries, looking for inconsistencies and slivers of newly remembered observations in the account.

"And there were no customers in the place or other employees?" Chapman asked. This was a new question.

Greg shook his head. "There was one other employee working today. He was out making a delivery, then taking lunch. After the ambulance left, I called him and told him to go home. No sense him coming back to work with all this going on."

Chapman looked up. "We still might want to talk to him. What's his name?"

"Aziz Hajjar," Greg answered. "I have one other employee, but she's on vacation."

"No customers?"

"There was one when I came in," I offered. "I think Chris called him Mr. Fujita."

Greg nodded as he took another drink of water. "Mr. Fujita came in to have some flyers copied for his church. It was for a mailing, I think. A copy-and-fold job."

"He must have left right before it happened," I said. "Chris should know when he left, but he wasn't there when the shooting happened."

"This Fujita come in often?" Chapman asked.

Greg gave it some thought and nodded. "Off and on. He also has the menus for his restaurant done here when he updates them, but usually he brings in stuff for his church — sometimes him, sometimes his wife."

Chapman looked up from his notes. "Do you know where his restaurant is?"

"Yes," Greg answered. "It's called Golden Sun Sushi."

"You mean the little place painted bright yellow over on Goldenwest and Warner?"

Chapman asked. When Greg nodded, Chapman added, "I know it. My partner and I grab lunch there once in a while. They have great lunch specials."

Chapman jotted more notes, then looked up again. "And the victim, this Burt Sandoval, was he a regular customer?"

Both Greg and I shook our heads, but I let Greg answer. "Again, we'd never met Burt until last Saturday," Greg told Chapman. "He helped us rescue the dog in that parking lot."

"Marla Kingston's dog, wasn't it?" Chapman asked for clarification.

"Yes," Greg confirmed. "But he had disappeared from the crowd by the time the police showed up. Then today he called out of the blue and asked to meet me here at the shop."

Chapman's face was a blank canvas except for a flicker in his left eye. "If you didn't know him until last Saturday, how did he know where you worked?"

I took this question. "Greg was wearing a ball cap with the name of the shop on it Saturday, and one of the newscasts mentioned Ocean Breeze by name."

"But you didn't exchange contact information, email addresses, stuff like that?"

"We did with the cops on the scene, but

with Burt only our names," I answered. I paused, then remembered something. "But Burt was on the videos people shot of us on Saturday. You know, the ones that were all over YouTube and the news. At least he was until the police arrived."

Chapman absorbed the information. I could see from his face that it was being digested and sorted in his brain. "Why did he want to see you today?" he asked Greg.

Greg shrugged. "I have no idea. He just called and asked if I'd be around, then said he'd be here in about an hour. In the meantime, Odelia surprised me and dropped in."

This time Chapman zoomed in on me, sniffing out the possibility of new information. "You said you work in a law firm, is that right, Ms. Grey?"

"Yes, over by South Coast Plaza," I replied.

"That's a good drive on a weekday. Do you often drop in on your husband in the middle of the work day?"

"Not often," I said, wondering how much to tell the detective. My being put on leave was none of his business, but it did have something to do with the Kingstons and therefore, in a roundabout way, to Burt Sandoval. I glanced over at Greg, who was watching me. "I had this afternoon off and decided to see if Greg had had lunch yet." I couldn't tell if Chapman bought that or thought there was more to the story. He was more difficult to read than a Chinese newspaper.

"We should tell him, Odelia," Greg said. "Just in case." I fidgeted in my seat.

"I'm all ears, folks," Chapman said, leaning back in his chair with his bottle of water as if settling in for a good campfire yarn.

Seeing how uncomfortable I was, Greg took the reins. "My wife was put on administrative leave today because Kelton Kingston threatened her job after what happened on Saturday."

Chapman straightened up, looking at me with more interest. "You work for Kingston?"

I shook my head, but it was Greg who answered. "No, she doesn't, but he's a client of her firm. First he wanted to sue us, but when he found out she worked for his lawyers, he insisted that they fire her."

"And they did?" Chapman sounded surprised.

"No," I said. "They put me on paid leave until they could sort this all out. They're hoping Kingston will cool down and forget about me."

Chapman put down his water and picked up his pen, hovering it over his notes again. He stabbed at the paper a few times before saying, "And who can verify this?"

"Michael Steele," Greg told him. "He's one of the partners and Odelia's supervisor." Greg picked up his phone, tapped the face, then turned it toward Chapman. "You can reach him at this number. We talked to him just before the shooting." Chapman wrote down the information.

I looked out the window of Greg's office. I could see crime-scene workers gathering evidence around the shop's threshold and in the parking lot. Yellow crime-scene tape cordoned off the parking lot. I also spotted a couple of news vans. *Great. We'd be on the news again.*

I looked back at Chapman. "You don't think this had anything to do with Kingston, do you?"

"Who knows," Chapman said. He closed his notebook. "Could be a number of things totally unrelated to this past Saturday. Could be something only Sandoval was involved with — someone with a grudge who followed him here. But we can't ignore that you were threatened and Sandoval shot on the same day. Maybe Kingston found out who he was and threatened him too.

Maybe Sandoval wanted to warn you." He looked at Greg. "Did Sandoval sound anxious or upset when he called you today?"

Greg dug back in his recent memory. "Not that I could tell. In fact, he sounded kind of casual, like if I'd said I was too busy to see him, he'd have been okay with it."

This wasn't making sense to me. "Kelton Kingston is hardly citizen of the month, but do you really think he'd kill someone over his wife's dog? Seems like overkill, doesn't it?" Greg shot me a judgy look at my questionable choice of words.

"It does on the face of it." Chapman stood up, finished with the questioning. "But people kill for the oddest reasons, and Kingston was sure ready enough to bury you and your career over the dog, wasn't he?"

EIGHT

After the cops left, Greg told Chris to shut everything down; they were closing for the day. Chris was clearly happy to comply. He'd never seen a man who'd been shot before, and it had shaken him to his core. Greg assured him that everything would be back to normal in the morning. Chris didn't look so sure about that, and neither was I, but he went about the business of turning off the equipment to close down.

Greg said goodbye to me at the door. The parking lot was still cordoned off, but the police were letting people remove their cars now. "I'll be right behind you, sweetheart," Greg said. "When I get home, let's go out to eat. We'll have an early dinner since neither of us have had lunch."

My stomach was growling, reminding me that he was correct, but my head was on Burt Sandoval. Why would he want to speak to Greg? Why would someone shoot him?

Had it been something only involving him or was it connected to Saturday? Maybe he was mixed up with unsavory characters who had followed him here and saw an opportunity to take him out. Did he have a record? Was that why he'd left the scene on Saturday when the police arrived?

"Does that sound good to you, Odelia?" Greg asked, his voice breaking through my thoughts. "Or would you prefer I bring home Chinese food?"

I shook off the sticky web of questions in my head to answer. "Let's do Chinese," I told him. "I'd rather stay in."

"You got it," he said with a tired smile. He lifted his chin up, and I bent and kissed him. It made me feel a bit better. Whatever was going on, Greg and I would see it through.

"Do you want me to take Wainwright?" I asked. "That way he won't have to sit in the hot van when you go in for the Chinese food."

"Good idea." Greg called to Wainwright. The old dog trotted out of the office to the front of the shop.

"Come on, boy," I told the animal. "You're going home with me." Wainwright looked reluctant. It wasn't that he didn't trust my driving, but he hated to be away from Greg unless I was taking him on a long walk. I patted my leg. "Come on, Wainwright. Time to go home." This time the dog wagged his tail and followed me out the door. It was still too hot for a walk, but maybe later I'd take him down to the beach a few blocks from our home. We usually took our walk in the morning, but this morning Greg had gone to work earlier than usual.

When I got home I checked on Muffin and Dumpster, then thought about calling Mom. The last thing I wanted was for her to accuse us of having "fun" without her when she saw tonight's news. But then I thought twice about the call. Mom was out of town, and this probably wouldn't go beyond local news. We could bring her up to speed once she got home and this had blown over.

I'd washed a load of towels in the morning and thrown them in the dryer just before leaving for work. The washer and dryer were located in a closet with folding doors at the end of the hallway leading to the guest room. I scooped the dry towels into a plastic clothes basket and carried it to the living room. The towels needed folding, but I was tackling the chore more to keep busy until Greg got home. After folding one bath towel, I aimed the remote at the big TV on the wall opposite the sofa and searched for news. It was still a little early for the local news to start, and after finding none, I turned off the TV and turned on some music. In the meantime, Muffin had hopped into the clothes basket and made a nest in the clean towels. I looked down at the little cat. "Sorry," I apologized as I pulled another towel out, dislodging her, "but unless you're folding these suckers, you're in the way." She gave me her disgruntled meow and left the basket in search of more quiet sleeping quarters.

I was putting the folded towels away when my cell phone rang. Grabbing it off the counter, I saw from the display that it was Mom. She'd texted me when they'd arrived in Branson yesterday, and I'd heard nothing since. No news with her usually meant good news. It was impossible that she had heard about Burt's murder since it hadn't even hit our news yet. "Hi, Mom," I answered, trying to keep my voice normal. "How's the trip going?"

"Pretty good," she answered. "Alma got hives last night at dinner, and one of the dancers at a show this afternoon tripped and nearly fell off the stage."

"Is Alma okay?" I asked, concerned about the plump elderly woman who'd recently moved into Seaside.

"Yeah, she's fine. She had some meds with her for it, and today she was right as rain." There was a pause. "The real question is how are you and Greg doing?"

"We're fine," I lied. Well, it wasn't really a lie. Greg and I were okay physically, just shaken to our marrow, and I was on administrative leave, but there was no way Mom would know about that.

"Yeah, really?" Mom prodded. "Then why aren't you at work today?"

Everyone knows that mothers have eyes in the backs of their heads, but from nearly two thousand miles away? I held the phone out in front of me and stared at it. Mom is the one who should go into the research business, not me. "I took a half day off," I said, returning the phone to my ear. I paused briefly, then added, "Do you have a tracker on me or something?"

"No need," she scoffed, "not when all your shenanigans are splashed all over the internet."

"I have no idea what you're talking about," I insisted.

"You never were a good liar, Odelia."

"The thing with the Kingstons will blow over in time, Mom." *At least I hoped it would.* "You don't need to worry about that."

"I'm not talking about that," Mom said with impatience. "Who's the dead guy at Greg's work?"

I nearly dropped the phone. "You know about that? It just happened, Mom. Are you psychic or something?"

"Turn on your computer and look up the Human Stain on YouTube. She has a video of it already posted." Mom paused. "I'm looking at it right now. I'm telling you, she has a thing for Greg. She's stalking him or something."

The hair on my arms stood straight up. "Hold on, let me grab my laptop." My laptop was in the bedroom, where I'd left it recharging last night. I dashed in, nearly tripping over Muffin in the process, snagged it, and brought it out to the kitchen table. Quickly, I fired it up, impatient with the time it was taking. I put Mom on speaker and set the phone on the table.

"So who's the dead guy?" Mom asked again while my computer went through its startup routine. "At first I was so worried it might be Greg, but I knew you'd call me if something happened to him."

"You got that right, Mom," I assured her. "It was Burt Sandoval." I drummed my fingers on the table with impatience. "The guy who helped us rescue the dog on Saturday."

"Really?" Mom asked with surprise.

"Yes, really." I filled her in on what we knew about the shooting, which wasn't much. "I'm thinking maybe this Holly person is following him and not Greg." Finally, my laptop was fired up and YouTube was on the screen. I went to the channel for the Human Stain and clicked on her latest video. In short order I was watching police cars and an ambulance in front of Ocean Breeze. Cops were working to set up crime tape and interviewing bystanders.

"But in her other video she was focused on Greg," Mom said.

"True, but maybe that was to throw off anyone looking at the video. You know, make it look like she was fixated on Greg when she was really watching Burt."

"Huh," Mom grunted. "I hadn't thought of that, but you may be right."

"Whoever took this must have been standing in front of the payday loan place across the street," I said. The video continued chronicling the activities, including the eventual hefting of the gurney holding Burt into the ambulance and its departure. "How long does this go on?"

"Not much longer," Mom replied. "It

ends right after they cart him away."

Something didn't jive. I stared at the screen. Another video was queued to start right after the last one. It was a rock music video. I paused it and tried to shake loose what was not fitting. Then it hit me. "Mom," I said into the phone, "when Burt was taken away by the ambulance, he was still alive. He died at the hospital. So how did you know he was dead?"

"It says so in the description of the video."

I punched some keys. The rock music video disappeared and was replaced by the one I'd just watched. Beneath it the description read: *Shooting in Huntington Beach 6/17/17. Victim did not make it.* There were a couple of comments from viewers, mostly calls for gun control and/or a stop to violence. Some applauded her journaling of the reality of the streets. There was one comment that even suggested she was the shooter for the purpose of getting ratings. I took note of the person making the comment. It was someone with a handle of Dire Consequences.

The Human Stain. Dire Consequences. Both were pretty negative in their tone. I was betting, like Holly, Dire Consequences was also young. Were they really this jaded? Disappointed in the world in general or just trying to get attention? For being such a recent post, the video had an amazing amount of comments already. Most of the commenters used what appeared to be real names with real profile photos, though Dire Consequences had used a depiction of the grim reaper as his profile pic. But whatever the tone of the comments or who made them, Holly did not reply to any of them.

"Do you see the description, Odelia?" Mom asked.

"Yes, I see it. I was reading some of the comments. That one from Dire Consequences was pretty cold."

"He's kind of a stinker," Mom said. "He's a video journalist like the Human Stain, but he's very negative and his videos are meant to shock, unlike hers, which show both the good and the bad of the world around us."

I leaned back against my chair, wanting to refocus on my little part of the planet instead of the overall human condition. "At least this video didn't catch Greg or me on tape."

"Yeah," Mom said, her voice trailing off into silence, like she'd run out of steam.

"Mom, you still there?"

"Just thinking," she replied, "about what you just said. You and Greg aren't in this video. Was she waiting across the street to

107

catch a glimpse of Greg or was she really following poor Burt? I wish we could see the footage filmed before this piece."

Mom was right. Holly could have been standing across the street for either reason. I was twisting a clump of hair around a finger, something I did when I was nervous or thinking, just as Greg ran a hand through his hair for the same reason. I tucked the hair behind an ear, knowing what I needed to do. "I think Greg and I should tell the police about this video," I said to Mom. "If there was earlier footage, it might contain something the police can use to catch Burt's killer."

"It also wouldn't hurt to tell them just in case this Holly person is stalking Greg. You can't be too careful these days."

I shivered at the thought of my husband having a stalker. "You're right, Mom. I'll talk to Greg as soon as he gets home." Wainwright ran to the back door, causing me to jump, as if a stalker were breaking in right that minute. Wainwright's tail was wagging excitedly and he was whining instead of barking, his wet nose pressed against the glass of the slider. Greg was home.

NINE

I ended the call with Mom and went out to help Greg. As soon as I opened the back slider, the heat hit me like a slap. I took the Chinese food from him and carried it into the kitchen while Greg said hello to Wainwright. The dog stood in front of Greg, holding a knotted piece of rag in his mouth. It was one of the dog's favorite toys. Wainwright was far from dumb. He knew Greg couldn't resist his big brown hopeful eyes. Greg turned and went back outside, a happy dog behind him. When they both came back into the house, Wainwright went straight to his water dish and Greg straight for a cold beer. Just a few minutes of playing in the oppressive heat had done them both in.

I hadn't done anything with the food except to set it on the counter before heading back to the table and my laptop. After his first long gulp of beer, Greg asked, "Aren't you hungry, sweetheart?"

"I am, but I want you to see this first." He rolled over to the table and I turned the laptop so that we both had a good view of the screen. "After you watch this, we can discuss what to do about it over dinner."

"That's the Human Stain woman," he noted as he grabbed some napkins from a dispenser on the table and mopped sweat from his forehead. "What's she up to now?"

"Just watch," I told him as I hit the play button.

Together we watched. At first, I don't think it registered with Greg what we were looking at, but soon I heard a sharp intake of breath, followed by "Hey, that's the shop!"

"That it is," I confirmed, "and from today, while we were both inside watching Burt Sandoval die."

When we got to the end of the video, Greg replayed it two more times. "From the angle, she had to be standing in front of the payday loan place," he said, turning to me.

"That's what I think too." I got up and pulled two plates from the cupboard and two forks and a couple of serving spoons from the cutlery drawer. Usually we eat Chinese food with chopsticks, but I wasn't sure we had the focus for it tonight.

"How did you find this?" he asked.

I placed the plates and utensils on the far end of the table from the laptop. "Mom called right before you got home. She subscribes to the Human Stain, and the link to this video showed up in her email a short while ago." I began taking the food from the plastic bags and setting the dishes on the table. Greg had gotten our usual favorites: pork fried rice, Mongolian beef, spicy eggplant, and shrimp with vegetables. We always got plenty because we both loved leftovers. I placed the containers on the table and stuck a serving spoon in each.

"Dinner is served," I announced as I grabbed a handful of napkins and put a couple next to each plate. "Would you also like water or iced tea with dinner?"

With his eyes still glued to the laptop, where he was once again viewing the video, Greg waved the hand holding the beer, indicating that was all he needed for now. I went to the fridge and poured myself a tall glass of iced tea. I took a seat at the table and started spooning eggplant onto both our plates. "We have to discuss what to do about this," I told Greg. Muffin had come out of one of her secret napping spots and was begging at my feet. I stuck a finger into the shrimp sauce and held it down toward her. She sniffed it a few times before turning her back, declaring it inedible. Muffin did this at every meal. It wasn't that she wanted what we were eating; she seldom did. She was just nosy and wanted to know what it was. Greg hated when she did it. Wainwright had better manners. He only begged when Greg wasn't home because he knew I was a soft touch. The dog was in his bed, watching everything. He wouldn't have turned his back on what I was offering. He would have licked it off my finger and right up to my elbow.

Greg finally turned from the laptop and repositioned his wheelchair in front of his plate. I had already dished a bit of everything out for both of us. He picked up his fork, not even noticing the missing chopsticks, and held it aloft, suspended like he was a wax figurine cast in an eating pose.

"What?" I asked him. "Did I forget something?"

He lowered his fork, setting it down on his plate. "I was just wondering, was she following me or Burt?" he asked.

"That's what Mom and I discussed," I told him. I took a bite of the eggplant. Even lukewarm it was delicious. I swallowed and dug into the Mongolian beef. I hadn't realized how hungry I was until I'd tasted the first few bites. Now I wanted to tunnel through everything on my plate. Greg didn't say another word but picked up his fork again and was tackling his food. Once each of us reached a point of slowing down, we got back to the discussion.

"So you and Grace are both wondering if the Human Stain was following Burt and not me?" Greg asked between a couple of small sips of beer.

I nodded and spooned more shrimp onto my plate. "If she was following you, wouldn't there be more videos of you? She seemed fixated on Burt's situation today. The video ends right after the ambulance leaves." I glanced over at my husband. "Why? Are you disappointed that you might not be the object of her affection?"

He laughed. "No, sweetheart. The last thing I need is a stalker. But as for the video, who knows what she has that hasn't been uploaded? Depending on how long she was standing there, she might even have recorded the shooting."

"That's also what Mom and I discussed — that and calling the police."

Greg tipped his beer back and drained it into his mouth. "Yeah," he said when he was done. "We need to contact Detective Chapman."

"How about the Long Beach Police too?"

I asked. "If she got Maurice's rescue on tape, she might have earlier footage of Burt on that day too."

"Good thinking," Greg agreed. "And how did she get the news of Burt's death so quickly? Did she call the hospital? Follow the ambulance? I don't think the hospital would have given out information like that, especially since it concerns a murder."

"I wondered the same thing," I said between bites. "It hadn't even made the news by the time she'd posted her video."

Greg took the rest of the shrimp and scooped it onto his plate. It was always the first dish to go. After shoveling a heavy forkful into his mouth, chewing, and swallowing, he asked, "Do you think maybe Marigold could have something on her? After all, don't you have to put in some personal information when you set up a YouTube channel?"

Marigold is a magic search engine available only by subscription, and even then only to those who know about it. It doesn't exactly operate in the deep dark web where nefarious activities of all kinds take place, but it's not crawling on the surface with banners and ads announcing its presence. You have to be referred to it by another user to even know it's there. It can pull information on anyone or any company that already has a presence. If someone is totally off the grid, living under an assumed name and not using day-to-day things such as credit cards or a registered cell phone, I doubt much would be found. When Marigold generates a report, it seems to pull information from public records that are not easily attainable and certainly not conveniently located in one spot. And some of it may not be public but gathered from servers that the gremlins who operate Marigold have accessed, legally or illegally. It was the most valuable search site that Barbara, the contract researcher, had given me access to when she retired.

"You're right," I said. "That information could be blocked from the public but might be required and stored in the company's records." I took a drink of tea. "All we know about the Human Stain is that her name is Holly. No last name or birthdate or even city," I told Greg, "but it might be worth a try." I got up and moved to the chair in front of my laptop.

"Finish your dinner, sweetheart," Greg told me. "It can wait a few minutes. So can calling the police."

"True, but sometimes the Marigold searches can take up to an hour or more, depending on the availability of the information. I want to at least get it started." I quickly accessed the site and started a search for the Human Stain. I put California in for location and checked female for gender. Usually you would only tag gender for searches on individuals, but I thought I'd give it a try since she used the Human Stain as an online moniker. Done with that, I scooted back to my place to finish my meal. "Besides, I want to know as much as possible about this person before we call the police. If the report comes back with nothing, we're in the same spot we are now. If it reveals something, we can be armed with that."

Greg chuckled. "And how are you going to explain how we know what we know if Marigold does provide more info?"

I had just speared a piece of Mongolian beef but hadn't gotten it into my mouth when his words stopped me. It was a delicate path we'd walked before. I don't know if Marigold is legal or not, but I did know that it was a lot like Fight Club or Las Vegas. What happened in Marigold stayed in Marigold.

"We don't have to share everything we learn, if anything," I told him and popped the juicy savory beef into my mouth.

"True, but if she knows something about

Burt's murder, then we need to be honest with the cops so they can find the shooter."

"There's one comment on the video that asks if she's the murderer," I noted.

"What?" Greg asked in surprise. "You're kidding."

"Nope. He suggests she did it for ratings. Mom says the person who posted that isn't very nice and his videos are pretty dark and ugly. Could he be saying that to throw dirt on Holly?" I paused, then voiced the next thought in my head. "Or do you really think someone, not necessarily her, could do something evil for ratings?"

Finished with his food, Greg pushed his plate back. "Chris and I were talking about this recently, long before we knew about the Human Stain. He's helping one of his friends with his YouTube channel. It's a cooking channel. It's a huge business these days, just like TV."

"Really?" I asked with surprise. "I mean, I know those videos are popular and some people doing them are becoming celebrities, but a business?"

"You bet a business. A lot of those YouTubers are making a living doing those videos. The more subscribers you have, the more money you can make from sponsors and other contributions. Chris is very interested in working on the production end of his friend's channel. It's like filming a TV show for many of those people, complete with lighting and cameras. The big ones are not just sitting in front of a webcam talking, although some make videos with selfie sticks and the like. It just depends on your audience."

"Huh. Where have I been?" I asked, more to myself. Because of my job I'm used to using business technology, but a lot of the new, popular stuff was passing me by like a too-crowded bus at rush hour.

"Getting older, sweetheart, just like me," Greg laughed. "Not all the YouTube stars are young, but most of them are. They've tapped into a whole new way of getting their products, services, and themselves out there without going through traditional routes. And I say, good for them."

"Do you think Holly, the Human Stain, is earning a living from this?" I asked.

Greg loaded his plate and mine onto his lap and pushed back from the table. "Who knows, but I'll bet she's making something with all those followers." He rolled over to the sink and started rinsing the plates to put into the dishwasher.

"Do you think she has other videos with you in them?" I asked as I ferried the uneaten food to the kitchen and started packing it up for the fridge.

Greg shrugged. "I doubt it. Grace subscribes to her channel, and I think she would have noticed if I showed up in any before now, don't you? Your mother doesn't miss much."

I nodded. The bus might be passing me by, but Mom was riding it right up front. Once her granddaughter Lorraine had set her up with an iPad, there was no stopping Mom, and she eagerly explored and learned about the internet and its offerings. "Yes, that's true. But maybe we need to look through some of them to see if Burt shows up in any others, especially the more recent ones."

Now it was his turn to nod. "Now that's a very good idea." After putting the dishes in the dishwasher, Greg dried his hands and rolled over to my laptop. "We can do it now, while we wait for Marigold."

I refreshed my iced tea, and this time Greg indicated he wanted one. I brought both glasses over to the table and settled in to watch a lot of videos. All that was missing was some popcorn.

Starting with the video of the dog rescue, we watched it again, taking note that Burt was on it but not there later, after the police arrived. Greg rolled over to the counter, where he picked up a notepad and pen we kept there for messages and grocery lists. First he wrote down the date of the video showing Maurice's rescue, followed by a couple of notes about Burt not being in the video once the police got there. I was glad Greg was doing the note taking since his handwriting was much better than mine.

We moved backwards through the Human Stain's video library. Between the video taken today and the one with the dog was a short piece filming a mural being created at a small public park in Westminster by a local artist. The video just before the one with the dog chronicled a peaceful march by food service workers, mostly Latinos, that moved slowly up Wilshire Boulevard. I remembered hearing about the march on the news. They were protesting low wages and lack of benefits. The way the video was shot, it looked like Holly was on the edge of it, then moved into the march itself, following the wave of humanity up the busy corridor. The audio recorded a continuous chant by the marchers. There was no sign of either Burt or Greg, though I didn't expect to see Greg in these other videos.

Videos weren't posted every day, just a couple times a week, and seemed well edited, catching events of everyday life in Southern California, both political and cultural. There was a short series on the homeless in Orange and San Diego Counties, spotlighting a serious problem that people usually connect only with Los Angeles County. We scrolled backwards, viewing about a dozen videos, and found no sign of either Greg or Burt on any of them. My senses were almost dulled when something caught my eye.

"Did you see that?" I asked Greg.

"That?" he said, pointing at the screen. "It's another rally or protest."

"Yes," I said, pausing the video. "But pay attention to what the video is about." I moved the slider on the video to backtrack about a minute, then hit continue.

In silence we both watched, eyes glued to the action on the screen. I hovered the mouse over the pause button, just waiting to capture what I had seen or thought I had seen. Maybe I was seeing something that wasn't there, desperate to find something — anything — that could be a link. "There!" I said, stopping the action. "Right there, on the stage."

Greg studied the screen, first without his reading glasses, then with them, finally deciding without gave him a better view. "Is that Kelton Kingston?" he asked.

"I think so," I said. "In fact, I'm sure of it. The title of this video is *Fighting the Rape of Local Wetlands.* Remember several months ago when Kingston Industries was trying to get permits to develop some of the wetlands that had dried up in the drought?"

"Yes, I do. It was on the news, then quieted down," Greg said. "Did he ever get the permit? I don't remember."

I shook my head. "No, he didn't." What I didn't add was that Kingston had lost his bid for the permit in spite of my firm's best efforts to obtain it for him. Most of the work had been handled in the LA office, but Steele had been fuming about it. He may seem like a money-focused capitalist on the outside, but under Steele's Armani suits beats the heart of an environmentalist. "Before it was denied he held a press conference, trying to sell the idea to the general public to calm down the protests. Trying to explain why it would be a good thing to develop that land."

"So he was pissing on them and calling it rain," Greg said with a glance my way.

"Basically, yes." I stabbed at the screen of my laptop. "I think this was that press conference. See the press and cameras closer to the stage, with the protesters in the back? And on the stage next to him is his wife, Marla." The power couple stood next to each other, Marla slightly behind Kingston. Kingston was a tall, slender man with thick, dark hair and a jutting chin. Since he was pushing seventy, I was pretty sure his hair was either a dye job or a weave.

"Yeah," Greg said, "I can see it now that I know what I'm looking for."

I looked at Greg. "Maybe Holly wasn't following you or Burt. Maybe she was following Marla Kingston."

Greg leaned back in his wheelchair to give the matter some thought. "But why Marla and not Kingston himself?"

I shrugged. "Who knows?"

"And if she was following Marla on Saturday, why was she surveilling the shop today?"

Another shrug from me.

We scrolled through a dozen more videos and found a couple more with the Kingstons in them. Mostly it focused on Marla Kingston, but sometimes they were together at an event. All of the videos had a barely veiled political comment in the title.

"Is she stalking the Kingstons?" I suggested.

"I'm not sure a few videos of public personalities like this would be considered stalking," Greg said. "I think it would depend on what else she has that she hasn't published online. This looks more like she's using them to make a point, like making them the poster kids for greed, which isn't that far from the truth."

A notice of an incoming email popped up in the lower-right corner of the screen. I clicked over to it and saw it was from Marigold with my report on the Human Stain.

"Okay, the report's in," I said to Greg as I opened the attachment to the email. "Let's see if there's anything worth while."

The report was short. Very short. The Human Stain was listed as a business with a P.O. Box in Long Beach. "Her mailing address is in Long Beach," I pointed out. "So she can't live too far from us, at least not in Ventura or Van Nuys. And there's no photo. Sometimes Marigold will provide a photo."

"Good location to work from since she seems to cover LA, Orange, and San Diego counties in her videos," Greg said. "Anything else?"

"The report says it's a business and the owner's name is Holly West." I sighed. I'd never seen such a short Marigold report. "If you remember, on YouTube there is a message button where you can send her a message, but at least here we have a Gmail account. No phone number, cell or otherwise."

"So what now?" Greg asked. "Should we send her an email and ask her what in the hell she's doing?"

"Not yet," I said. "Let's run a search for Holly West in Los Angeles County."

"Not Long Beach?" Greg asked.

"Just because she has a mailing address in Long Beach doesn't mean she lives there," I told him. "I'd prefer to cast a wider net."

He nodded in agreement. "See, sweetheart, you're good at this. You could find work researching if you don't go back to the firm."

I started a new search, indicating Los Angeles County as the location, and sent it off. Finished, I stretched and purged my mind about the possibility of not returning to T&T, at least for the time being. "And now we wait."

"That's not the fun part," Greg said as he went to the cupboard where we kept the animals' food. He gave Wainwright his dinner and dished some cat kibble out for Muffin. "Come here, you little mooch," he said to the cat. While Wainwright dug right in, the cat sauntered over to her bowl like it was beneath her. "You better hurry," Greg told her, "or Wainwright will gobble up his *and* yours."

Years ago, before I met Greg and we adopted Muffin, I had a surly cat named Seamus. I kept kibble out for him all day and he grazed at will. Once we moved in with Wainwright and Greg, I had to feed Seamus on a schedule with the dog or put his dish on the counter. If I didn't, the dog would devour both dishes. Seamus didn't like being on a schedule, but it was either that or starve. He learned to eat all his breakfast and dinner when served. We were already on that schedule when Muffin came to live with us.

While Greg was doing pet duty our doorbell rang. Wainwright stopped eating and ran for the door, barking. When he got to the door the barking turned to whining; there was someone he knew on the other side. I pulled open the door to find Dev Frye.

"Surprise," Dev said in his gravelly voice. He was dressed casually in a knit shirt and jeans. Dev is a really big man. Not fat but tall and solid like a brick building. I threw myself into his arms for a hug while Wainwright danced around his legs.

"Let the man get in the door, Odelia," Greg said, laughing. He had wheeled up to

126

the door and was awaiting his turn to greet our friend.

"Yes," I said, "come on in where it's cool." I backed away, and Dev stepped into our home and pumped Greg's outstretched hand with gusto. I closed the door and ushered everyone back to the dining area as I offered Dev something cool to drink. He and Greg both took a cold beer.

"What a nice surprise," Greg said. "Why didn't you tell us you were going to be in town for a visit?"

"Did Bev come with you?" I asked as I handed each man a cold brew. I went back to refresh my iced tea.

Dev took a swig from the bottle. "Bev didn't come with me," he answered. "I moved back."

Greg and I exchanged wide-eyed looks. Beverly was a doll, but their relationship wasn't always stable. She hated Dev being a cop and he hated not being one. After he retired from the force, he'd had a rough time finding interesting work up in Portland.

"Okay," Dev said, "since I can hear the big question in your silence, I'll skip the formalities. Bev and I broke up again, but this time it's for good. I just didn't like living in Portland."

"Hey, man," Greg said, "we're happy to

have you back, no matter what the reason, but we're sorry about Bev."

"Thanks," Dev said. "Me too."

"What about your house?" I asked, knowing Dev had rented out his home when he left town.

"My renters left in June, right after school was out, so I told my daughter not to lease it again, that I was probably coming home. I got back last weekend to find she'd cleaned it and had it painted, and all my furniture that was in storage was moved back in."

"Sounds like she was also happy to have you back," I said with a smile.

"Yeah, her husband and kids too," Dev said with a chuckle. "It's nice to be missed." He took another drink.

"Are you going to try to get back into police work?" Greg asked.

"Not really. I'm a bit long in the tooth for that, but I have some interesting options, one of which is to go into a PI partnership with a former cop from LA who has been gumshoeing it since he retired. His name's Jeremiah Jones. We've been kicking around pooling our resources and putting out a shingle together. I'd cover Orange County and he'd cover Los Angeles. We'd handle big cases together."

"That sounds perfect," Greg said with enthusiasm.

"Well, nothing's finalized yet," Dev told us. "We're going to meet up next week to hammer out some details and see if a partnership makes sense." He paused. "I just came from having coffee with Andrea Fehring. I wanted to run the idea past her since she has a good feel for things like this."

"And what did Andrea say?" I asked. I had taken the chair in front of the laptop and kept my eye on the screen for the search on Holly West.

"She's all for it. She says Jeremiah's a good man with a solid reputation, a widower like me." He grinned. "Quirky, she said, like me. She thinks we'd make a good team."

"Fehring actually called you *quirky*?" Greg asked with a chuckle.

"That she did." Dev took another drink from his beer. He leveled his blue eyes at the two of us but remained silent.

"What are your other options?" I prodded.

"Well," Dev began, then paused. I could tell he was weighing his words. "Well, let's just say when I told Clark I was returning to California, a friend of his got in touch with me and offered me an opportunity." Another pause. "Or should I say a friend of yours?" He winked at me.

"Are you saying that Willie Proctor offered you a job?" Greg asked, his eyebrows arched high in surprise.

As for me, my mouth dropped to my knees. Willie was a friend, yes, but he was also a felon on the run. My brother Clark, also a former cop, worked indirectly for Willie in one of his legitimate businesses that on the surface had no connection to Willie. Clark assured us that all of Willie's businesses now were legal, even if he wasn't. Years before Willie had embezzled money from an investment company he owned, leaving his clients high and dry and broke. He's since paid back all the money, but he's still a wanted man, living in the shadows. We see Willie and his wife, Sybil, from time to time, and he often comes to our aid with his interesting connections. He's like Batman but with the feds after him.

"The man himself called me," Dev told us. "Said he could use someone like me in his organization. Swore it was totally on the up-and-up. Said I'd work with Clark in security."

"And?" I asked as the suspense made my heart flutter. In spite of my great affection for Willie, I wasn't sure I wanted Dev working for him. I worried enough about Clark, but Clark had flirted with the dark side of legality before, when he was a cop. To my knowledge, Dev was a total straight arrow. He might be more flexible now that he didn't have a badge, but I didn't think he'd be as flexible with the law as Willie might need. "What did you say?" I asked.

Dev laughed. "Calm down, Odelia. I told him I'd think about it but that plan A was going into business with Jeremiah. Willie said to give him a call; a job would always be waiting for me."

"That sounds like Willie," Greg said with a grin. "He takes care of the people he likes and respects."

Dev turned the bottle in his hands around several times. "Now, back to Andrea. She told me you two are up to your asses in crap again."

"None of this is our fault," I said, my jaw set.

"It never is, is it?" Dev said rather than asked.

"Not true, sweetheart," Greg said, correcting me. "I did break the glass on Marla Kingston's car."

"But what about the dead guy at your shop, Greg?" Dev asked. "How is that fitting in?"

"You already know about that?" I asked with surprise. Was everything instant knowledge these days?

"Andrea told me about both," Dev answered. When we remained silent, Dev added, "You didn't think a murder in Huntington Beach with the shooter still at large would go unnoticed by other local forces, did you?"

Greg and I exchanged glances, then Greg turned to Dev. "Got a little time on your hands right now?"

Dev raised his beer bottle in our direction. "I'm retired. I've got a beer, and it's cool in here. I've got nothing but time."

"This might take a while. Are you hungry?" I asked. "We just finished Chinese food, but there's plenty left." I got up from the table. "I can heat it up for you."

"Sure, but don't bother heating it up," Dev said. "Just give me a carton and a fork and I'm good. That's how I eat leftover Chinese at home." When he caught my doubtful look, he added, "Seriously. Just the food and a fork, Odelia."

Greg laughed. "That's how we usually eat leftovers here too."

"Yes," I agreed, "but Dev's company."

"I'm hardly company." He got up from the table. "But I am going to use your guest bath." He started down the hall while I pulled out the leftover Chinese food and a fork.

When Dev returned, he said, "What's with the duck in your tub?"

"I won him in a poker game," Greg said proudly. "His name's Dumpster."

"We're holding onto him for a few days," I quickly added, "then he's going to live with a friend who has lots of other animals."

"Seems about right for you two," Dev said as he retook his seat at the table. He picked up the fork, opened the closest carton, then stopped. "This is kind of how we met, isn't it? The three of us discussing a case over Chinese food. It was at Odelia's condo in Costa Mesa, wasn't it?"

Greg and I looked at each other, both of us remembering back many years. The case was the murder of my friend Sophie London. I was the executor of Sophie's estate, Greg was a witness to her death, and Dev was the investigator. Greg and I didn't believe it was suicide, as initially determined, and had joined forces to lay out our suspicions to Dev over a meal of Chinese takeout. Before her death none of us had known each other. Now I was married to Greg, the condo was long sold, and Dev was an important part of our lives.

"Seems like yesterday," Greg said. "One

of the saddest and happiest moments in my life." Greg took my hand and squeezed it as I squeezed back tears.

TEN

While Dev ate, we told him all about the Kingstons and Burt, my leave from T&T, and our concerns about Holly West.

"So you're not sure who this West woman is following, if anyone?" Dev asked as he wiped his mouth with a napkin.

"No," I told him. "We haven't gone through all of her videos, but it looks like there are more starring the Kingstons than of Burt or Greg. So far we've only seen Greg in one of them."

"We're looking into Holly West a little more before calling the police," Greg told him. "But we'll definitely give them a call tomorrow."

"Are you using that magic search engine you have?" Dev asked me.

I nodded.

He chuckled. If you didn't know Dev, you'd think he was clearing his throat. "I hope when I go into the PI biz you'll share that source with me."

"I'm pretty sure Clark knows about it too," I said. "I think Willie's people use it sometimes, along with their other mysterious contacts."

I heard a tone and glanced at the laptop. My magic search engine was notifying me that the search on Holly West was complete. I cut my eyes to Greg. Both he and Dev were watching me.

"Go ahead and open it up, sweetheart," Greg told me. "Dev can help us decide what to do if it turns up anything disturbing."

While I opened and read the report, Dev moved the empty food containers to the kitchen counter and washed his hands.

"There are three Holly Wests listed for Southern California," I reported. "One is older than the one we're looking for, and it looks like she moved to Northern California a few years ago. Another is a high-school student. The third has the same Long Beach P.O. box we found."

"Like Goldilocks and the three bears," Dev noted with a half grin. "One's too old. One's too young. The third is just right."

I read more. "The one in Long Beach was born May 16, 1991," I reported. I did the math in my head. "That means she's 26." There wasn't much more information in the

report. "It says here her mother'
Jane Newell. Father is Jordon Wes
reading. "Oh, how sad," I said, "he
passed away about just two months

I looked over at the guys. Dev was looking at me with interest. Greg was looking at me like he'd seen a ghost.

"What's the matter, Greg?" I asked him. "Are you feeling okay?"

"What were her parents' names again?" he asked.

I looked at the report and read the names. "Jane Newell and Jordon West." I looked back at him.

Dev was now watching him too, and with his cop-trained eyes. "Do you know them?" he asked.

Greg nodded. "I do, or did back in college. At least I knew Jane Newell. I've only heard about Jordon West, and that was from Jane." He took a deep breath. "And you're sure Jane's deceased?"

"Was she an old college flame?" Dev asked.

"Sort of," Greg said after a long pause. "We kind of dated off and on during my senior year. She was a junior at the time. She left school mid-year and I never saw her again." He pushed his wheelchair away from the table and toward the fridge. He ed it and grabbed himself another beer. ou want another, Dev?"

"Sure," Dev answered.

Greg turned to me. "How about you, Odelia?"

"Will I need a beer?" I asked, concerned about where this was going.

As an answer, Greg pulled three beers from the fridge and brought them to the table. When he set one in front of Dev, Dev pushed it aside and got up from the table. "On second thought, maybe I should shove off so you two can talk about this in private."

Greg and I were staring at each other, neither of us speaking. Whatever this was, it was huge. Greg's eyes were nearly wet. I couldn't read the emotion behind them, which was rare. He was definitely upset but not angry. Behind his obvious agitation I saw sadness and concern.

"I'll let myself out," Dev said. "You know how to reach me if you need me."

Without taking his eyes off of me, Greg called to Dev as he made his way to the front door with Wainwright as an escort. "Thanks for coming by, Dev. Nice to have you back." At the door Dev gave the dog a good scratching behind the ears before exiting. "We'll fill you in shortly."

When the front door closed, I twisted the

cap off my beer and took a sip. It was icy cold and tasty, especially after the salty, spicy Chinese food. "So is Holly West following you after all?" I asked Greg.

"She might be, or it could be a coincidence." He took a long pull from his fresh beer.

I snorted. "If Dev were still here, he'd say there are no *coinkydinks.*" I took another sip of beer, worried about what was coming next. Greg and I had shared with each other some of our more important relationships in our pasts, but the name Jane Newell was new to me.

"Like I said," Greg began, "Jane and I dated in college off and on for a short while. We liked each other but there was nothing serious on either side. We were more like occasional bed buddies. She abruptly left in her junior year, and I never saw her again."

I got up and paced the kitchen, finally stopping and leaning back against the counter to face my husband. "Do you know why she left school."

"Yes," Greg answered, his voice low. "She left because she was pregnant."

I took another drink. This time I didn't sip but chugged back nearly half the bottle at one go. College girls got pregnant all the time, but something in my gut told me this was different. Without warning, the beer that went down came back up like a foamy geyser. I slapped a hand over my mouth and turned toward the sink just in time to expel it down the drain. When I was finished, I swished some water around in my mouth and wiped my face with a nearby dishtowel.

"Are you okay, sweetheart?" Greg asked. I nodded as an answer, still unable to speak.

"So is Holly West your daughter?" I asked, finding my voice as I turned back to face him. My eyes burrowed into his, looking for the truth.

"I don't know, Odelia. Jane told me the baby wasn't mine when she left. She said it was this Jordon West's baby."

"Did Jordon West go to school with you guys?"

Greg shook his head. "Not that I know of. In fact, I have no idea who he is, just that she claimed the baby was his." We were both silent, then Greg said, "I'm so sorry, Odelia. I should have told you, but Jane wasn't that big a part of my life and I knew she dated other guys, so I accepted her word that the baby wasn't mine." His jaw tightened. "While I can father a child with my injury, tests have shown that I don't have the best swimmers when it comes to sperm, so it was easy to believe."

I took a deep breath, then another. When we first met, I knew that Greg wanted children — not desperately, but he certainly wouldn't have thought it a bad idea. I'm ten years older than Greg and don't want children; frankly, I'm not that fond of rug rats. Don't get me wrong: I actually love children — other people's children. I've just never wanted my own. When we married, Greg had put the idea of having kids aside. I knew about his low sperm count and knew it was one of the reasons he easily accepted us not having children. Had we both wanted them, with my age and his issues, we probably would have had to jump through medical hoops to try, and even then there would have been no guarantee.

Now, here was a young woman who might be his daughter. I had mixed emotions about the possibility. Part of me was jealous in a weird way, worried that by coming into our lives she would upset the apple cart. Greg and I had a wonderful marriage. It wasn't without its bumps and bruises, but we were as close as opposite halves of Velcro, and the union was way better than I had ever expected any marriage to be, at least any marriage I would have. I was also pleased by this offspring possibility. Greg would have a child. It would be a piece of him that would go on in the world, like a healthy seed sprouting into other plants, providing Holly West wasn't some psycho.

"Are you thinking now," I said to Greg in a slow, deliberate voice as I formed the bones of my question, "that maybe Holly found out that she is your daughter and was following you for that reason?"

He sucked down some beer before answering. "It's a possibility. Seems strange that she was at the grocery store and at my shop, doesn't it?"

I nodded in agreement. "Yes, it does."

"But there were no other videos of me," he pointed out.

"That we know of," I added. "She could have hours of you that she hasn't posted."

I went back to my laptop and the report on Holly West, checking it for more information. "Rather than calling the police right away, let's get to the bottom of this first on our own," I told Greg. "There's a phone number on the report. Should we call or email her?"

"Phone," he said. "Stuff like this should be handled by phone or in person. Since we don't have an address for her, it looks like the phone will have to do."

"I agree." I jotted down the information on the pad Greg had been using earlier and

142

held it out to him. "Now seems like a good time, doesn't it?"

"Sweetheart," Greg said to me, taking my hand along with the paper, "I'm so sorry about all this."

I squeezed his hand. "I won't lie, Greg, I'm totally thrown by this, but whatever happens, whoever this Holly girl turns out to be, I am with you a hundred percent. Remember that, even if I get kind of cranky about it."

He smiled, and the love in his eyes nearly shattered me into a thousand little pieces. I'd meant what I said about being with him on this, and I knew he'd have my back if the tables were turned.

Greg's phone was on the counter. I got up and handed it to him. "Do you want some privacy?"

He shook his head. "We're in this together. I'm counting on that."

I watched as he punched in Holly's phone number, half hoping he got voice mail, half hoping the number was disconnected. Just for security, Greg blocked his identity before calling. Some people won't answer blocked calls, but for his first try, he wanted to give it a shot.

Greg put the call on speaker and held the phone between us. It rang three times, then a soft female voice answered, "Hello."

Time stood still in our kitchen for what seemed like an eternity but was really just a few seconds. I swear I could hear the digital clock on the microwave move.

"Hello," she said again.

Greg cleared his throat. "Is this Holly West?"

"Who's asking?" The voice might have been soft, but there was a defiant edge to it.

Greg and I locked eyes, then he said, "My name is Greg Stevens, Holly. I knew your mother, Jane Newell, a long time ago."

Nice start, I thought to myself. *Keep it soft and subtle.* I gave Greg an encouraging smile. There was silence, but she didn't end the call. With my eyes I encouraged Greg to continue.

"Holly, are you following me?" he asked, his voice turning tight and demanding.

No! Don't put her on the defense so soon. I wanted to kick Greg, but he wouldn't have felt it. Instead, I widened my eyes at him and shook my head like Wainwright shaking off water.

"What?" Greg asked silently with expanded eye sockets. My normally smart hubby was clueless.

Holly disconnected. No big surprise.

"Well," I said, "that could have gone better."

"Oh yeah?" Greg asked, his voice challenging. "Just how would you have done it?"

"I wouldn't have asked her right off the bat if she was a stalker, that's for sure." I got up from the table and started pacing the kitchen.

"Yeah, I kind of jumped the gun on that," Greg admitted. He ran a hand through his hair, his face dark with frustration. "So where do we go from here?"

I was wondering that myself. "The police really need to view any video taken prior to what is on her YouTube channel. We should talk to her and ask her to come forward on her own."

"Maybe she already has," Greg said.

I stopped pacing and leaned against the counter again, weighing that possibility. "Most decent people would go to the police," I said, "if they had any information on someone's murder." I paused. "Unless they were doing something wrong at the time they were filming that video," I tacked on. Inside, I was hoping this Holly West was a nice person, not just because there was a slim chance she might be Greg's daughter, but also because she was for sure the daughter of an old friend of his.

"Holly was at the store filming and at the shop filming," Greg said. I could see he was working out the possible angles of Holly's civic responsibility. "I don't think she could be charged with stalking unless we filed charges — unless she was afraid of being found out in the first place."

"But," I said, holding up a finger to make my point, "who knows what else she might have been doing on her own or for someone else? Maybe she knew that Burt was going to talk to you and what about. Maybe they even knew each other. It's possible."

"The police may have already seen the video," Greg said. "It is out in the public view. If they have seen it, I'm sure they would be tracking her down to get the entire thing."

"True." I moved back to the table and took my seat. "But all they would get for information on her is her first name, like we did, unless they have access to private information on her. If they have something like Marigold that farms information or a special access just for law enforcement, they still may not have anything more than we do, which is just a last name, telephone, and a mailing address."

"Was that P.O. Box address a real post office box or a mailbox place?" Greg asked.

Turning back to the computer, I copied the address from the Marigold report and pasted it into the Google maps page. It popped up the location. I clicked on the street view feature and inspected the address and the buildings around it. "It looks to be a private mailbox place," I reported. "If the police only have this address for Holly, they'd go there to get more information on her. At least that's what I'd do."

"But that's private. The police might need a warrant to get them to cough up her full contact information, unless they can convince the people running it to do it without a warrant."

"We could asked Dev about this," I suggested, "or Clark." Antsy, I got up and grabbed the beer on the table that had been meant for Dev. I held it out to Greg. "Will you be wanting this?"

He looked at the beer in his hand, then at the one in mine, and shook his head. "Nah, I've had enough." He gave his phone a thoughtful look. "Speaking of which, since Clark hasn't called since the thing with the dog, I'm guessing he doesn't know yet about Burt's murder. You know he'd be all over this, and so would Willie, at least with warnings to stay out of it. Maybe we should call him and give him a heads up?"

"If Clark doesn't know yet, he'll know soon enough," I said with a roll of my eyes. Clark had called the night of the dog rescue. Mom had not only told him about it but sent him the link to the video. "My mother knows. Dev knows. Andrea Fehring knows. It's just a matter of time before the hotline rings on Clark's end in Arizona."

I shuttled the unopened beer to the fridge. As soon as it was stored, I turned back to Greg with an idea. "How about calling Holly again," I suggested, "without the block on your phone."

"I hardly think she's going to answer the call," Greg said, draining his beer. "And if she did, what should I say? I don't want to bungle it like I did before."

"You don't really need her to answer it," I told him. "Leave her a message asking if she has anything on the video about Burt's death or right before Burt was shot that might help us or the police figure out what happened. Leave your number and mine, and ask her to call one of us. Assure her it's all we want." I paused, then added with a shake of an index finger in his direction, "Say nothing about her following you, and do not ask why she was there."

"I've already spilled the beans about knowing her mother," Greg said.

148

"True," I said. "And if I were Holly, I'd be wondering how you linked me to Jane Newell in the first place. But let that go for now," I advised. "Let's just focus on information that can help the police find Burt's murderer."

Greg shrugged. He gathered up the empty beer bottles from the table and brought them into the kitchen. I took them from him, gave them a quick rinse, then dropped them into our recycling bin for glass. While I did that, Greg rolled back to the table and picked up his phone. With a look in my direction for support, he unblocked his number and called Holly again. As we expected, it went straight to voice mail. Greg calmly left the message I suggested. We didn't know if it would yield anything, but it was a start.

With another idea in my head, I returned to the table. Sitting down, I quickly typed something, then closed down my laptop. "I just told Marigold to run a search on Jordon West," I told Greg. "He might be able to lead us to Holly."

"Not a bad idea."

I held out my hand to Greg and he put his into mine. It was warm and strong. "I know this is going to bother you until it's resolved," I told him. "It's going to bother both of us. So how about I snoop around at that mail place tomorrow while you're at work? You never know what I might be able to shake loose."

He added his other hand to mine and gave it a squeeze. "I don't know, sweetheart. We don't know what's behind Burt's death. Until we do, it may be dangerous."

"I'll just ask a few questions. Tell them I'm Holly's aunt or something and see if they buy it. Who knows, she might even come in to collect her mail."

"What about the police?" he asked.

"What about them?" I asked in return. "They probably have as much information as we do or should have, which isn't much. So it's not like we're withholding anything. If something new comes up, we'll call them."

"I guess asking a few questions won't hurt, although it might spook her if they tell her someone was asking about her." He removed his hands from mine, picked up his phone again, and placed a call.

"Who are you calling?" I asked him.

"My cleaning crew," he said. "I just realized they will come in tonight to clean the shop and see that puddle of blood. I don't want them blindsided by it."

"Should you maybe hire a special cleaner

for that?" I asked. The people who cleaned Greg's shop also cleaned most of the other stores in the strip mall, along with several others in the area. The cleaning company actually had several crews that worked at night cleaning local businesses on a rotation. They took care of Ocean Breeze, dusting and wiping down machines and counters, washing floors, and scrubbing the bathroom and kitchen once a week every Monday. In between, Greg and his employees took care of the trash and kept things tidy. Some of the businesses used the cleaning company more than once a week.

Greg shook his head. "I think they've had experience with stuff like this before, but I'll let Jaime make the call on how to handle it."

While he placed the call and chatted with Jaime Morales, the owner of the cleaning company, I decided to get ready for bed. It was still pretty early, but I was exhausted. After a quick look in on Dumpster, I went to our master suite and washed my face, brushed my teeth, and put on a nightgown. Muffin was already curled up on our bed when I finished. I slipped between the sheets, nudging the bed-hogging cat with one leg until she moved enough for me to stretch out. I'd been settled for about ten minutes with my Kindle, although I was having trouble keeping my mind on my reading, when Wainwright trotted in with Greg rolling in behind him.

"I was right," he said. "Jaime says he has two guys who are trained in hazard cleanup. He'll send one over with the usual crew tonight to clean up the blood."

Greg likes to watch the evening news when we get ready for bed, but we were tucking in much earlier than usual tonight. He aimed the remote at the TV mounted on the wall across from our bed, then seemed to think twice about it. He tossed the remote on the bed. It landed near me. "How about finding us a movie to watch tonight while I get ready for bed?" he suggested. "A stupid movie that will make us laugh."

I had a couple of choices ready when he finished cleaning up and slid into bed next to me. Instead of starting one of the movies, I turned to him. "I really want to stake out the mailbox place tomorrow, Greg."

He turned his upper body so that he was facing me. With a couple of fingers, he pushed a thick clump of my hair away from my face. "Instead, why don't you do what Steele suggested and call Zee and plan something with her?"

"You don't think I can handle talking to a couple of people without you?" I narrowed my eyes at him, which made him laugh. Not the response I was hoping for.

"It's not that, sweetheart. It's just that we've had a couple of really bad days in a row. Hell, if I didn't have so much going on at the shop, I'd play hooky and do something fun with you." He leaned over and kissed me. "Call Zee and have some fun with her. Have you even told her about what happened at the office yet?"

I hadn't and knew she would be unhappy not being one of the first to hear it. I looked at the clock on the nightstand. It wasn't too late to call the Washington home. Picking up my cell phone, which was on the nightstand charging, I called Zee and made a date for lunch. She was thrilled, and since I normally didn't work on Tuesdays, she didn't ask why I had the day off. I could also tell by our short chat that she hadn't seen any news reports of Burt getting shot in front of Greg's shop. I decided to save that conversation for tomorrow.

"There," Greg said after I ended the call. "Don't you feel better already?" He aimed the remote at the TV and started one of the movies I'd picked out — a buddy road trip movie that never failed to amuse us. We'd seen it so many times that between the two of us, we could probably recite the entire dialog.

"Yes," I admitted as I snuggled next to Greg. "You and Zee are the two people in the entire world who can always make me feel better."

He kissed the top of my head. "Not your mother?" he asked with a laugh.

"Humph," I said with mock disgust. "You're funnier than the movie."

ELEVEN

Zee's fancy Mercedes sedan was in the shop, so I drove to Newport Beach and picked her up for our lunch date. We decided to go to one of our favorite places in Laguna Beach that overlooked the ocean. There were also a lot of shops along PCH — Pacific Coast Highway — where we could wander after, providing it wasn't too hot.

On my drive from Seal Beach to Newport Beach to pick up Zee, I was half kicking myself for making the lunch date. What I'd said to Greg last night was true. Next to him, Zee was the one person who could bring me comfort and calm me down, but now I was antsy to talk to the people at Holly's mailbox place and even antsier to speak to Jordon West, her father. The search results had come in from Marigold during the night, and I'd read them over breakfast after returning from a morning walk with

Wainwright. Greg seemed to have forgotten about my ordering the report on Jordon. He was anxious to get to work after losing more than half a day the day before, and he wanted his world set right again for his clients and his employees. He'd kissed me goodbye and bundled Wainwright into the van almost as soon as we'd returned from our walk.

There were about a dozen Jordon Wests living in Southern California. To narrow them down, I made the assumption that the Jordon West I was looking for might be about Greg's age, give or take a few years. That left me with two candidates. If neither panned out, then I'd widen the net a bit on the age. The same went for geographic choices. Just because the Jordon West I was looking for lived locally over twenty years ago didn't mean he still did. We live in a mobile society, with people following jobs and significant others to new locations all the time. Of the two hopeful candidates, one lived in Costa Mesa, the small city wedged between Newport Beach and Huntington Beach. The condo I owned before marrying Greg had been located in Costa Mesa, right on the border with Newport Beach. The other lived in Westminster, a city not far away that bordered Huntington Beach.

The one in Costa Mesa was about fifty years old and had teacher listed as his occupation. The photo that came with the report showed a man with a thin, angular face and small eyes, and must be fairly current as the man in the photo matched the given age. The report gave his address and phone number, and also noted that he was married with two sons in their twenties. The Jordon West in Westminster had nothing listed for his work. His age was listed as fifty-two, but the photo was of a man who appeared to be much younger, barely college age. I found it odd that there wasn't a more current photo. Nor was there any work history or family information, not even a phone number. Either way, I planned on tracking down both. Something about Westminster nagged at me, but I couldn't quite place why.

Zee and I were almost done with our lunch by the time I'd filled her in on everything that had happened since I'd last spoken with her. We'd both ordered salads. She'd had the chicken salad with cranberries and goat cheese, and I'd had a Chinese chicken salad with teriyaki dressing, mandarin orange slices, and crispy wontons. For dessert we were splitting a piece of key lime cheesecake. I put the first bite of the pale green goodness into my mouth and moaned. "Gawd, that's good. Perfect for a hot day."

We were on the patio of the restaurant but were shielded from the sun by a large awning. A soft breeze came in off the ocean, giving welcome relief from the heat.

Using her fork, Zee snagged a bite of the cheesecake. She'd been unusually quiet during my narrative of the past few days. "I don't know," she finally said just before the bite landed between her full, glossy lips, "which event to comment on first." She clamped down on the dessert, chewed slowly, and swallowed. If she didn't hustle, my stress-eating habit might inhale the remainder of the cheesecake before she got to her second bite.

With great restraint, I put my fork down and turned my head toward the sea. The sky was such a bright blue, it didn't look real — a color someone chose from a paint chip and splashed across the sky with abandon, without any shading or blending. Even the tint of my sunglasses didn't diminish the clarity of the color. I have a pair of topaz earrings this shade of blue. Greg bought them for my birthday a few years back. Come to think of it, the stones were called sky blue topaz.

I heard "Earth to Odelia," the words digging through my random thoughts like a shovel until they hit pay dirt in my brain. I turned to find Zee looking at me, her large brown eyes wide with worry as they peered at me over the top rim of her sunglasses. "Are you okay?" she asked once she had my attention.

I nodded. "Yes, I'm okay." I picked up my fork and, using its side, sliced off another bite of cheesecake. "Steele is pretty sure this will all blow over and I'll be back at my desk next week or the week after, although Greg isn't keen on me going back. He's not happy with the way they're handling this and thinks maybe it's time for me to make a change."

"Do *you* want to make a change?" she asked.

I popped the bite of cheesecake into my mouth. Unlike the other bites, this one tasted sour and gummy on my tongue, its original wonderful flavor turned rancid by my concerns. I put my fork down and took a drink of my iced tea to rinse away the bad flavor. "I don't know," I said, and was surprised by how weary my voice sounded to my own ears. *Why* I was surprised was a surprise in itself. Since this chain of events began on Saturday, I hadn't slept well, yet it wasn't until this very moment, sitting here in the warm sun with my best friend, that I felt my body sag like a sack of dirty laundry. I beat back my weariness with an imaginary bat. I had things to do after lunch.

After Greg had left this morning, I ran a Marigold report on Burt Sandoval. Funny how in all the hullabaloo over Holly West, we'd forgotten him, the dead guy. His report was longer than either Holly's or her father's. He lived in Torrance, a small city a few miles north of Long Beach. He was divorced and the father of two boys and a girl, all grown. The report didn't list their whereabouts. Burt was originally from Santa Rosa, and it looked like he'd been down in Southern California since his divorce five years ago. According to the report, he was forty-eight years old — a year younger than Greg, although he looked older. The report listed that Burt worked for a company called Church Construction, also located in Torrance. Given Burt's substantial size and strength, I could see him easily working in that field, but it raised another question. If he was employed, what was he doing meeting up with Greg in the middle of a Monday? Perhaps they couldn't work in the oppressive heat. I'd made a note to contact someone at Church Construction when I had the chance. It went on my mental to-do list, right along with contacting Jordon West one and two.

"I've lost you again," I heard Zee say. "You've been staring at that cheesecake like you half expected it to grow legs and scoot off the table."

I looked up at her. "I'm sorry, Zee. I guess I'm not very good company today."

"Nonsense," she said, dismissing my weak apology. "You have important, pressing things on your mind. Are you really worried about your job or is it something else — that girl, maybe? Are you worried that she might be Greg's daughter?"

A short, sharp snort escaped my lips. "All of the above, although it really wouldn't be a problem for me if Holly did turn out to be Greg's daughter. Weird, yes, but not really a problem, unless she's some kind of psycho."

"Like if she were the one who shot Burt?" Zee suggested. I'd told her about the accusation in the YouTube comments.

"Yeah, something like that," I admitted. "We have a lot of possibilities. She could have been there stalking Greg and taking the video or maybe she was stalking Burt and was the one who pulled the trigger." I

161

paused, my mind travelling to my memories of mixed horror and odd affection for Elaine Powers, a notorious hitwoman who went by the street name of Mother. "You know, like Mother."

Zee took a very deep breath and leaned back in her chair. "Like you need another hitwoman in your life." Zee had never understood my feelings for Elaine. I barely understood them myself. But in spite of her murderous ways, I'd actually liked her. Not how she made her living, of course, but her, the person she truly was under all that crime.

"I doubt Holly West is a hitwoman," I said. "She could be, but I doubt it. She appears to be more the type to hunt and shoot people with her camera." I paused and looked back out at the beach. A tall shirtless man was walking his dog, a rambunctious, large puppy, who didn't care about the heat, just chasing the waves and the gulls. "But the question is, was Holly there to film Greg or Burt? Or was she there stalking Marla Kingston? She had several videos of events featuring the Kingstons."

"Let me come with you," Zee said, surprising me.

"What?" Now it was my turn to peek over the top rim of my sunglasses.

"Let me come with you," she repeated.

"Where?"

Zee's sunglasses were still halfway down her nose. Over them, she rolled her large eyes at me like I was having a senior moment. "You know, when you investigate."

"What makes you think I'm investigating anything?" I asked with firmness. I received another eye roll, this one more pronounced.

I picked up my glass of iced tea, took a long drink from the straw, and paused before answering. "Okay, it's true," I finally confessed. "I do plan on checking out a few people who might be able to give me some information. Might as well make use of my time since I can't go to the office, and since this woman has some long ago possible tie to Greg, even indirectly, I want to know more about her."

"I knew it," Zee said. She pushed her sunglasses back up the bridge of her nose and gave me a smug smile, then dug back into the cheesecake.

While she went back to chowing down on the dessert, I studied my best friend. She and I are about the same size and age. Her skin is the color of fine dark chocolate. Her eyes, two deep pools of chocolate pudding, dance when she's amused and shoot killer lasers when she's angry. In the last year she'd started cropping her tightly curled hair close to her scalp and stopped coloring it. It was now a soft, cushy salt-and-pepper carpet. I'd happily take a bullet for her if I had to, which brought me to my next concern.

"Seth doesn't like it when you play detective with me," I said. It was the truth. A few years back, Zee's husband had all but put our relationship in a timeout because of flying bullets.

She put down her fork and dabbed her mouth in a ladylike manner with her linen napkin. Then she stared at me with those laser eyes of hers. I looked down at her mouth, pursed now like a plump cherry. When wiping her mouth, she hadn't smudged a bit of her lipstick. I've always marveled at women who could do that. They can eat and drink and wipe their mouths, all without mussing their lip gloss. If I'm not careful, after I eat I look like a clown who put on his lip color while drunk. I looked up again. The lasers were gone. Her dark eyes were now wet.

"What's the matter, Zee?" I asked with concern. "Does it really mean that much to you to come with me?"

She nodded a little, then switched gears, her head now going side to side. "It's not to help you, Odelia, although I do want to do that. It's for me." A single tear ran down one plump cheek. "I've been banished from my grandbaby!" More tears flowed. She picked up her napkin and dabbed at them on her cheeks and under her sunglasses without removing them.

"What do you mean *banished*?" Hannah, Zee's daughter, had given birth to an adorable baby girl the summer before. It was Seth and Zee's first grandchild, and Zee was spending almost as much time on the East Coast with Hannah and her husband as here with Seth. The news of her exile wasn't a complete surprise. Zee was a super mom and sometimes a helicopter mom and sometimes simply too much of a mom, even to me. They also had a son, Jacob, who was attending law school at Stanford. "Who put the travel ban on you going east? Hannah or Seth?"

Zee sniffed and tilted her head slightly to indicate indignation. Her mouth was tight. "Both. They called it an intervention," she said sharply. "Like I was some sort of drug addict. Can you imagine that?"

I was about to say something unpopular. I paused, weighing my options, but couldn't help myself. Zee and I have always been brutally honest with each other. After taking a deep breath, I said, "Yes, I can." In spite of the look of horror she gave me, I continued. "Zee, you raised a lovely, smart, strong daughter. She and her husband can handle the baby, and if they can't, they're also smart enough to ask for help, don't you think?"

Her pursed lips relaxed a tiny bit. "I suppose," she finally said.

"And I recall," I ventured, "way back when your children were very tiny, how much you resented Seth's mother interfering, not to mention your own mother." I took a long drink of my tea. "Trust me, Zee, you come by the 'hovering mother' bit honestly."

Her mouth relaxed, melting into a tiny smile. Finally, she blew out a long breath. "You're right. Seth even brought our mothers up as an example. They both about drove me crazy with all their advice. Seth's mother just about camped on our doorstep when the kids were little."

"And they did it out of love," I added. "Just as you're driving Hannah crazy with your love and good intentions. Just back off a bit. Do some volunteer work. Go back to selling cosmetics. Redecorate your house."

"Why do you think we're relandscaping our backyard? It gives me something to do, although it's nearly done. And I've been volunteering at church." She took a drink of her lemonade. "So now you see why I want to come with you. I need something to do." She pointed a lacquered nail in my direction. "If I have to attend one more ladies' church event with my mother, they'll be putting me into a padded room."

My best friend was begging for my help to keep her sanity. How could I refuse? "Okay. Okay. After lunch today, I was going to try and find a couple of people. They don't live that far away. One is in Costa Mesa and the other in Westminster. There was no phone number for the one in Westminster, but before I left to pick you up I called the one in Costa Mesa, but I only got a generic voice mail. He's a teacher, so he may be off for the summer."

"Or teaching summer school or traveling to Patagonia for a month," Zee noted.

"True," I agreed. "I left my cell number and asked him to call me. I also need to contact a construction company in Torrance about Burt Sandoval."

"Then let's get going," Zee said.

It was the shortest lunch date Zee and I had ever had.

TWELVE

We had gone to lunch around eleven thirty. By one o'clock we were on the 405 Freeway heading for Torrance, two plump middle-aged women in stylish capris and tops, toting designer handbags. Well, Zee carried an expensive designer handbag. I had my usual trusty tote with me.

While waiting for our check to be processed, we'd mapped out our plan of attack. Zee pointed out that if we started in Torrance, which was farthest away, and worked our way back to Orange County, we'd be heading toward home during rush hour instead of hopscotching from place to place. After Torrance we could hit Westminster, then Costa Mesa. If the teacher didn't get back to us by phone, we'd head to the address on the Marigold report. It was a good plan. I plugged the address for Church Construction into my GPS and away we went, heading north on the 405 Freeway.

Torrance is about fifty miles from Laguna Beach. Traffic on the notoriously busy 405 was heavy but not jammed. We'd gone about ten miles when I turned to Zee. "Do you have any antacids with you? I have some in my bag, but it's in the back seat."

"Sure." She dug around in her handbag and produced a small travel container of a well-known brand. After shaking a couple into my hand, I popped them into my mouth. "You okay?" she asked.

"I'm not sure if it was the cheesecake or the salad, but something is doing a conga in my stomach," I said after chewing the tablets.

"It's probably stress," Zee diagnosed. "Not surprising with everything going on in your life." She reached over and gave my knee a couple of comforting pats. "Don't worry, Odelia, I'm sure it will all work out with your job." I gave her a weak smile, hoping she was right.

"By the way," I said, changing the subject, "Dev is back — I think for good."

Zee looked surprised. "Did he and Bev break up?"

I nodded but didn't take my eyes off the road. "Yes. He's moved back into his house and is starting up a PI business with a friend of his in LA. He stopped by the house last night."

"I'm very sorry about him and Bev," Zee said with sincerity. "I liked her very much."

"Yeah, me too."

Zee snapped her head toward me and flashed a thousand-watt smile. "Hey, we can ask Dev to help with this stuff."

I carefully changed lanes to get past a slow-moving RV towing a small car. "I had the same thought this morning while reading up on the two Jordon Wests," I told her. "But I nixed it because you know how protective Dev can be. I don't need his nagging. Besides, he's busy getting settled in. But if we get stuck, he'll be a great resource."

A shiny black sports car came up on our right, in the slower lane, going well past the speed limit. After hugging the bumper of the car in front of it, the vehicle darted between me and the car in front of me like thread going through the eye of a needle. I would have made contact with him if I'd been going any faster. The car wasn't in front of me but a few seconds before it made a move to the next lane to our left, then wove its way to the far left lane. From there it darted in and out between cars and lanes, car by car, playing chicken with the traffic to move ahead.

"Look at the fool!" cried Zee as she clung to the hand grip just above the passenger's door. "He's going to kill someone."

I shook my head in disgust as I watched the car move forward, barely missing other vehicles. "You see that way too often on these roads, yet you seldom see them pulled over by the Highway Patrol for those tricks."

We made it to Torrance in good time and found a parking spot a couple of spaces down from Church Construction. It was a low white building located on the corner of an intersection on the edge of the city. A chain-link fence surrounded the property with a wide driveway and gate that was open. Before we could get out of the car, my cell phone rang. I recognized the number as that of Jordon West.

"Is this Odelia Grey?" he asked after I said hello.

"Yes, it is," I told him. "Is this Jordon West?"

"Yes, I believe you called me. What can I do for you? You said it was important — about someone named Holly."

I was thrilled that he called. Many people would have assumed it was some sort of sales call. I was going to say in my message that it wasn't a sales call, then figured a shady sales rep would pull such a stunt. Instead, I told him that I was trying to locate a Holly West and hoped he could help.

"Yes," I told him. "Thank you for calling back, Mr. West." Turning, I gave Zee a wide-eyed glance. "I'm trying to locate a Holly West. I was told her father's name was Jordon West and that he lived in Southern California."

"You've got the wrong Jordon West here," he told me. "I have two sons, no daughters."

I tried another avenue. "Did you ever know a woman by the name of Jane Newell? That's Holly's mother. It might have been about twenty-five years ago."

There was a short silence on the other end, then he answered, "No, sorry. I don't recall anyone by that name."

"Well, thank you for your time," I told him cheerfully, although I was a bit disappointed.

"Struck out there?" Zee asked.

"Yes," I told her as we prepared to get out of the nice cool car. "He said he didn't know Holly or Jane. Of course, he could have been lying, but I don't think he was. But if the other Jordon West doesn't pan out, I may revisit the teacher."

We entered the construction company

through the large gate and made our way to a door marked *Office.* We could see that the driveway led to a large open yard containing a couple of neatly parked trucks with the company's logo on the side. A large building, painted to match the office, was in the back with two large garage-style doors, both closed. When we opened the door to the office, we were greeted by a soft bell and lovely air conditioning. The office was a large room containing a couple of basic chairs and a very large desk on which were several neat stacks of papers and a laptop. There were only two windows, both with security bars. One faced toward the front entrance and one faced the back, giving a wide view of the work yard. To the far right of the desk, I spotted an open door through which I could see another desk. On the clean painted walls hung enlarged photos of beautiful home kitchens and bathrooms, some with before-and-after shots. Another showed a room addition in several stages of progress, ending with the final product. A couple were photos of stately homes. Zee stepped over to the photos to examine them, and I wondered if she was getting ideas for her next project to keep her busy.

A woman who looked to be in her forties emerged from the back holding a ream of copy paper. She didn't move toward the front desk but leaned against the doorjamb as if the paper were a heavy load. "Can I help you?" she asked. She was slender with a long, narrow face, her dark blond hair secured in the back. Perched on her nose were a pair of glasses with fire-engine red frames. The glasses were the only bright color present in her ensemble, which included khaki cargo pants and a white T-shirt with the company logo. Her skin was tanned, her face lined, and her arms strong. She looked like she'd spent more time doing construction work than in an office.

"We'd like to speak to the owner," I told her.

"And this is about?" she asked, still standing in the doorway leading to the back area.

I looked at Zee. We both shuffled uncomfortably where we stood.

"Do you have a renovation you'd like us to handle?" the woman asked. "That's our specialty: home renovations." She took a few steps forward and set the paper on the desk. She looked at us expectantly, her mouth straight as a ruler and just as stern. Up close, I could see dark circles under her eyes, barely hidden by the lower rim of her glasses. I got the feeling she didn't greet clients face-to-face very often, if at all, and was feeling put upon by our presence.

"No," I stammered, wondering how much to say.

"We'd like to see the owner," Zee piped up in her soft but authoritative mom voice. "Are you one of the owners?"

The woman sized up Zee, then me. "No, I'm not," she replied. "What is this about?"

"We'd like to discuss that with the owner," Zee pressed.

"Look," the woman said, her tired eyes zeroing in on Zee, "if you're selling something, hit the road. We're busy here."

I took a step forward and placed my tote bag on the seat of the single chair facing the desk. It was a subtle sign that we weren't going anywhere. "We really do need to speak to the owner," I told the woman. "We're not selling anything, but it is important. It's about one of your employees."

"I'm the office manager. Is this about Burt?" she asked, her voice gaining more of an edge while the hard line of her mouth drooped at each side.

"Yes," I answered, "it is. Did you know Burt Sandoval?"

She waited a long moment before answering, then said evenly, "Of course I did. He worked here for several years."

"Like five years?" I ventured, remembering that Burt had moved to Southern California right after his divorce.

"Something like that." The office manager leveled her eyes at me. "From looking at you, I'd say you're not the police. Besides, they were here early this morning. Who are you, and what do you want?"

Before either Zee or I could answer, the door to the office opened and in strode a tall young man. He had brown skin, thick black hair, and wore an air of confidence as easily as his jeans and company T-shirt. He tossed a curious smile our way, then addressed the woman. "Donna, if you don't need me, I'm heading out to the site — finally." The last word was said with a hint of weary frustration.

Donna looked from us to the young man and back at us. It was clear she was weighing which path to take. "Ben," she said, addressing the man, "these woman are asking about Burt."

He turned to give us his full attention. "I'm Ben Church," he said. "What can I do for you?"

"I'm Odelia Grey, and this is Zee Washington." I shot a glance at Donna, then asked, "Can we talk in private?"

He nodded. "I can give you a few minutes, but that's about it. I've been tied up here most of the day with the police and need to get to the work site to check on things."

"We'll try to be quick," Zee told him.

Ben Church led us through the open doorway to the other office. The desk here wasn't nearly as tidy as Donna's. On the wall was a huge calendar with various names of projects scrawled across it. It looked like currently there was only one, the *Sanderson Kitchen,* but in two weeks the *Weinberg Remodel* was due to start.

"Sorry about the mess," Ben told us. He removed a stack of papers from the one visitor's chair and indicated for one of us to be seated. Zee took it and Ben offered me the only other seat, the desk chair, which I took. He shut the door and leaned against a short two-drawer file cabinet. "What interest do you have in poor Burt?" he asked.

I cleared my throat. "You know the place where he was shot?" I asked.

Ben shrugged. "Some strip mall in Huntington Beach is what the police told me."

"Yes, that's correct," I confirmed. "But specifically, it happened in front of my husband's business, Ocean Breeze Graphics. Burt stumbled into Ocean Breeze and nearly died on the floor in front of the customer counter."

Ben straightened and his large dark brown

177

eyes widened. "Oh, wow! I'm so sorry to hear that. Were you there?"

"Yes, I was," I told him. "We did our best to keep Burt alive until the ambulance came. We were told he died shortly after arriving at the hospital."

"Yes," Ben said with a nod. "That's what the police told me today. So very tragic." He took a deep breath. "But why are you here? The police covered almost everything we could tell them. Did you know Burt?"

"Kind of, sort of," I said. "My husband and I only met Burt on Saturday in the parking lot of a grocery store in Long Beach. He helped us out with a . . . um . . . problem."

"Burt was a good guy, always ready to help someone. He'll be missed around here." Ben settled back on the edge of the file cabinet.

"Did the police mention Saturday to you at all?" I asked.

He nodded. "Yes, you're talking about that guy in the wheelchair breaking into Marla Kingston's car, aren't you?"

"That was my husband," I told him.

"The cops showed me the video," Ben said. "They wanted to know if I knew of any reason why Burt would be in Long Beach."

Zee stirred. "Long Beach isn't that far from Torrance," she said. "Nothing odd about someone from Torrance going to Long Beach."

Ben turned to her. "That's what I told them. People in SoCal drive all over, one city to the other, several times a day. But they wanted to know if I knew of any specific reason why Burt might be there, like visiting a girlfriend or maybe doing some freelance work — stuff like that."

"And what did you tell them?" I asked.

Ben shrugged. "That to my knowledge, Burt didn't have a girlfriend. As for the freelance stuff, my guys are always picking up odd handyman jobs when they're not working for us." He paused. I thought he was going to say something else, but he changed his mind.

"On Monday," I said, "Burt tracked my husband down at his shop and set up a meeting. He said he needed to talk to Greg about something. Burt never said what, and he was shot as he arrived for the meeting. Any idea why he might want to talk to my husband?"

Ben Church swayed his handsome head back and forth. "None at all."

"And why wasn't he at work on Monday?" asked Zee.

"As I told the cops, Burt had asked for a few days off this week. He said he had some personal business to take care of." Again Ben shrugged. "We're in a short lull right now, finishing up a project, but we will be gearing up for a couple of big ones in a few weeks, so I gave it to him. He had the time coming anyway."

Zee reached out and picked up a photo from the desk. "Is this a family business?" she asked, turning the photo toward him.

"Yeah," he answered with a smile. "My dad actually runs it, but he took advantage of our slow period and took my mom on a cruise for their anniversary."

"Does he know about Burt yet?" I asked.

"No, not yet," Ben replied. "I didn't want to bother him on his vacation. He and Mom aren't able to get away that often. They'll be back this weekend. I'll tell him then or if he calls."

"Did the police talk to anyone else here at Church Construction?" I asked.

Ben nodded. "Yeah. I know they spoke to Donna out front when they were here this morning, and the foreman from the project site called to say that two detectives showed up on the site to talk to the guys. He asked if it was okay and I told him yes, as long as it wasn't all at once. The cops must have gone straight there from here."

"Did you talk to a Detective Conrad Chapman?" I asked.

"Yeah, that sounds about right." Ben pushed off from the file cabinet and glanced at the desk. From a spot near the phone, he picked up two business cards and read them. "Yeah, Chapman and his partner, Emilio Suarez."

"Yes," I said. "That's who spoke to Greg and me yesterday."

Ben put the cards back down on the desk. "Now, if you ladies will excuse me, I really do have to get to the site and see if things are back on track."

He escorted us out to the front door. Donna wasn't anywhere to be seen. At the threshold Zee stopped to study one of the photos on the wall again. It was a collage of several photos, including a front shot of a mansion, though most photos were of the pool and guest house area. "Isn't that one of Kingston's homes?" she asked. "I recognize it from an article in a home magazine awhile back."

Ben glanced at it. "Yes, that's in Beverly Hills," he said. "We remodeled both the pool house and guest house about two years ago. I understand that they've since sold the property."

I turned and looked at the young man, who seemed unfazed by what Zee had uncovered. "Did Burt work on that project?"

Ben looked at the photo, his brows knit together. "He probably did. He's been a part of our regular crew for several years now."

"So he and Marla Kingston knew each other?" asked Zee. I had to hand it to her, she was good at this. "Did you tell the police that?"

Ben ran a hand down the side of his face and cupped his chin while he considered the question. "No, I didn't. I'd forgotten about this job." He brought his hand down and studied the photo. "But I doubt Burt and Mrs. Kingston ever had any contact. Usually with properties of this size and stature, we deal with the architect and a staff member, like the property manager. We seldom deal directly with the owner. They are usually travelling or staying at one of their other homes while we work on the job. And even if an owner did interact with us directly, it would mostly likely have been with my father or me."

That made sense to me. I couldn't see Marla or Kingston themselves running out to the pool house to check on drywall, especially Marla.

"Did you work this project?" I asked.

He studied the photos again, then shook his head. "No, at least not until the end. As I recall, I was overseeing the finishing up on another one. I think it was a place in Malibu — a smaller job. My dad is very hands-on when it comes to these bigger clients."

I held out my hand to Ben Church. "Thank you for your time, Ben. I appreciate it." After we shook, he and Zee shook hands.

Before leaving, I dug into my purse and produced my T&T business card. Before I left this morning, on the back of a couple cards I had jotted down my cell number in case I needed to leave my contact information with anyone today. Just before handing it to Ben, I caught a movement out of the corner of my eye. I turned just in time to see Donna press herself up against the wall just inside the door by her desk. I held out the card to Ben.

"If you think of anything that might help us figure out why Burt landed on my husband's doorstep yesterday, please contact me."

Ben took the card and nodded.

Thirteen

As soon as we were in the car, Zee asked, "Did you see that woman skulking around, eavesdropping?"

"You caught that too, huh?" The car was an oven. With the driver's door open, I turned on the engine and set the AC on full blast to try to force some of the hot air out. "I wonder what her story is? Or if she's just nosy? I would love to have talked to her, but it seemed like an imposition at that moment. She wasn't exactly friendly. Maybe I can call her later."

"Ben Church seems like a nice young man," Zee said. "Do you think he's right, that Marla Kingston and Burt Sandoval probably never met during that job?"

"He did seem nice, also genuine," I said. "Not bad on the eyes either."

Next to me, Zee huffed at my comment. "Odelia! He's just a few years older than my Jacob."

184

"Well," I said with a chuckle, "I don't have a son, and Ben Church is a bona fide looker." I shut the driver's door. In the few minutes in the car, I could already feel sweat forming on my forehead and the heat baking my body like a doughy dinner roll. "I may be old and married, but I'm not dead." I punched the address for the next stop, the one in Westminster, into my GPS.

After checking traffic, I pulled away from the curb and thought about Zee's question. "But I do think it's possible that Marla and Burt never met at that remodel job. Marla didn't seem to recognize Burt on Saturday." I paused as something from my memory emerged from the muck. "Then again," I began and drifted off, leaving the thought incomplete as I merged into traffic, following the instructions from the GPS to get back onto the 405 Freeway.

"Then again what?" asked Zee, who'd turned in her seat to look at me.

"I was just thinking about something Marla said in the parking lot. It was right after she came screaming up to her car." Zee waiting patiently while I pieced together my memories of that moment into a whole thought. "When she came up to the car," I continued, "she immediately pointed at Burt and asked him if he'd broken her window."

"Did she call him by name?" Zee asked.

I shook my head as I came to a stop at a red light. "Not that I recall. I dismissed it as racial profiling. Here was a white man in a wheelchair, a middle-aged white woman, and a bulky Latino with tattoos, but she immediately zeroed in on the Latino and accused him of the damage." I turned toward Zee. "Is it horrible that I jumped to that conclusion about Marla?"

Zee lowered her sunglasses so that I got the full effect of her laser-hot eyes. "I'm a black woman living in Orange County, Odelia. Did you really need to ask me that? Women like her always make those ignorant assumptions." She pushed her glasses back up. "Remember just a few years ago when we were at that day spa in Newport Beach?"

I smiled tightly. "I remember. We were sitting in the lounge in the women's section waiting for our facial appointments."

"Yep, and some ditz very much like Marla Kingston breezed in and mistook me for one of the spa's staff, even though I was wearing a robe." Zee huffed and puffed. "She asked me to get her some extra towels. And when I refused, she informed me I was definitely not getting a tip and complained to management." Zee crossed her arms

186

across her chest, clearly still angry by the memory. I was there. It wasn't pretty, and, I confess, such things never happen to me. I've been treated poorly because of my size but never for my pasty complexion.

"Yes, but look on the bright side," I said, tossing her a grin, hoping to calm the waters. "The spa manager was so mortified by that woman's behavior, she comped both of our facials and threw in pedicures."

"Humph," came from my passenger's seat.

When the light turned green, I moved through the intersection. "For argument's sake," I said, moving on with my thoughts, "let's say Marla wasn't profiling Burt and she did recognize him from the job. It still wouldn't explain why they were both there and why she jumped to the conclusion that he might have been the one to break into her car. After all, the job Church Construction did for the Kingstons was two years ago."

"I agree," Zee said as she unfolded her arms and relaxed. "Unless Burt and Marla had an ongoing relationship over the past two years, I think it's unlikely she'd remember him."

"Unless," I added, "they'd had a run-in of some kind when he was working the job."

"True," Zee agreed, "then she might

remember him, but if they did have a run-in, she would be the type to report it to the company, and I'd think Ben Church would have remembered that."

"Excellent point," I agreed. I glanced at Zee. "You're pretty good at this detective stuff. Who knew?" I laughed.

"Please, Odelia," Zee said with a little laugh of her own. "I raised two kids. I'm an expert at interrogation and getting to the bottom of things."

We rode along in silence for a bit. Just before getting onto the freeway's on-ramp, Zee said, "I think we're heading down the wrong path here, Odelia."

"No," I told her, "this is the way back south to Westminster. Even without the GPS, I'm sure of it."

"No, not the way back to Orange County. I think we're taking the wrong tack with Burt and Marla."

"I'm all ears."

"Instead of asking why Burt was in that parking lot on Saturday, maybe we should be asking why Marla Kingston was there. Burt lives in Torrance. It wouldn't be that out of his way to be at a grocery store in Long Beach. But if memory serves me, the Kingstons' primary residence is in Newport Coast, and I'll bet they also have a home in either Beverly Hills or Bel Air. Long Beach is about midway between both of those properties."

"So she could have taken a potty break on her way to one or the other," I suggested, "or stopped to buy some water or tea or something."

"True," Zee said. "Did you see her with anything in her hands?"

I thought about that. "No, I didn't. She just had her purse. So maybe it was a potty break." I studied the road and checked out the map on my GPS. Slowly I began moving to the right and exited the freeway.

"Where are we going?" Zee asked.

"To the scene of the crime," I told her. "It's not too far from here."

For once I was happy that the 405 was running slow. If not, we would have been long past the turnoff we needed to get to the shopping plaza. As it was, I was able to exit the freeway and maneuver on city streets to get to the little shopping plaza I knew well.

At the rate we were going, we may never get to check out both Jordon Wests today, but I was following my nose and my nose was saying Zee was right. What was Marla Kingston doing at the shopping plaza nowhere near one of her homes? Not that there is a law against it, but I would think that most high-end shoppers would not end up in Long Beach at a shopping plaza that served the neighborhood.

The plaza that held the grocery store was set up in an L-pattern with a huge parking lot in the middle. The grocery store anchored the longest side. On the short side was a drugstore belonging to a national chain, and between them were various small businesses. I parked my car in the parking spot in front of the grocery store next to the spot where Marla's car had been on Saturday. The actual spot was currently occupied by an old white Toyota.

Leaving the ignition on for the AC, I looked around at the shops between the two anchor stores and spotted a nail shop and a greeting card store on the short side. On the long side was a pizza place, a clothing boutique, and a dog groomer. In the elbow, a chain coffee shop was wedged between the nail shop and the dog groomer, joining the two sides of the plaza. A few small tables and chairs were out in front of the coffee shop.

"It makes sense," I said to Zee, "that Marla may have felt it would be okay to leave her dog in the car if it was just for a quick in-and-out. It's not right by any means, but it makes sense. It doesn't take long for an animal or small child to become distressed in a vehicle in extremely hot weather."

Zee was also checking out the stores. "Maybe she went into that Starbucks to use the bathroom or to buy a drink."

I wasn't convinced. "Marla had parked her car here," I said, pointing to the spot on my left. "She wasn't carrying a drink when she returned to her car. And if she was going to go to Starbucks, especially on a hot day, she would have parked closer, don't you think? She was wearing ridiculously high sandals."

"Unless she needed to go to the grocery store too," Zee suggested. "Or maybe she used the restroom in the grocery store?"

I replayed the scene of Marla screaming and tottering up to her car in my head. "I don't think she was coming from the grocery store."

On my phone I opened up the Google app, clicked on the images tab, and searched for an image of Marla Kingston. After picking one that was a fairly current headshot, I saved it to my phone.

"What are you doing?" asked Zee.

"Saving a photo of Marla to show to some of the shop people."

"Great idea, Columbo," Zee said with a grin.

I shook my head and grinned. "Columbo didn't have a cell phone. But think how much more he could have done with one?"

I turned off the ignition and reluctantly got out of my cool car. Zee climbed out of the passenger's side and joined me by the rear of the car next to mine.

"I'm pretty sure," I said, pointing off to the left of the market, "that Marla came from the left of the store, from one of those shops. "We were standing about here, and she was screaming long before she reached us, so we all turned to see what the ruckus was about."

"That meant she had to be inside one of those places when the dog was being rescued," Zee said, shielding her eyes with a hand above her sunglasses. "If she'd been outside, she would have noticed people standing by her car long before the glass was shattered. We're not that far from the front of the market."

"Exactly," I confirmed. "So that leaves the pizza place, the boutique, and the groomer. She couldn't have been at the groomer because she would have taken Maurice with her. And I doubt Marla is into greasy pizza."

"You never know," Zee said, looking at

me. "With that misogynist husband of hers, maybe she sneaks in some of her favorite foods at out-of-the-way places so he doesn't rag on her about getting fat. You've heard some of the things he's said about women."

"I hadn't thought of that, but it's a possibility." I started walking toward the line of shops. "Let's start with the boutique. I think that's our best chance."

The clothing boutique was called Kelly's Fashion Corner. In all the years I'd been shopping at the nearby supermarket, I'd never noticed it. As soon as we entered, a light bell sounded. The shop was crowded, with racks of clothing against walls painted a soft blue-green and with several round racks down the middle, and it was blissfully cool inside. I pushed my sunglasses to the top of my head and started looking around, Zee on my heels. Besides nicely displayed clothing, there were shelves and tall narrow rotating racks displaying various accessories. Everything was cute and well-presented and moderate in both price and quality — definitely not the sort of place Marla Kingston would shop. Near the back was a small glass display case, behind which a pleasantly plump woman was bent rearranging jewelry in the case.

"Be with you in a sec," she said in a cheerful voice without looking up.

A few seconds later, satisfied with the positioning of several bracelets and necklaces, she looked up and greeted us with a smile. "Hello, ladies. Can I help you find something?" She was mid to late forties with light brown hair cut into a chin-length bob. Her face was round and friendly, her cheeks two dots of rosy blush the same color as her lipstick. Around her neck glasses hung from a sparkly chain of multicolored stones.

"I hope you can help us," I answered back with my friendliest voice. "Were you working this past Saturday?"

"Why, yes, of course," she answered. "I'm Kelly, the owner. I'm here every day but Sunday, 10 to 6, except I close on Saturday around 4."

I produced my phone and showed her the photo of Marla. "Was this woman in here this past Saturday?"

Kelly slipped her glasses onto her face and examined the photo. "Humph," she said once she'd removed her glasses. "Hard to forget a piece of work like that."

"Was she in here?" I asked again. "Around noon or so?"

"Oh yes, she was here about that time," Kelly said. "I remember because I usually grab a quick bite to eat between 11:15 and

194

11:45. I don't have any employees, so if it's quiet, I eat in the back with my feet up and listen for the front doorbell. I get a lot of customers from those large office buildings across the street, so I like to be free from about noon until 2 during the week. If it's very busy, I wait and eat later. Saturdays can be dead or very busy; hard to tell." She tapped my phone, which I still held out between us. "This one came in just before 11:30."

"Are you sure?" Zee asked.

"Positive," Kelly replied. "It was very slow this past Saturday. It usually is on very hot days."

"Did she buy anything?" I asked, thinking maybe Marla made a small purchase that would fit into her handbag.

"Nope," Kelly said. "She roamed the store, pulling out this and that, but I don't think she was really interested. When I asked if I could help, she waved me away like I was a servant." Kelly paused. "Frankly, I think she was waiting for someone and ducked in here to keep cool."

"Why do you say that?" Zee asked.

"Because she kept glancing out the front window," Kelly explained. "She'd wander around, pick something up, then saunter to the window and look out, like I was too stupid to notice."

"Do you know who she is?" I asked, showing her the photo again.

"I sure do," Kelly answered with an uptick to her tone. "She's that annoying Marla Sinclair from that tacky TV show. The one who married that creep Kelton Kingston. I watched that show a few times before I got tired of their snotty attitude toward us common folks." Kelly studied me. "Hey, didn't I see you on the news? Aren't you one of the people who rescued that poor dog of hers?"

I nodded. "Actually, it was my husband who smashed her car window."

"Well, your husband deserves a medal, in my opinion," Kelly said with authority. "Who in their right mind leaves a poor animal in a car in heat like this?" She shook her head. "If she'd brought it in here, I'd have understood."

"Did she ever make contact with anyone while she was in here?" I asked. "Or place a call or anything like that?"

Kelly shook her head gently from side to side. "Not that I noticed. She'd pick up a blouse or something, pretend to be looking at it, then go to the window and look out. Then she'd discard the item, pick up another, and go through the same motion. She did that for almost thirty minutes." She took a breath in her narrative and came out from behind the counter. She started straightening a table of neatly folded knit shirts that did not need straightening. "That woman touched these things like they had vermin. If she ever comes in again, I'm going to ask her to leave."

"Do you know what caused her to leave?" Zee asked. She'd been fingering some light, summery scarves.

Kelly looked up from the table. "I believe it was the smashing of her car window." She went to the front window of the shop and gazed out. "She'd picked up another garment and brought it back to the window right here. She wasn't here but a few seconds when she dropped what was in her hands and ran straight out the door." Kelly turned back to us. "I tried to see what was going on, but I couldn't see much except a crowd starting to form. One of the kids from the pizza place dashed over there, then filled me in on what had happened when he came back. Later that night my husband and I watched it on the news." She paused. "I do hope they took that poor dog away from that horrible woman. Do you know if they did?"

I shook my head. "I don't think so, but

Marla Kingston did get a hefty fine for leaving him in her car."

Zee held the scarf in her hand toward Kelly. "Kelly, I'll take this. I think my daughter would love it."

"Aw," the proprietor said with a smile, "please don't feel obligated to buy something just because I'm answering your questions."

"I'm not. I really do think this would look lovely on Hannah," Zee told her. "She just had a baby, and it would be nice for her to get a gift not baby-related."

"Alrighty then," Kelly said, clearly pleased. She took the scarf to the back counter to ring it up.

While Zee and Kelly were transacting business, I stood by the window and looked out toward the parking lot where my car was parked. I couldn't see it clearly because of the other rows of cars, but the parking row was angled just enough for me to note that it was my car through the gaps of other parked vehicles. I could see the car parked next to me more clearly, but not by much. On Saturday, that's where Marla's Mercedes would have been parked. But even then, looking out this window on Saturday, Marla would only have been able to see a crowd gathering, not what was actually going on.

But a crowd would have been enough to alarm her into leaving the shop and rushing toward her vehicle.

After thanking Kelly, Zee and I left the shop and stood outside under the awning protecting the storefronts. "What do you think?" Zee asked. "Do you think Marla was waiting for someone?"

"Sure sounds that way," I said with a slight rise of my shoulders to show I wasn't 100 percent sure. "She could have been waiting on someone but keeping out of sight and keeping cool in Kelly's place. Maybe she kept checking out the window to see if Maurice was okay, although at this distance she'd never be able to monitor his condition."

"Do you want to check out the other places?" Zee asked as she tucked the small bag with the scarf into her handbag.

"No," I said, turning to scan the other businesses. "It seems like she might have gone only to Kelly's. You know, maybe she was going to meet someone at Starbucks but was keeping an eye out for him or her."

"Maybe someone she's cheating on Kingston with?" Zee suggested. "It would make sense why she would pick a place this far away from one of her homes." Zee and I both turned our heads toward the coffee shop, which was right next door to Kelly's. The clothing store would be a perfect place to scout out anyone heading in or out of Starbucks.

"Feel like an iced coffee?" I asked her.

Zee smiled. "Lead the way."

Starbucks wasn't very busy. A few tables were occupied by people with laptops. Zee and I laid claim to two of the upholstered chairs by the entrance. While she held down the fort, I went to the counter to order our iced drinks.

"I asked the girl at the counter if she recognized Marla's photo," I said when I returned with the drinks and took my seat, "but I struck out. She wasn't here Saturday and never recalled seeing her any other time."

We were kicked back in our comfy chairs, enjoying our iced coffee drinks and tossing out possibilities, when someone I recognized entered the coffee shop. It was a young guy, late teens or early twenties, but this time he didn't have a skateboard with him. He went straight to the counter and ordered his drink. Without a word to Zee, I got up and went to the counter.

"I'll pay for his order," I told the girl at the counter.

The kid turned to check out his benefactor, and I saw a flicker of recognition in his eyes. "Remember me, Charlie?" I asked.

He nodded. "Yeah, from Saturday. You and the guy in the wheelchair rescued that dog." He turned back to the cashier. "If she's paying, throw in a couple of those big cookies and bump my drink up to the largest size." The girl looked at me and I gave her the okay.

After paying and waiting for Charlie to get his cookies, we moved over to stand in the area where the drinks were picked up. "Can I ask you a couple of questions, Charlie?"

He shrugged. "Sure, you're paying." He pulled one of the cookies out of the bag and took a big bite. I glanced over at Zee, who was only a few feet away and watching us.

"Do you hang around here a lot?"

Charlie shrugged. "Enough. Don't live very far away."

"You know the woman whose dog we rescued?" I held up my phone with Marla's photo. "This one. Have you ever seen her here before Saturday?"

He studied the photo while taking another bite of the cookie. "Don't think so." He looked up at me. "She's some famous bitch, isn't she?"

"Sort of," I said. "But you don't recall seeing her around before?"

"Nah." The barista called Charlie's name and he picked up his drink. It was an iced something topped with whipped cream and drizzled with caramel sauce. "Don't think I've ever seen her before Saturday. Why you asking?" He stuck a straw into his concoction and took a long drink. He was taller than me by several inches. Sweat and heat radiated from him.

I took a second to think of something to say. "Her husband is making things difficult for my husband and me because of the broken car window."

"But even the cops said you were in the right with that," he said.

"I know, but that isn't stopping them from harassing us."

"So why ask if she hangs out around here? It's a free country. She can be anywhere she wants to be." He polished off his cookie.

Charlie had a point. Marla Kingston could be anywhere she wanted to be, so my explanation seemed lame. I wasn't sure about telling him that I was trying to put Marla here for a reason, to try and link her somehow to Burt Sandoval. I wasn't sure I wanted to bring up Burt.

"True," I told him. "I guess we're just grasping for straws — anything to get

Kingston off our backs."

His eyes brightened. "You looking to blackmail them to stop bugging you? That could be cool. I could get into that."

"No, no," I quickly said. "Nothing like that." It was a bit scary how eager this kid was to jump on the blackmail wagon. "We are just trying to see if she's done this before." It was a lie and not a very good one, but it was all I had up my sleeve at the moment. "Do you work around here or are you off from college or something?" I asked. It was a deflection, but also I was curious. Charlie was at that awkward age. He was either on the tail end of high school or recently passed it and waiting out the summer to move on to the next phase in his life. Like before, he was dressed in beach clothing — board shorts and a T-shirt — but except for the sweat that all of us were wearing, his clothes were clean. It looked like he took decent care of himself. He could also still be living at home.

"Got a summer job working nights," he said without enthusiasm. "Nothing great, but it'll do until school starts. You know, make a few bucks. Then I'm off to Santa Barbara for college in the fall." That information told me that he was about eighteen. "If I do see the crazy bitch," he continued, "do you want me to call you or something?"

I thought about giving him my contact information but changed my mind. Not that I was worried he'd use it, but he seemed the type to become too enthusiastic, and not in a good way, should something come up.

"No, that's okay," I told him. "I don't think she'll be back."

Charlie grunted and left, and I returned to my seat next to Zee. "Who was that?" she asked as soon as I sat down.

"His name is Charlie. He's the kid who took the video Saturday that showed up on the news." I took a long pull off my iced coffee. "I was hoping maybe he'd seen Marla here before, but no such luck."

"Unless she came to this plaza a lot, people probably wouldn't notice her," Zee said.

"Ha," I scoffed. "Marla Kingston is hardly an incognito type of personality. She'd stick out like a sore thumb in this place. She did Saturday the way she was dressed and acting." I finished my coffee. "Just to be thorough, let's show her picture to the other shops in this place."

No one in the other businesses remembered seeing Marla. Striking out, we picked up a couple of bottles of cold water from our last stop, the drugstore, and returned to my car.

"Westminster, then home?" asked Zee.

"First I'd like to swing by Holly's mailbox place," I said, unscrewing the top from my water bottle. I took a drink and set the bottle into one of the cup holders in the console. "It's not that far from here." I turned to her. "Do you mind?"

Zee took a swig from her own water bottle. "Not at all. Lead on."

The mailbox place was an independent business, not one of the big chains. The name of the place was Your Office. In addition to mailboxes and mail forwarding, it offered all kinds of business assistance, like packing and mailing packages, notary services, office supplies, and even computer time rental. It was in an old building that housed two other small businesses — a computer repair shop on the bottom floor next to it and a small accounting firm taking up the top floor. The floor of Your Office was scarred linoleum and the walls needed painting, but it was clean and the inventory neatly displayed. To one side was a bank of individual mailboxes, small ones on top with larger ones on the bottom. To the left of the space was a service counter. A young black man was seated behind it reading a graphic novel. Both his head and his face were clean shaven. A loose black T-shirt covered a thin but wiry body. He glanced up with sharp eyes when we approached. Close up, he didn't look much older than Charlie.

"Can I help you?" he said. He put the book down but remained in his seat.

"I have this address for someone and didn't realize it was a mail place," I lied. "I was hoping to speak with her in person."

"A lot of people use our address as theirs," was his response, delivered in a bored voice.

"Can you tell us," Zee chimed in, "if a Holly West has a mailbox here? Maybe we simply have the wrong address."

The young man eyed Zee and then me, then said, "I'm sorry, but we don't give out the names of our customers. Most use a box for a reason, get my drift?" Zee and I glanced at each other. We both got the drift, and it was one I'd expected.

Zee dug a twenty-dollar bill from the depths of her bag. She smoothed it and set it flat on the counter but kept her fingers on top, holding it down tight. She looked at the man but said nothing.

Again, he looked at both of us. "But there are two of you."

I got that drift too. Reaching into my tote,

I dug out a twenty of my own and set it on the table next to Zee's. "That should buy information and you keeping your mouth shut about our visit here," I told him.

The guy leaned forward. "That last part will cost you another twenty."

It was Zee's turn to lean in. She removed her sunglasses and latched her eyes onto his. "Didn't your momma ever teach you that greed is one of the devil's tools?"

He leaned forward more, their dark faces close, their eyes unflinching. "Only thing my momma taught me was to grab what you can when you can from whoever you can." He leaned back, keeping his eyes on Zee. "I'll bet that's not what you taught your kids, is it?"

Zee reached into her bag for her wallet, but he stopped her with, "No, I want the other twenty from her." He jerked his chin in my direction. "The white lady."

With a nod to Zee, I pulled out another twenty, glad I'd hit the ATM before picking her up this morning. "There," I said putting it on the counter. "So what do you know about Holly West?"

He scooped up the three twenties. "Tough chick but kinda cute. She comes in once a week to pick up her mail. Every Wednesday around 6, just before we close."

"Never any other time?" Zee asked.

He shrugged. "Not that I can tell. She could come in after hours. Our clients all have a security code that lets them into the box section. But I don't think she comes in except on Wednesday."

I glanced back at the bank of mailboxes and noticed for the first time the sliding gate that ran from one side of the front door to the short wall next to the boxes. When extended, the gate would cut off the inventory and counter from the box area and front door, allowing customers access to only that area when the place was closed.

"Why don't you think she comes in after hours?" I asked.

"Because her box is always full until Wednesday," he told us. "I put the mail in the boxes every day, Monday through Saturday. She don't get much, but her box is never emptied until Wednesday night. Starts clean on Thursday."

"And you said she's a tough chick," I said to him. "Does that mean tattoos, piercings, stuff like that?"

"Nah," he said with a slight shake of his head. "I've never noticed anything like that. I mean, she's not gangsta or anything like that." He paused. "It's more her attitude. She's not very . . . um . . . approachable.

You know what I mean?"

"You mean," Zee said, "that you hit on her and she rejected you, right?"

For the first time, the guy smiled. "Hey, like I said, she's cute. Pretty long hair, got that half Asian, half white thing going on. You know. But man, she's cold. Whenever I speak to her at all, I mean, even for business, she doesn't talk. Just gives you this steely look that can freeze a man's balls."

Back in the car, I called Greg and put him on speaker. When he answered, I asked without any lead-in, "Hi honey, was Jane Newell Asian?"

"Yeah, she was," he said. "Korean. She was adopted when she was a baby. Why?"

"The guy at the mailbox place just told us that Holly West is half Asian, half white, so I wanted to check that out with you."

There was quiet on the other end of the line, then, "Who is the other half of the *us,* Odelia?"

"Me," chimed in Zee. "I'm helping out Odelia a little bit." An audible groan came from the phone.

"Gee, Greg," Zee shot back at the phone, "tell me how you really feel."

There was a slight chuckle from the phone. "You know I love ya, Zee, but Seth is going to have our heads if anything hap-

209

pens. You know how he feels about you chumming along with Odelia on this stuff."

"I do," she replied, "but nothing is going to happen, and I'm a grown woman. I don't need my husband's permission to hang out with my best friend." She took a breath. "Besides, that last incident was not Odelia's fault."

"All right," Greg said, "I'm just pointing out a fact. Have you girls found out anything?"

"Little threads here and there," I told him. "Not much more. And those threads don't tie together at all. There's a Jordon West in Costa Mesa, but he says he's not related to Holly West. We're on our way to check out another Jordon West who lives in Westminster, then I'm dropping Zee off and heading home. I'll give you a full report over dinner."

"Sounds good," he said, "although you're going to be right in the thick of rush hour. You're already facing the start of it now."

"Well," I said, "it can't be helped. We're on a roll of checking off the obvious leads."

"Since there's no leftover Chinese food from last night and you might be late, how about I pick up a pizza for dinner?"

"Sounds good to me," I told him. "Half and half?"

Again Greg chuckled. "Half and half," he assured me. My husband loves pineapple and ham pizza, which I dislike. I'm a purest: I prefer pepperoni. In all our years of marriage, this is one of the few things we haven't been able to compromise on. Both of us like green peppers, mushrooms, and onions on our pizza, so our usual order is half and half with the veggies on both sides.

FOURTEEN

Usually when I head someplace new, I like to check it out on Google — not just on the map, but also through the street view feature. I like to know what the building looks like before I get there so I can identify it easier instead of looking for street numbers that might or might not be visible. I didn't do this with Jordon West number two's address, though, and as we pulled up in front of the address Marigold had given me, I wished that I had.

We pulled up in front of a sprawling two-story building that took up the corner of a busy street and stretched down a small side street. It was an older building, solid looking but in need of a paint job. Small patches of dried grass bordered it, with scrappy low hedges hugging the building just below window level. The main entrance was on the side street.

Pulling up in a loading area in front of the

place, I leaned across Zee for a better look at the address numbers painted across the front door. "This can't be the place, can it?"

"Does the address match the one you have?" Zee asked.

I double-checked. "Yes, the address matches."

The two of us stared at the sign attached to the wall next to the front door: *Bayview Assisted Living.* "I don't think there are any bays around here for anyone to view," Zee noted.

I put the car in gear and moved it to a curbside parking spot just up from the main door. After we both took swigs from our water bottles, we opened the door to the heat and slogged our way into the air-conditioned lobby of Bayview Assisted Living.

The lobby was small, with a few cheap vinyl chairs gathered together in one corner. To the left was a smaller room with glass walls. Inside, a few people in wheelchairs were watching something on TV. It looked like a rerun of an old sitcom. There was another room next to it with glass walls facing the reception area. On the other side was another glass wall that looked out onto what appeared to be a small courtyard. A few people were in this room, most sleeping in wheelchairs or on regular chairs. A couple of staff members in colorful uniforms were scattered in the rooms, talking and helping the patients.

We approached the L-shaped reception desk and were greeted by a young woman with pale skin and blond hair worn in a ponytail. She was wearing a cheerful uniform top like the other staff members. Her name tag announced her as *Debbie.*

"Hi, Debbie," I began as soon as we made eye contact. "We're looking for someone and were told he might be here."

"A resident," she asked, "or an employee?"

Now there was a good question. "I'm not sure," I replied. "This address was the only one connected with him. His name is Jordon West. Do you know him?"

There was no mistaking the look of surprise Debbie cast my way, then turned on Zee. It was as if we'd asked if the Easter Bunny lived there under an assumed name.

"Um," she said, "yes, I do. Are you relatives?"

I shook my head. "No, we're actually trying to locate his daughter, Holly West. We're hoping he can help us."

"His daughter?" she parroted. "Are you sure you have the right Jordon West? Because I don't think he has a daughter or any family."

Zee stepped forward. "We understand that this might be a delicate matter," she told the young woman in a soft, even voice. "Is there someone else we can speak to, Debbie? Like maybe the manager of this place?"

Still in shock, she nodded. "Sure, Celeste is here — I mean, Mrs. Jackson. She's in charge of the facility."

"Will you see if she has time to see us?" Zee asked. "It shouldn't take long."

Debbie picked up the phone on her desk and poked in three numbers. She spoke in a low tone into the receiver, just loud enough that we could hear her telling the other person someone was there to see Jordon West. There was a slight pause on Debbie's side, then she said, "That's what I said. They're here to see Jordon West." I looked over at Zee and she cocked an eyebrow in my direction.

Debbie put her phone back into the cradle. "Mrs. Jackson will be out in a minute," she told us.

Before we could barely reply with a thank you, a door behind the reception area opened and out came a very tall black woman dressed in tailored navy pants and a peridot blouse — Zee's favorite color. Her copper-colored hair was intricately braided and wound around her head, making her appear even taller. She had a wide open face, small dark eyes, and high cheekbones to envy.

"I'm Celeste Jackson," she told us, "the manager of Bayview Assisted Living. May I help you?" She stayed behind the counter and did not offer us her hand.

"I'm Odelia Grey and this is my friend Zee Washington," I told her. "We're looking for Jordon West. Does Mr. West live or work here?"

Instead of answering, Celeste Jackson opened a short gate built into the counter and ushered us behind the desk and into her office.

"Are you family or some sort of legal representative?" she asked once we were seated in the two plain visitor chairs across from her desk and she was seated behind it.

"Neither," I answered honestly. "We're trying to locate a woman named Holly West. Her father is Jordon West."

Celeste leaned forward. "I seriously doubt our Mr. West is the man you're looking for," she told us in a businesslike voice. "I'm pretty sure he doesn't have a daughter. He's been living with us since he was seventeen years old."

"Living here?" I asked without hiding my surprise. Most of the people we'd seen in the public rooms were quite elderly and sick. "What's wrong with him?"

Celeste weighed her words carefully. "I shouldn't tell you this, but since you're about the only people who have shown an interest in that poor man in nearly thirty years, I will tell you that he came to us after being in an alcohol-related vehicle accident when he was seventeen."

I felt my eyes pop open at the information. "So the Jordon West who lives here is a vegetable?" I blurted out.

"Odelia," I heard Zee softly chide me.

Celeste smiled at both of us with great patience. "Mr. West is not in a vegetative state, but he is greatly incapacitated. He can't talk beyond grunts and a few mangled words, but he can hear quite well and respond with his eyes. He's also a quadriplegic. I understand it was a very bad accident. He was lucky to have survived at all."

"My husband is a paraplegic," I told her. "How extensive are Mr. West's injuries?"

"Outside of wiggling a couple of fingers on his right hand, he can't move at all from the neck down," she told us.

"And he's been that way for thirty years?" Zee asked.

"Yes," Celeste said. "So you see, I doubt he is the father of the woman you seek."

"But what about his family? Where are they?" I asked, grasping at straws. "Maybe he fathered a child in his teens, before the accident."

"Mr. West has no one but his mother. Shortly after Mr. West came to us, she moved out of state."

"And who pays for his care?"

"A trust managed by a law firm, but his mother hasn't been to see him since she left the area," Celeste said. Her voice changed from businesslike to sad touched with anger. "But that's about all I can tell you, so if you don't mind, it's almost dinnertime, which means we're quite busy." She stood up, signaling we should too.

"Can we see Mr. West?" Zee asked as the three of us neared the door.

"Why?" Celeste asked. "Don't you believe me?" She squared her shoulders, which straightened her to her full intimidating height.

"Oh, no, it's not that," Zee quickly said. "It's just that if he hasn't had a visitor in all this time, I think it's time he did have one." Zee glanced at me. "Or two. We'll only stay a minute or two, I promise."

Celeste thought about the request a few

beats, then smiled. "I can see no harm." She turned and opened a different door than the one we'd used before. "Although he does have lots of friends among our staff. He's quite intelligent and loves to listen to audio books and watch movies. We're all quite fond of him."

She led us down a sparkling clean corridor smelling of disinfectant. "Our facility is quite old and privately owned," she said, "but we keep it in tip-top shape." At a wide door, she stopped. The door was open, showing a very large room with floor-to-ceiling windows that looked out onto a courtyard filled with small plants and rose bushes and a couple of benches. Judging from the direction of the room, I was betting it was the same courtyard I'd spotted earlier off the other room by reception. There was a large hospital bed against the center of one wall, and a nice flat-screen TV was mounted on the wall across from it. Below the wall was a bulletin board with a lot of photos pinned to it. The TV was off, but soft classical music was coming from somewhere. In front of the window a large industrial wheelchair faced the courtyard.

"Jordon," Celeste called brightly, "I have some company for you." She walked up to the wheelchair and came around to face the person in it. "Would you like some company?" She smiled down. "I thought you might." She waved us over.

"This is Odelia and Zee; they wanted to meet you," she told the person in the wheelchair.

I looked down to see a middle-aged man, shrunken and crippled by his injuries. His head was shaved bald and his skin was waxy. He drooled slightly as he smiled up at us. His mouth of misshapen teeth worked but nothing much came out.

"See, Jordon is wiggling his fingers," Celeste told us with a smile. "He's pleased and wants to shake your hands."

Zee went first. She took the hand with the moving fingers in her hand and gently squeezed it. "I'm so happy to meet you, Jordon." I was next and did and said the same.

We stayed just the few promised minutes, during which Jordon, through his active fingers, had Celeste show us what book he was currently listening to — the blockbuster bestseller *The Help.* "He loved the movie and wanted to listen to the book," Celeste explained. "The local library got us a copy for him. We do a couple chapters a day, don't we, Jordon." His eyes danced in agreement.

He started gesturing with his mobile

fingers and a couple of strangled sounds came out of his mouth. Celeste smiled and pulled a cell phone from her pocket. "He wants a photo with the two of you," she told us. "It will be printed out and pinned to his wall of friends over there." She gestured toward the bulletin board. Zee and I were happy to comply.

Before we said goodbye, both Zee and I squeezed Jordon's fingers again.

Celeste walked us to the front door and this time offered her hand. "I'm happy you wanted to visit Jordon. He loves people, and I'm sorry he's not the person you thought he might be."

"That's okay," I told her. "It certainly wasn't wasted time at all. It was a pleasure meeting him. My husband is quite active in both paraplegic and quadriplegic sports. Would it be possible if I brought Greg by sometime to visit with Jordon? I think he'd like to meet him. In fact, would you be so kind as to send me that photo?" I held out one of my cards with my personal cell number on the back. "Just text it to this number."

Celeste took the card and nodded. "A visit would be very nice, Odelia," she said with a genuine smile. "But please call ahead because some days Jordon isn't feeling as well as he was today. Today was a good day."

As we started out the door, I said to Zee, "I doubt he dated Jane Newell."

"Excuse me?" I heard a voice behind me say.

Zee and I turned to see Celeste Jackson eyeing us with curiosity. "I apologize for eavesdropping, but did you mention Jane Newell?"

I felt the hair on my neck stand up at the thought that maybe the trip to Westminster would yield something in our search. "Yes," I confirmed, turning back around.

Celeste opened the door to Bayview and beckoned us inside. From the lobby she escorted us back into her office in silence, where she made sure both doors were shut securely. "What does Jane Newell have to do with your questions?" she asked once we were all settled back in our previous seats.

"Did you know Jane?" Zee asked.

"Years ago," Celeste answered. Unconsciously, she rolled a pen back and forth across her desk without taking her eyes from us. "She worked here years ago."

"She worked here?" I echoed.

Celeste nodded. "I wasn't the manager back then, but a nurse. Jane was a college girl who worked here part-time." She looked uneasy, like she wasn't sure how much to tell us.

"Jane is dead," I announced, hoping that would erase any privacy concerns Celeste might have. "She passed away about two months ago. She was the mother of Holly West, the young woman we're trying to locate. As I said before, a Jordon West is listed as Holly's father. My husband knew Jane in college. She left her junior year because she was pregnant."

The pen stopped rolling, trapped under Celeste's sturdy fingers like a squished bug. Celeste leaned back and looked out her single window. Her window didn't face the cute courtyard but the street, and it had security bars on the window. "It can't be," she said more to herself than to us. "It just can't be. It's impossible."

"What can't be?" asked Zee, who was sitting at attention, her total focus, like mine, on Celeste, waiting for more information to dribble out.

Celeste turned around to face us again. "As I said, Jane Newell worked here. She was a nurse's aide. I don't believe she was here very long, a few months maybe, but during that time she became quite close to Jordon. They were both young, and when her work was caught up, she often read to him or took him out to the courtyard for some sun. He was devastated when she left. She did visit him a few times over the years, but then the visits stopped. That's why I remember her so well." Her mouth took a turn south.

"During her visits she never brought along a child, a little girl?" Zee asked.

"Not that I remember," Celeste replied. "Of course, I wasn't here for all of her visits, and back then I was a nurse and not the manager, so sometimes my schedule changed and I worked nights." Celeste shook her head. "But it's impossible that he fathered her child."

"As I said," I told her, "my husband is quite active with athletes with serious challenges. Many of them have children — natural children. Many are quite capable of erections."

She shook her head again, "But Jordon isn't. That's one function that did not survive his accident."

"Did Jane leave her job here on good terms?" Zee asked.

"As I recall, very good terms, even though it was a short time. She was kind of distant emotionally. Except for Jordon, she didn't make any close friends here, even though she was well-liked. She did her job, spent time with Jordon, then one day gave notice. It didn't surprise anyone. Aides came and went regularly since for most it's just a part-time job and not that well paid." She paused and studied the pen trapped under her fingers. "One thing we all thought was odd was that she chose to work here. It was obvious that she was very bright and had never done any work like this before — you know, caring for people, cleaning up their messes, physical labor. Not that she didn't do it well, she did, but I think at first it was tough for her." Celeste smiled at the memory. "But she fooled us all and quickly became quite good working with our residents and doing the manual labor."

"If she didn't have experience, why was she hired?" Zee asked.

"Like I said," Celeste explained. "There's a big turnover on part-time aides. We often have jobs open but few applicants. I'm sure the manager at the time saw Jane as a pair of willing hands with a good attitude."

I stood up. "We've taken up a lot of your time, Celeste. Thank you for being such a help. For some reason, Jane Newell put Jordon West down as the father of her child, and with her being dead, we may never know why. Since Holly has never visited him, she might already know he's not her father." I reached out my hand. Celeste stood up and shook it with warmth.

"I hope you understand," Celeste said, still holding my hand, "that a lot of what I disclosed today about Jordon is confidential." I nodded my understanding.

"I like Celeste," I said once we were back in the car. I drank some of my water. It was warm but wet.

"Me too," Zee said, taking her own drink. "She didn't have to tell us all that she did. I got the feeling she was so happy someone, anyone, was taking an interest in poor Jordon."

"Can you believe his own mother doesn't even visit him?" I asked with disgust. "Just sends money for his care through a trust. What a heartless bitch."

"Sadly, stuff like that happens all the time," Zee said, putting on her sunglasses. "For some parents it's too much seeing their child in such a condition. Others are just selfish." She sighed. "At least they have the money to give him care."

I shrugged. "Or that trust was set up with insurance money after the accident. Jordon enjoys a pretty big private room. It can't be cheap, even in a moderate place like that. But either way, at least he's in a decent place. It's not fancy, but it's clean and they clearly care for their patients."

From Bayview Assisted Living we easily found the freeway and headed home. We were in the thick of rush hour now, and the freeway moved like sludge.

"I was thinking," Zee said. "What if Holly is Jordon's daughter?"

I glanced over at her. "You heard what Celeste said. He's impotent."

"I read a novel years ago about a woman, a nurse, who did it with a patient who was pretty much in a vegetated state because she wanted a baby."

I looked at Zee as if she'd sprouted three heads. "Are you kidding me?"

"No," Zee said, looking at me. "She raped this guy who was near death and got pregnant by him."

I looked straight ahead, trying to wrap my head around this information. "That's icky," I finally declared. "And it was fiction." I gave a few shakes of my right index finger in her direction to make my point. "And, don't forget that Celeste said that Jordon is impotent. I'm guessing in this novel, veggie man was not."

FIFTEEN

"The World According to Garp," Greg told me as we ate our pizza. "It's by John Irving."

"What?" I said, my mouth half full of pizza. Greg had brought home our usual pizza order, and I'd thrown together a nice salad. We were washing it down with a couple of cold beers while I filled him in on my day's activities, ending with the visit to Bayside Assisted Living and Zee's remarks about fictional conception.

"That's the novel that's from," Greg said. "Haven't you read it?" He took a drink from his beer bottle.

I love to read, but my husband is a super reader, polishing off a novel almost every week, even with his busy schedule. Still, it surprised me that he knew that reference. "Apparently not," I said. "I think I'd remember a little thing like that."

Greg laughed. "It's how Garp is conceived in the book. His mother, a nurse, straddles a dying patient to become inseminated."

"She raped him, you mean."

He nodded. "Yes, it was rape, considering he was in no shape to give his consent."

I popped a grape tomato into my mouth and popped it with my back teeth, letting the cool, tangy juice saturate my tongue. "Do you think that's possible in Jordon's case? We were told he's impotent, but could he have, you know, risen to the occasion if properly motivated?"

"I doubt it if he's in as bad of shape as you say. And I'm sure the medical staff at that home would have noticed any erections over the years refuting the diagnosis. After all," Greg said with a sly wink in my direction, "sometimes we guys have no control over our junk's response."

We were halfway through dinner when I brought the subject up again. "A lot of our friends in chairs have kids. Were all of them conceived naturally?"

Greg nearly choked on the pizza he was about to swallow. "Gee, I don't know, Odelia. Should I take a poll at the next basketball game?"

"Smart ass. I just thought maybe you guys talked amongst yourselves — you know, like us women."

He took a drink of beer while he considered the question. "I do happen to know of guys who cannot conceive through regular means because of their injuries, so it is done via artificial insemination. That's probably how we would have done it if we'd wanted children, even though I can get an erection."

I nodded. "So do you think Jane would have done something like that?"

Greg put down his beer and wiped his mouth with a napkin. "No, I don't. First of all, taking a sample like that would have taken time and a plan for proper storage, not to mention impregnating herself. I would think the odds are against it being successful." He paused. "I think Jane got pregnant by someone else and for some reason put down Jordon's name on the birth certificate."

We were both quiet, but our eyes met. I was the first to say what was obviously on both of our minds. "So you could still be Holly's father."

"It's a possibility. Maybe Jane just wanted a child to raise by herself, like in the book, without any paternal strings."

Greg picked up another piece of ham and pineapple pizza. "All this has brought back a lot of memories," he said. "I met Jane during her sophomore year. It was at a mixer. That summer she got some fancy internship at a big company." He put the pizza slice down on his plate without taking a bite. "She was quite excited about it. She still had the position when she returned to school that fall and was even more excited by it, though it didn't leave her much time for anything besides school. I only saw her on occasion, but I do remember that several months before she left school, she seemed different, distracted, and I hardly saw her. I assumed she had a regular boyfriend. She eventually told me that she'd quit the internship and was working at a rest home."

"That's quite a big change. Did she say why?" I asked.

Greg looked off, past the table, as he remembered. "She said the job with the corporation had become boring, and she wanted more hands-on experience with real people." He picked up the slice again. "A few months later, she was gone."

"Celeste described Jane as kind of distant emotionally but nice," I told him. I pushed my plate away.

"Yeah, I would agree with that. She didn't share much with me, even though we saw each other off and on for almost two years. You'd think we'd get to know each other in all that time, but all I knew was that she was from South Korea and had been adopted by a couple in the Midwest when she was a baby." He took a bite and chewed before continuing. "The sad thing is, she was orphaned twice. Once in South Korea as a baby and then again here the summer before college."

My hand instinctively when to my heart in empathy. "How tragic."

"Yes. Her adoptive parents were killed by a drunk driver — at least that's what she told me. She had no other family." He took another drink of his beer. "Sometimes I think she chose me to be her part-time lover because she sensed I was a safe place. We liked each other but weren't in love. I was lonely. She was lonely. Neither wanted an attachment at the time or made demands; it worked. And it wasn't wham, bam, thank you, sir. We'd talk about movies, books, or school. Sometimes she'd cook me a meal at her apartment. But when it came to her private thoughts, she was very guarded. She was also very smart. When you looked into her eyes, you could see the gears moving. She wasn't exactly manipulative; she was nicer than that. But I got the feeling she played chess with her life in her head. Making moves and planning the next. She didn't have a lot of friends, just friendly acquaintances."

"Celeste at Bayview said Jordon's injury was due to drunk driving, but I don't recall her saying if he was at fault or someone else." I started picking at the label on my beer bottle. "You don't think that's a connection, do you?"

He shrugged as he polished off his pizza in several big bites.

"Well, tomorrow I hope to meet up with Holly," I told him as I picked the label clean off my bottle.

"You mean stalk her?" he asked.

"You say that like it's a bad thing." I shot Greg a half-curled lip in jest. "Since the mailbox guy said she shows up around their closing time, I thought I'd hang out there starting around five."

"And what if she comes later?" Greg asked.

"Then I wait. He said she always picks up her mail on Wednesday evenings, even if it is later."

"If I didn't have a big job to finish tomorrow, I'd take off early and go with you," he said.

"That's okay. Zee wants to tag along again." I smiled. "She's very good at this and very good with people."

"I'm not surprised." Greg closed the pizza box. Putting it on his lap, he ferried it over to the kitchen counter, got out some plastic wrap, and started wrapping the leftover pizza. "Since you'll be late, I can heat this up for dinner tomorrow. I might be late getting home myself."

I carried over the salad bowl and prepped it for the fridge. "Good idea," I told him. "I sort of promised Zee that she and I would go out to dinner after our stakeout. Seth is out of town tomorrow night. He has to fly to Sacramento tomorrow morning."

Greg winked at me. "You girls just stay out of trouble and keep me posted."

SIXTEEN

There really wasn't much to do the next day until Zee and I left to stake out the mailbox place in Long Beach, so I drove myself nuts trying to figure out how all the players fit together — or even if they fit together at all. The more likely possibility was that the person who killed Burt had no connection to the dog's rescue or to Holly's birth puzzle. And there was also the possibility that Burt's murder had absolutely nothing to do with either, but I didn't have enough information on Burt to link him to a personal issue that would have gotten him killed.

They all seemed like entirely different things, so I set out with several packs of colorful sticky notes that I found in our home office to try to make some sense of it. I cleared off our kitchen table, intent on using it as a large bulletin board. Using the neon pink sticky notes, I wrote *Holly West* on one and stuck it on the table to the far left at the top. I used a bright yellow sticky note for Burt's murder, wrote his name at the top, and stuck it at the top of the table in the middle. On lime green notes I wrote *Marla Kingston* and placed that note at the top and to the right of Burt's name. Those were my columns. I left a small corner of the table open for us to use for meals.

Next, I took a blue note and on it drew one long horizontal line in the middle with two arrowheads. At the top I wrote *dog,* signifying Saturday's dog rescue. I stuck that note between Holly and Burt's columns to show that they were both at that event. I did the same to another blue note and stuck it between the columns for Burt and Marla, showing they were also there and that it was a common denominator for all of them. I took another blue note and drew another two-way arrow. At the top of this I wrote *OB* for Ocean Breeze and positioned it between Burt and Holly, then another blue one but with *home remodel* at the top and placed it between Burt and Marla. Then I took more pink notes and wrote *Greg, Jane,* and *Jordon* at the top of each one separately, and stuck those to the table under Holly's name. Under Burt's another yellow note was pressed into service with a heading of *who killed him?* Finally, I took a pink note and on it noted *Greg — Burt — Kingston all on videos,* then filed that under Holly's column. Turning to Marla's column, I stuck a green note there with a heading of *who was she waiting for?*

I wasn't any closer to an answer, but I now had them sorted out, which helped me sort them in my mind. Standing, I looked down at the table, instead of across it, and took it in as a whole. What they all had in common was being in the grocery store parking lot on Saturday and being filmed by Holly for her YouTube channel.

I got up and paced the kitchen. Without more information I was stymied, so I went and took a shower. I was halfway through shampooing when an idea occurred to me. Quickly finishing up, I wrapped a towel around my dripping body and went in search of my laptop. I found it on the coffee table in the living room and quickly turned it on. What I wanted to see again was Jordon West's Marigold report. Before, all I'd wanted to know was his whereabouts. Now I wanted to read whatever was there about his family.

According to the report, his father was deceased and had been for quite a while. Doing the math, I came to the conclusion that his father had passed away when he was a very young teen, possibly just a few years before his accident. His mother's name was Doris West Hoffman. *Hoffman.* She'd probably remarried at some point. I ran a request for a Marigold report on Doris West Hoffman and went back into the bathroom to dry off and do my hair and makeup, hoping there would be a quick turnaround on the report.

When I was done dressing the report still wasn't in, so I busied myself straightening up the house. Jill from the office called to ask me how I was doing. She'd heard nothing about my status but did report that Steele was crankier than usual. She also told me that when clients called for me, they were being told I was out of the office for a couple of weeks on vacation. That made *me* cranky. Jill was checking my office email for anything of importance and had a couple of questions on some client matters. I had been checking my firm email too, happy to see they hadn't taken away my connection to the office server. I gave Jill directions on how to handle the couple of minor things that had cropped up.

Greg called to see how I was doing and told me to let him know immediately if I made contact with Holly West. During his call the Marigold report came in. I assured Greg he'd be the first person I'd call after we contacted Holly. I love my man, but I was really eager to get to the report and was half reading it while on the call with him. He was talking about something we had planned for the upcoming weekend when I cut him off.

"Greg, something's come up," I told him.

"You okay?"

"Yes, I'm fine," I assured him, "but I ran a report on Jordon's mother this morning, and it just came in."

"Anything jump out at you?" he asked with interest.

"Oh yeah," I said as I read the report. "Celeste told us yesterday that Jordon's mother had moved out of state shortly after his accident and had never been to visit him since. According to this report, she did move out of California back then, but she moved back to California four years after that. She's been living in Aliso Viejo all this time."

"And hasn't been to visit her son?" Greg asked, his tone incredulous.

"Not according to the manager at Bayview, who I don't think has any reason to lie to us."

It was quiet on the other end of the line,

239

then Greg asked, "You're going to Aliso Viejo today, aren't you?"

"Damn Skippy I am! Wouldn't you?"

"Just be careful, sweetheart. Do you have a phone number for her? Maybe you should call her first."

"No way," I said, half of my brain plotting my visit south. "I'm betting this woman is hiding something to be pulling this nonsense. I think a sneak attack would be best." Actually, I wanted to face down a woman who had abandoned such a sweet son just because of injuries. Renee Stevens sure hadn't, and because of her, Greg had turned out to be a wonderful man with a great life after his accident.

"Then make sure you take Zee with you, at least," he said. "And send me the report so I'll know where you're heading."

After emailing the report to Greg, I called Zee. There was no answer at her home, so I called her cell. She picked up on the third ring. "I need to go to Aliso Viejo," I told her quickly. "It turns out Jordon's mother has been living there for many years."

"So she didn't move out of state?" she asked, her voice low.

"No, she did," I reported, "but she moved back shortly after." I glanced at the clock on the microwave, judging my time, calculating the drive down and back. There would be plenty of time to make it back to Long Beach to stake out the mailbox place if I left soon.

"What do you expect to get from her, Odelia?" Zee asked. "I doubt if she knows anything about Jane and her son. That happened long after she checked out of her son's life."

"True," I said. "She may be a mother not visiting her son out of the inability to deal with what happened, or maybe she knows something. My gut is telling me the latter. Seriously," I pushed, "my Spidey sense is telling me it will be worth the drive."

"When are you leaving?"

"Right now," I told her as I decided which shoes to slip into — sneakers or sandals. "I can swing by your house and pick you up on the way."

"Gee, Odelia, I can't," Zee told me, still keeping her voice low. "I'm at my mother's, helping her prepare for a ladies' tea this afternoon. I dropped Seth at the airport this morning and came straight here. I promised Mom I'd help. Can we do this tomorrow? I'll be back home in time for our thing with Holly tonight."

I was disappointed but understood. "Sure. I don't think Jordon's mother is going anywhere. It looks like she's lived in the same place for a long time."

"How about I pick you up around four thirty," Zee said. "I'm using Seth's car today. I can swing by instead of you coming down to Newport Beach, then back up to Long Beach."

"Okay," I told her half-heartedly. "That makes more sense. Give your mom a big hug for me."

"Speaking of which," Zee said, "Mom wants to know when you and Greg are available for a Sunday dinner. She says it's been too long since she's seen you two. And she wants Grace to come too."

Pearl, Zee's mom, was in her seventies, like my mother, and was one of the most gracious women on the planet. And a damn good cook, especially her cornmeal biscuits and roasted chicken. My mother, a fine baker in her own right, had once pressed upon Pearl to teach her how to make the biscuits, and Pearl had agreed. Mom's were good, but Pearl's were still better. There was simply something magical about Pearl's touch in the kitchen.

"Tell Pearl we'd love to. As soon as Mom's back from her trip, we'll coordinate a date." I glanced again at the clock. I now had hours to kill if I didn't go to Aliso Viejo.

"And I'll see you later."

"So you're okay with doing Aliso Viejo tomorrow?"

"Yeah, we can do it tomorrow," I assured her, struggling to keep the disappointment out of my voice.

Once off the phone, I returned to my tabletop of notes. I stared down at them, looking for something I might have missed. I picked up a pink note, wrote on it *Doris West Hoffman?* and stuck it directly under Jordon's note in Holly's column. I looked over the pieces of colorful paper again. Picking up a fresh green note, I wrote on it *videoed by Holly at protest* and placed it in Marla's column to denote that Kingston and his wife had been videorecorded earlier by Holly. I'd forgotten that until this moment. I scanned the tabletop again, hoping another tidbit would wave at me from inside my brain, but nothing did. I returned my eyes to the new note under Jordon's name. *Doris West Hoffman.* The three words taunted me, pulled at me, challenged me.

Less than fifteen minutes later, I was in my car heading for Aliso Viejo. On my feet were my trusty white Keds.

SEVENTEEN

Aliso Viejo is located in the San Joaquin Hills about thirty miles south from where I live. Before leaving the house, I'd quickly looked up Doris Hoffman's address on Google maps. It was a two-story home in a housing development of nice homes on tiny lots, built side by side up and down the street like houses lined up on a Monopoly board. Each house was different but still the same. The Hoffman home was painted a cream color with dark taupe trim and had a three-car garage. I was pleased to see it was not located in a gated community.

Although I'd told Zee the trip to Aliso Viejo could wait until tomorrow, the more I stared at Doris's name on the tabletop, the more it yelled *yoooo-hoooo* at me, begging for my attention. I figured if the trip was a bust, all I'd be losing was time and a bit of gas. These days I had a lot of time on my hands. And if it was a bust, I would be back home in time for Zee to pick me up at four thirty. If it proved fruitful, I could call Zee and tell her to go home and I'd pick her up, since Newport Beach was just north of Aliso Viejo and on my way back. Easy peasy.

I wasn't sure yet what I was going to say if I did manage to catch Doris Hoffman at home. I wasn't even sure of my plan of attack. On the way there, I weighed the option of going up and ringing her doorbell over the option of sitting in my car and watching for signs of life first. It wasn't as hot today as it had been, but it was warm enough that sitting in a car was not an appeasing thought, especially if I wasn't sure if the woman had a job and would be working. By the time I pulled up in front of the address on the Marigold report, I had decided on the direct approach.

Ringing the doorbell triggered the barking of dogs. Not big dogs like Wainwright but the yipping of a couple small dogs. In short order they were directly on the other side of the door, scrabbling and barking like they wanted to tear my face off. Then I heard footsteps and a woman ordering the dogs to quiet down. They did. Good. They were small and well trained. There was a peephole in the door. From the delay in answering the bell, I figured whoever had quieted the dogs was on the other side checking me out. I tried to position myself so that she could see me and hoped I looked presentable and nonthreatening in my navy capris and white summer top.

I must have because the door finally opened, revealing a woman in her early sixties in black yoga pants and a bright yellow tank top. She was slender and fit, with a long, narrow face with fine lines around her mouth and eyes, where I could see a bit of Jordon in her. Her hair was pale gold and clipped at the nape of her neck, which she dabbed with a small towel. She looked like she'd just finished a workout or I had disturbed her in the middle of one. At her feet were two tiny white terriers. One watched me with alert brown button eyes while the other was lying down, bored with the stranger at the door.

"Can I help you?" she asked with mild annoyance.

"Are you Doris Hoffman?" I asked back.

"Yes, what do you want?"

"My name is Odelia Grey," I told her. "I want to talk to you about your son."

"My son? Is George okay?" Now she looked alarmed.

George? Then I remembered that the Marigold report listed three children for

Doris: Marissa, George, and Jordon. Jordon had been the eldest.

"No, sorry," I said quickly. "I meant your son Jordon, the one involved in that tragic accident nearly thirty years ago. Alcohol-related, wasn't it?"

She'd gone from annoyance to alarm and was now rounding the corner back to annoyance. "If you're with Mothers Against Drunk Driving, I already give to you annually." She started to close the door.

"I'm not with MADD," I told her. "I want to talk to you about him."

"Why?" she asked, her body tensed. "Jordon is dead."

"Really? Because I spoke to him yesterday, and he sure didn't seem dead to me. In fact, in spite of his injuries, he appeared to be thriving."

At this point I expected the door to be slammed in my face, but instead it stayed partially open while Doris weighed my words. Finally, she said, "Who are you, and what do you want?" This time her question held menace.

"I'm Odelia Grey," I repeated. "I'm checking into a strange turn of events that happened to my husband and me this past weekend. During that checking, I came across two women named Holly West and

Jane Newell, a mother and a daughter, which in turn led me to your son Jordon."

"That's impossible," she hissed. "You have the wrong Jordon West. My son has been a vegetable since the accident, and if you really did see him, you know that."

"I admit," I said, keeping my eyes locked onto hers, "that his injuries are extensive and tragic, but he's not a vegetable at all. He's charming and well-read and pretty happy, and even communicative in his own way. But you'd know that if you ever bothered to visit him."

She narrowed her eyes at me. "So that's what this is. You're some kind of social worker who tracked me down to plea on behalf of my crippled son. Did that home he's in send you? Well, you're wasting your bleeding-heart breath because I decided a long time ago that it was best for this family if Jordon died, and that's what my other kids think happened — that he died after we moved."

"Did you have a funeral for him?" I was now curious about the web of lies this woman had been weaving for over two decades. I was angry at her and felt sorry for her at the same time.

"Leave before I call the police," she threatened. A car drove down the street behind me. She looked up, taking note of it, but I didn't.

"Listen, this has nothing to do with Jordon being alive or dead, but someone put his name on a birth certificate saying he fathered her daughter, and this is connected to me in a roundabout way. I want some answers."

"Go," she said again. "You know nothing about me." She pointed a finger at my face. The nail was neat and trim and painted a soft pink. "And I'm telling you right now that you're going to stir up a shitload of problems for yourself if you don't stop butting into something that's none of your business."

Now there's a threat I've heard before — many times.

I straightened my shoulders and ignored her threat, as I do most threats thrown in my face. "What I know about you, Doris West Hoffman, is that you moved with your other children to Spokane shortly after your son's accident. There you married Alex Hoffman, a small-time CPA," I said, ticking off points learned from Marigold. "You moved back to Southern California four years later, after divorcing Hoffman." I lifted a hand and swept it over the front of the house. "And you live here, in this million-dollar home, without any visible means of support, unless Hoffman gave you a bundle in the divorce, which I doubt, seeing he was small potatoes." I actually didn't know that about Hoffman but thought it was worth a shot. I returned to looking her in the eye. "You can slam that door if you want, Doris, but trust me: I smell a juicy story here, and I *will* get to the bottom of it."

If Doris Hoffman had looked down, she would have seen my knees knocking. I can talk a big game, but inside I'm a pile of melting Jell-O.

While she pondered my counter threat, I quickly produced my cell phone. "Would you like to see a picture of Jordon?" I pulled up the photo Celeste had texted to me and held it out toward her. Doris looked down at it. Her eyes showed initial shock. Seconds later they started tearing up. *Bingo!* The picture had hit some maternal nerve that wasn't quite dead.

Slowly, the door started opening wider, and without a word Doris invited me in.

Eighteen

I followed Doris through a formal living room to a great room that took up most of the back of the home. The huge area was sectioned off by tasteful furniture into a family room and informal dining area. To the far right was a long counter with tall stools that divided the dining area from the kitchen. The entire back wall of all three sections was made up of French doors leading to a patio and a pool area surrounded by grass. Along the back and side stone walls tall shrubs provided more privacy. The lot wasn't that big, but good use had been made of it. The dogs had followed us to the back of the house and were now curled up together on a large doggie bed.

I had been right about her working out right before I arrived. On a huge TV screen a yoga video was set on pause and a yoga mat was laid out on the floor in front of it.

"I'm sorry I disturbed your workout," I told Doris.

She waved off my comment as nothing. "It was almost over anyway."

She directed me to a U-shaped sofa. I took a seat on one of the short extensions and she took a seat to my left on the middle section. She grabbed a bottle of water that was set on the coffee table and took a long drink. She offered me nothing. After a second long drink, she said in a voice that chilled me to the bone, "Did he send you?"

"You think Jordon sent me here?" I asked, surprised.

"Well, that's a possibility I hadn't considered," she said, "but it hardly looks from that photo that Jordon has the capacity to do something like that."

I prickled at the way she was putting down Jordon. I'd only met him, but she was his mother. Yet I was his only advocate in the room. The near tears of a few minutes ago were gone, turned off as easily as a faucet. Was Doris Hoffman really that cold? "As I told you, your son is hardly a vegetable. He has limitations, but his brain functions quite well."

She got up from the sofa and went to a wall unit I hadn't noticed before. On it were books and knickknacks and bushels of photos in frames. She plucked out two photos and brought them back to the sofa. She held them out to me. I put my phone on the coffee table and took the photos. In one were three children — a teenage boy and two toddlers, a boy and a girl. The second photo was an action shot of the teen running down a grassy field in pursuit of a soccer ball.

Doris sat back down. "That's my son. Jordon was smart and funny. A sweet kid with a bright future. He was on his way to UCLA on a soccer scholarship."

"Your other two children are much younger," I observed. "Were they from a different marriage?"

She shook her head. "No. When I had Jordon I had a hard time with the delivery. The doctor said the odds of me getting pregnant again were almost nil. When Jordon was twelve, my husband and I got a big surprise: I became pregnant with twins. Once we got over the shock, we were delirious with joy. Even Jordon was excited. Just months after this photo was taken," she tapped the one with the three kids, "my husband suffered a heart attack and died. He'd hardly been sick a day in his life, but one day on the golf course he dropped dead, leaving me with a teen and two kids barely out of diapers."

I felt tears welling in my eyes. It was a tragic story. Not that uncommon either. People in their prime often had heart attacks with no warning, usually caused by a defect they never even knew they had. "I'm terribly sorry," I said to Doris, meaning it. "Truly sorry. And then a few years later to have Jordon cut down. It must have almost killed you."

"Honestly, I thought I was in hell when Jack died, but to lose Jordon was the real hell." She reached out and lightly touched the soccer photo. I wanted to tell her that she didn't lose Jordon, but I didn't think she needed reminding at that moment. "A hell that still continues," she added. "I told the young ones that Jordon had died. They were so young when it happened that there was no need to have a fake funeral or anything. It's what they believe to this day." She smiled and now touched the photo with the three of them. "George is in law school up north. Marissa moved to London last year to take a job in fashion marketing. I'm very proud of them both."

I was realizing that Doris Hoffman would have nothing to tell me that could help me. She was a grieving mother, perhaps even trapped by guilt. My Spidey sense had been off. Maybe the heat had warped it or maybe the stress of not having my job had tipped it off balance. But I didn't want to get up and leave. Something held me to the sofa.

"Who was the *he* you thought had sent me, if not Jordon?"

She looked at me funny, then quickly looked down. "I don't recall asking that."

"You specifically asked if *he* sent me," I told her. "I thought at first you meant Jordon, but now I know you didn't. Who is the *he* you thought sent me?"

Instead of answering, she picked up my phone. The screen had gone dark and the phone had locked as part of its security system. "May I see the photo of Jordon again?" she asked.

I took my phone and unlocked the screen using my thumbprint. It instantly lit up. I opened Jordon's photo and gave Doris the phone. She studied the photo. "He still has the same warm eyes." There was a catch in her voice.

Before I could stop her, she turned off the phone. I was worried she was going to destroy it, but she didn't. She just turned it off and held on to it. "What are you doing?" I asked. "Give me my phone back."

"I had to make sure it was off," she said, still clutching it. "I needed to make sure you're not recording this. Who knows, maybe you're a reporter, and all that about you and your husband is BS. He warned me that someone might start snooping around and connect us. I guess he got some bad press recently, and that always stirs up his enemies — and here you are, right on cue."

"Who is *he*?" I asked in frustration.

"The man who put Jordon in that wheelchair, that's who *he* is."

My mind was reeling. "Wait a minute," I said, both of my hands raised in "stop" mode. "I was told Jordon was injured in a DUI accident. I assumed he'd been drinking. You know, a crazy kid out with his friends."

"Jordon never drank," Doris said, getting defensive. "He was hit by a drunk driver."

I fell back against the sofa, a hand slapped against my mouth in surprise. "That's why the trust, isn't it?" I asked when I found my voice. "He's being supported by the settlement from the accident when you sued the driver of the other car."

"We didn't sue. It never went to court, and the police reports say that Jordon was at fault. *He* saw to that. It was all done behind closed doors in private." Her lower lip trembled. "He told me if Jordon shouldered the blame and we took the settlement

— which was astronomical — and didn't drag him into court or the news, he'd make sure Jordon was cared for until he died, and that I would be supported until I died." She looked me in the eye. "If we didn't take the deal, he said we'd end up with nothing. He said he'd make sure of that. I believed the bastard. I still believe he'd ruin us if he felt the need."

Tears started running down her cheeks. She picked up the towel she'd dropped on the coffee table and dabbed at her face. I wanted to reach out to her, to give her comfort, but didn't get the feeling it would be welcome.

"I sold my son, Odelia. I sold the light of my life for a life of comfort for the rest of us. That's why I can't bear to visit him. I live with enough guilt without seeing it in the flesh." She looked up at me again and I saw that her grief was real and as deep as a cavern. This woman had been suffering a long time in silence. I wondered if I was the first person to hear this story.

"But what could I do?" she continued. "I was a widow working a dead-end job to support three children. Jack owned his own small business, but when he died I found out he'd gotten us deep in debt trying to keep it afloat. We lost everything. When Jordon was in that accident, I knew he'd never be the same boy he'd once been and that his future was gone. So I traded doing the right thing for doing what I felt was best for my other two children."

"Did your second husband know about this?" I asked.

She gently blew her nose into the towel. "No, he knew nothing about it. I told him the money came from the accident and my first husband's insurance. When we married, I insisted on a prenup and I kept the funds separate, saying it was for my children's future. Dave Hoffman is a sweet guy and understood." She snorted softly. "Too sweet for the likes of me. I was bored and withdrawn, and he was frustrated trying to make me happy. After two years of marriage, we went our separate ways. He remarried shortly after I moved back here with Marissa and George. We don't keep in touch at all."

"So who is this guy who hit Jordon?" I asked. It had to be someone in the public eye, a politician maybe.

"I can't tell you that, Odelia. If I do, it will all go away, including Jordon's support. And I can't destroy the life I built for the other children. They can never know I lied to them."

"Don't you think they'll find out one day? Things like this have a way of leaking out."

She glared at me. "So you *do* intend to cause trouble?"

"I intend to cause no trouble," I assured her. "Like I said, some things happened to my husband and me this past weekend that led me to Jordon and to you. What you're telling me doesn't appear to have anything to do with our problem."

Doris took another drink of water. I was as parched as sand, but still she didn't offer me a drop. After she swallowed her water, she said, "What's this about some woman claiming Jordon is the father of her child? They told me he's totally paralyzed."

"We're not sure," I told her. "But we think some college girl who used to work at Bayview put his name down on the birth certificate."

Again Doris snorted. "She must be a gold digger after the money he lives on."

"No," I said with a shake of my head. "The child would have been born over twenty-five years ago, and she's not made a single claim on Jordon in all this time."

"And what does that have to do with you?" Doris narrowed her eyes at me.

"Well," I began, deciding to tell her a partial truth, "we think the child might be my husband's. The mother is someone he dated about the same time that she worked at Bayview. The mother of the child recently passed and we want to reach out to the girl, who we know is still local, but that's about it. I went to Bayside hoping to find out more."

"Interesting," Doris said, her guilt replaced by curiosity. "Most women would tell their husbands to forget about it — that he dodged a major bullet." Another soft snort of laughter. "Unless you intend to give this love child a poisoned apple."

I didn't find the reference to Snow White at all funny, especially with me in the role of the wicked stepmother. "Nothing of the kind," I said, getting to my feet.

I was dying of thirst and needed to pee, but I didn't think my request to use the guest bathroom would be met with courtesy. Doris Hoffman was on the edge, careening between hate, guilt, and paranoia like an Olympic bobsled bumping along on an icy run.

"If you'll give me my phone, I'll be on my way." I held out my hand for the phone. "I'm meeting a friend shortly. I need to call her."

She handed me the phone, and I put it into my bag. At the same time I pulled a card out and gave it to her as we walked to the front door. She opened the door for me as she glanced down at my card. I had one foot outside on the landing, one foot still at the threshold, when her eyes shot up from the card to my face.

"How dare you!" she yelled at me. "He *did* send you, didn't he? He's checking up on me, making sure I behave. Is he trying to get out of paying for what he did to my son? Trying to see if I would break the confidentiality agreement so he can stop the checks? Well, he'll have a fight on his hands, believe me." My ears were ringing with her shrieking.

"What do you mean, Doris?" I asked, surprised by her attack. "No one sent me. I'm telling you the truth."

"Then how did you find me if not through him?" Before I could respond, she screamed, "Get out of here!" She followed it up with a hefty shove, her palms squarely against my chest, just above my breasts.

I teetered on the one foot planted on the stoop, while the one that had been just inside the house went off kilter from her forceful thrust. The air filled with a strangled scream as I lost my balance and fell backwards. My arms flailed as I tried to grab for the wrought-iron railing and missed. I tumbled down the three brick steps and, with a cry of pain, hit the paved walkway.

I lay there crumpled and dazed. Everything hurt, but especially my left shoulder, which had taken the brunt of my fall. Above me, Doris was still screaming accusations while her two dogs barked and growled. As a final gesture, she flashed a middle finger and said, "Go back and tell him that!" Then the door slammed hard enough to rattle the front window a few feet away.

Slowly I started testing my limbs, making sure nothing was broken. Surprisingly, both legs worked fine, but I had some nasty scrapes on them, particularly my left one, which was bleeding from a gash just below the knee. I raised myself up using my right arm, which had received the least damage, and heard talking. Turning my head, I saw two elderly women, each with a small dog at the end of a leash, standing across the street. They were staring at me and talking to each other, but neither approached to see if I needed any help.

"Thanks for your offer to help," I called out to them. "But I'm fine, just a broken hip." They immediately took off.

My hip was not broken. Neither was my left shoulder, although it hurt like hell. I slowly got to my knees and used the railing as support as I got my feet under me, first one, then the other. It was then I realized that my tote bag had come off my arm and spilled across the walk. I spied my phone on the grass just off the path and stiffly went to it, but when I bent down to pick it up, I became dizzy and felt nauseous. I grabbed the phone and straightened again, then began feeling around my skull with one of my hands, wondering if I had received a blow to the head but was too stunned to feel it yet. I felt no injury there, so I gathered up my tote bag and its spilled contents and made my way to my car.

I was hurting but knew the pain would be much worse tomorrow. Maybe I should go to urgent care just in case I was injured more than I realized? Or maybe I should call an ambulance or an Uber? Instead, I put my keys in the ignition, started the car, and drove off to the nearest McDonald's. I still needed to pee and was surprised I hadn't wet myself in the fall.

NINETEEN

"I need to cancel our trip to Long Beach," I told Zee by phone once I was back in my car and heading home. "I fell down some stairs and am pretty banged up." Besides using the bathroom, I'd also picked up a large iced mocha. Every now and then I'd pick up the cold glass from the cup holder, take a sip, then hold it against my left shoulder. The cold felt good even through the fabric of my shirt, which was stained with dirt and some blood.

"Are you okay?" Zee asked with alarm. "Maybe you should go to the ER?"

"I'm fine," I assured her, "just bruised and scraped. I didn't land on my head, thankfully. I hate to miss staking out Holly, but I think I should go home and soak in the tub." Then I remembered that Dumpster was currently residing in our whirlpool tub. He'd have to be moved and the tub cleaned before I could use it, and I wasn't sure I was up for that. *Damn.* It looked like a long hot shower was going to have to do instead.

"Are you sure?" she asked.

"Yeah. If she runs true to form, we can track her down next Wednesday. I can't see that there's any rush in it."

"I meant, Odelia," Zee asked with frustration, "are you sure you don't want to see a doctor? I can come to your house and take you."

"Really, Zee," I said, "I'm fine." I wasn't really sure I was fine, but so far everything was working, just achy. "I'll be home soon and can relax."

"Where did you fall?"

I paused. I didn't want to tell her that I'd gone to Aliso Viejo anyway, without her, but I didn't want to lie about it either. "Um," I began. "In Aliso Viejo."

"Odelia Grey," Zee scolded, "did you go see Jordon's mother after you said we'd go tomorrow?"

"Maybe." *Oh, Gawd,* I groaned in silence. I was becoming my mother, the mistress of vague responses.

"Did you at least speak to her before you fell or did you fall before?" Zee asked.

"During," I told her. Traffic had slowed to a crawl. I wanted to click my heels together and be home, but even if I could, my legs hurt. "She kind of pushed me down her front steps."

"*Kind of* pushed you or *did* push you?" Zee asked, keeping up the interrogation.

"She definitely pushed me," I replied, "and hard, but it was after I talked to her." I took another sip of my coffee drink but this time put it back into the cup holder instead of against my aching shoulder. "She's not a very pleasant woman, Zee. At least not now, not after everything she's been through. She's in a lot of emotional pain, but something sent her over the edge right at the end. I never saw it coming." While stuck in traffic, I relayed to Zee my entire conversation with Doris Hoffman. When I was done, I was just minutes from home.

"That poor woman," Zee said, her voice soft and squishy.

"Yeah, and whoever did that to Jordon seems to be still tormenting her, constantly reminding her that everything she has or needs can disappear. She really thought I was some sort of spy sent to test her loyalty to the settlement agreement between them."

"So it's someone with a lot to lose," Zee said with disgust. "Someone rich enough to buy off most anyone." She paused.

"In Southern California, that could be a

lot of people," I said. "A celebrity, a politician, or even a foreign diplomat. I'd love to find that person and hang him by his thumbs. But one thing at a time."

"What were you doing when she went ballistic?"

"Honestly, Zee, we were done with our talk. I didn't learn anything about Jordon's link to Jane Newell." I ran the sequence of my visit with Doris through my tired, battered brain again. "She walked me to the door," I continued. "I handed her my card in case she wanted to talk again. Next thing I knew, my ass was hitting the bricks."

A bright light suddenly went on in my head. Right before she pushed me, Doris had looked at my business card. The memory of her twisted, angry face as she lifted her eyes from the card to me came crashing through my pain. "Oh my Gawd, Zee," I shouted into the phone secured to my dash. "It was my business card! She went nuts after reading my T&T business card."

"Why would that make a difference?" she asked. "Do you think she has a severe hatred for all things relating to law firms?"

"No, I think it's the trust," I said, piecing it together on the fly. "Celeste said that Jordon's expenses at Bayview were paid monthly by a trust handled by a law firm.

What if it's *my* law firm that is handling that trust?" I took a deep breath. "Maybe the bastard who hit Jordon is represented by Templin and Tobin. They represent a lot of important and wealthy people, especially in the LA office."

"Can you ask Steele about that?"

"I don't know if he'd be able to tell me anything. He wasn't there when this happened," I pointed out, "and even so, I doubt this is something known throughout the firm. This would have been handled on the QT." I quickly ran through what I knew about the firm's history. "In fact, I think Templin and Tobin, as a firm, was only a few years old at that time."

Zee became awfully quiet, and I wondered if she was thinking the same thing I was. "I know this is a reach," she finally said, "but what if the client turns out to be Kelton Kingston?"

"I just had that same thought myself, but it could be any one of our clients. And isn't Kingston quite public about the fact that he doesn't drink and never has?"

"I believe you're right about that," Zee said.

By the time I pulled into our carport and entered the back door, my left shoulder was throbbing. I immediately swallowed some ibuprofen along with some water. After giving Muffin a few pats with my good hand, I balanced an ice pack on my injured shoulder and went to work on my laptop. The firm hadn't deactivated my access to the firm's server, so I could still access records. Since the accident happened so many years ago, it was unlikely that those documents were stored in our current document management system, but I tried to find them by doing a word search of the system. Poking out letters with just my right hand, I first tried *Jordon West.* Nothing came up. Next I tried *Doris Hoffman,* then *Doris West.* Still nothing came up in my search. Striking out, I finally typed in *Bayview.* That produced a few documents and several emails, but they mostly pertained to a medical company called Bayview Vision out of Manhattan Beach. I knew that company because I'd done some corporate work for them, and they'd only become a client in the past year.

Each document listed had a date of creation, the person who created it, and a file number. File numbers consisted of eight digits. The first five represented that client's individual identification number within the firm. The last three digits represented the matter number under that client. Some clients may have only a couple of matter numbers. Others may have dozens. It all depended on how much work the firm did for them. Whenever a document was created or saved or an email sent, it was supposed to be filed on the system under the client's number and specific matter.

Scanning down the list of documents and emails the search had supplied, I noted that almost all pertained to Bayview Vision. Search results were listed in order of date of creation, the earliest at the top. About six months earlier, though, there were a couple of emails that had nothing to do with Bayview Vision.

I opened the earliest and read it: *Celeste Jackson at Bayview called to say they didn't get the check this month. What gives?* The email was from Templin's assistant to our accounting department in Los Angeles.

That same day the head of accounting wrote her back: *Not sure. Will look into it and let you know.*

Early the next morning, the head of accounting wrote a follow-up email to Templin's assistant: *Apparently there was a glitch in the system. Several monthly checks got screwed up and were never printed, including Bayview's. It will be hand-cut today and sent tomorrow. Should I call Bayview or will you?*

The assistant wrote back: *I will. Just make*

sure it gets out.

These four emails all had the same client and matter number, which I didn't recognize. I jotted the number down. The firm kept a master client number list on the system. I accessed it and did a search for the number. It popped up immediately. The client number belonged to Kelton Kingston. The matter description was simply stated as *Settlement.* The matter was opened about thirty years ago.

Next I went back to the main search engine for the document manager and poked in the client and matter number combination. Except for the four emails, nothing was stored on the system under that number, as I suspected.

Holy crap! Had Holly been following Marla Kingston on Saturday? If so, was she also following Kelton himself? Had she somehow discovered the truth behind Jordon's accident? Did she know Jordon wasn't her father or did she believe he was? But Celeste has said no one ever came to visit Jordon.

Now I wished I had gone to meet Holly. I looked at the clock. It was after six. Too late for that, and I didn't think I could drive. My head was killing me. Every bone in my body ached. The ibuprofen and ice were doing nothing to help my shoulder. When Greg came home soon after, he found me slumped over my laptop, sobbing.

As soon as he could understand through my gibberish what had happened to me, Greg bundled me off to the nearest ER, where I was poked and prodded and X-rayed. I told them I'd fallen down some steps while visiting a friend but didn't think it was all that bad. The doctor proclaimed I didn't have a concussion, nor was anything broken, but that I had badly torn my shoulder. We departed with my left arm in a sling and a prescription for painkillers.

Before the drugs could kick in and with Greg's help, I showered and crawled into bed. He laid next to me and held me while I told him about my visit to Doris Hoffman and my research on the firm's server.

"Wow," was all he said when I'd finished. "So do you think it was Holly West that Marla was waiting for?"

"Could be," I answered with a yawn. "But when we broke into Marla's car, the meeting didn't happen, and Holly simply filmed us with the dog."

"But what about Burt? How does he fit in? And why would someone shoot him?"

I shrugged, and pain shot through my shoulder. "Maybe he knew something and

Holly followed him to you and took him out."

"But why Burt?" Greg asked. "Why not go after Kingston directly?"

I had no idea, and it was the last thing I heard before drifting off into drug-induced bliss.

Twenty

I was disoriented when I woke up. Muffin had claimed Greg's side of the bed, and Wainwright, upon hearing my grunts and groans, came around to my side of the bed and nudged me with his nose. I tried to move, but it was impossible without protests from every inch of my body. I felt like I'd been in a bad car accident.

If Wainwright was here, Greg probably was too. "Greg," I called out. I called his name again and tried to get up. He rolled into our bedroom.

"Morning, sweetheart," he said. "How are you feeling?"

"Like I've been hit by a truck." I tried to roll to my side so I could swing my bruised legs around to the floor, but it was difficult without putting pressure on my bad shoulder, which was still in a sling.

"Here," Greg said, coming closer. "Let me help."

It took several tries and a lot of groans, but by holding on to his strong arms with my good arm, I was able to upright myself and get to my feet. From there I shuffled into the bathroom, and after that into the kitchen, where Greg had a nice hot cup of fresh brewed coffee waiting for me on one end of the table. With care I took a seat. The sticky notes were still where I'd left them, but Greg had shut and moved my laptop over to the counter and plugged it in to keep it charged.

"You did some nice work there," he said, waving toward the table of notes. "I didn't want to disturb them. Anything about Burt jump out at you?"

I looked at the notes. I'd only placed them the day before, but it felt more like a month ago. "Just that Burt, Marla, and Holly were all in the grocery store parking lot at the same time. That seems to be the only common thread for all three."

Greg grabbed a lime green note and a pen. On it he wrote Jordon's name and stuck it in Marla's column. I nodded. It was exactly where it belonged. We now had a connection between the Kingstons and Jordon. Was there also a connection between Holly and the Kingstons other than second-hand through Jordon?

"Burt might have met Marla once upon a time, but I don't see a current connection between him and the Kingstons," I noted.

"Maybe not, but if it's there, you'll find it," he said with confidence. "Just don't fall down anymore steps trying to find out."

"I didn't fall," I reminded him, "I was pushed." I adjusted myself in my seat. "It actually hurt less this morning once I got moving. Except for the shoulder."

"That shoulder is going to take a bit," Greg said. "Even when not wearing the sling, keep the arm folded and close to your body." He demonstrated how I should hold my arm. "No weight on the shoulder, like the doctor said. The aches and pains from the stiffness everywhere else will subside in time." He rolled closer and leaned in to kiss me good morning. "Mmmm, nice and minty."

"Yeah, at least I can brush my teeth with one hand." I adjusted the sling. It was a real nuisance but the shoulder did feel better with it.

"Do you want some eggs, bacon, and toast?" Greg asked. "You need to eat if you're going to be taking those drugs. I'll bet you didn't eat anything after breakfast yesterday."

I searched my memory. "Nothing except

for an iced coffee, but my stomach isn't ready for bacon. How about some simple scrambled eggs and toast?"

"You got it, sweetheart." Greg turned and rolled to the fridge to gather up the ingredients. "Just sit and relax."

I glanced at the microwave. It said it was after 10:00 a.m. "What are you doing still home?"

Greg cracked a couple of eggs into a bowl and added some milk. "I didn't want to leave until you were up. I wanted to wait and see how you're feeling." He started scrambling the eggs with a fork. "I'll stay home with you, if you like."

I shook my head just as the eggs hit the hot skillet. "No, I'll be fine, honey. As long as I can walk, use the bathroom, and feed myself peanut butter and jelly for lunch, I'm good to go. And you've been so busy lately."

He put two slices of bread into the toaster and went back to watching the eggs. "Then how about I go in just after lunch. That way I can get you settled." He moved the eggs around with a spatula. "Besides," he said, glancing over at me, "I called Steele. He'll be here in about thirty minutes or so."

I stared at Greg. "Why did you do that?"

"Because of what you found out yesterday

277

about Kingston," he explained. "He should know about that."

"That happened thirty years ago, Greg." My voice was thick and froggy. I took a sip of coffee, hoping the hot liquid would loosen it up. "And just because the firm set up that settlement and administers the trust payments to Bayview and Doris, it doesn't mean they did anything wrong. They were hired to do legal work as requested by their client." He was in the middle of scooping the eggs onto a plate. I heard the toast pop up.

"Seriously?" he asked, reaching for the toast. He slapped some butter on it, cut the slices in two and added them to the plate with the eggs. "They have no liability in this?" He rolled over with the plate of eggs and toast and a fork.

"Probably not," I answered. "Do you think criminal attorneys are responsible for their clients' crimes?" I looked down at the plate in front of me. The eggs were cooked just the way I like them: fluffy, with a lot of fresh ground pepper. I reached for the fork he'd set down on the table. "Law firms decide who they represent and who they don't. If they had a problem with the morality of this situation, it was then they should have made the decision. All this does is show what a rotten piece of work Kelton Kingston is. He's even a worse human being than we expected."

"But," Greg argued, "if he paid someone to cover up the facts of the accident, that's fraud, isn't it?"

"It's certainly something." I dug into the eggs. I didn't think I had much of an appetite, but as soon as they touched my tongue I became ravenous and shoved them in, along with the toast, while Greg cleaned up the kitchen. When I was done, I started to get up from the table.

"What do you need, Odelia?" Greg asked as he rolled over to get my dirty plate. "I can get whatever you need."

"What I need is to get dressed if Steele will be here any minute." I shuffled into the bedroom. I had stiffened up again, but moving my bruised legs helped them feel better.

After hearing everything, Steele pretty much told us what I'd told Greg earlier. He had no idea about the work the firm had done for Kingston thirty years ago but said it was still covered by attorney-client privilege. "And that means for you too, Grey," Steele warned. "You're still an employee of the firm and cannot speak of this to anyone. Do you understand?"

I nodded. We were in our living room.

Steele was dressed for the office but had left his suit jacket in his car. He turned to Greg. "That means you too, Greg. Odelia should not have told you this, but since she did, you need to keep your trap shut too. Saying anything implicates Odelia in a breach of confidentiality."

"But this is immoral," Greg protested. "Don't you agree?"

I could tell Steele wanted to say something other than what I knew was coming. "It doesn't matter what I think personally," Steele said. Yep, that's what I expected him to say, especially in front of Greg. "I'm an attorney of T&T," Steele continued, "and therefore one of Kingston's attorneys, even though I don't work with him and his companies directly."

"Then what good are you, Mike?" Greg shouted.

Whoa!

Steele straightened up in his seat on the sofa, and his handsome face grew hard. "I'm going to let that pass, Greg, because we're friends and because I know you didn't mean to say it. You're upset by everything that has happened in the past few days, and you're worried about Odelia."

"Speaking of which," I said, trying to join the party, "what's happening with my job?"

Greg was rolling back and forth in his wheelchair, clearly agitated. Muffin and Wainwright watched from Wainwright's bed like spectators at a tennis match. "I'll tell you what's going on with your job, Odelia," Greg said, his voice harsh but low. "There's no way in hell I'd let you go back to that place, not even to work for Mike. They've treated you like shit since this all began. And now this. I don't want you working anywhere that has any connection with Kelton Kingston. You deserve better." He looked up at Steele. "And so do you, Mike." He rolled back and forth again.

Steele stood up. "To answer your question, Odelia, nothing has been decided about your job yet. The partners are still hoping this will all blow over and Kingston will forget about you, and you can return to work unnoticed."

I looked at my boss, then at my husband. In spite of his rage, I knew when it came down to it, Greg would not stand in my way if I decided to return to T&T. He wouldn't be happy about it, but he also wasn't the type of husband to order his wife around. I looked back at Steele and hugged my bad arm to my side. "Steele, I don't know how I feel right now. I really like my job, but, like Greg, I'm upset about the firm being in bed with this horror show of a human being. I'm sure we have many clients that skirt the edge, but this, if it's true, is really heinous. Do I need to make up my mind right this minute?" I looked at the two of them, one then the other.

Greg didn't say anything, and I knew we'd be discussing this later. Steele gave me a weak smile. "Of course not, Grey. But know you are missed. By all of us."

He looked up from me and his eye caught on something. I followed his gaze. He'd noticed the notes spread out on the kitchen table. Our home has a very open floor plan for Greg's convenience. From the living room you can see most of the dining area and part of the kitchen, except for the bit hidden by a common wall. Steele walked over to the table and looked down at the notes, studying them. I was really glad we hadn't put down a sticker with T&T on it under Marla's column. I'd thought about it.

Greg and I joined him at the table. "I suppose you're going to say we can't look into the murder that took place at my shop on Monday," Greg challenged.

Steele turned and looked at Greg. "I don't know what you're talking about, Greg," he said with a slow smile. "All I see is a jigsaw puzzle. Lots of people enjoy working them."

Steele bent down and kissed me lightly on the cheek, something he'd only done a few times before in all our years of working together. One of those times had been on my wedding day. Another time was on his. This time it felt like goodbye.

Next, Steele held out his right hand to Greg. Greg eyed it, then took it, and the two men shook. "I would be very troubled if this changed our friendship, Greg."

"So would I, Mike," Greg said in agreement. "So would I."

Twenty-One

When Greg finally went to work, he decided to leave Wainwright behind to keep me company. He was still agitated from our meeting with Steele, so I was happy to have Greg gone for a few hours. Wainwright, on the other hand, was clearly depressed by the turn of events. Going to work with Greg was his job, and he was one employee who never asked for vacation time.

My whole body was very sore from the fall, in spite of there being no other major injuries beyond my left shoulder. It really did feel like I had been in a car accident, where the muscle pain was worse the next day from all the jarring and jerking. Greg told me to spend the day relaxing. He made our bed before leaving, a chore that was usually mine. Before leaving, he set my laptop up on the end of the kitchen table so I wouldn't have to do it, and he made sure I had enough iced tea and lunch fixings handy. Even in his surly mood he was considerate and concerned. It was almost to the point of suffocating. Loving, but suffocating.

My cell phone rang. It was Mom. We talked a few minutes, but I didn't tell her about my fall. She would be home this weekend and I could fill her in then. Greg and I also decided this morning not to tell Clark because he'd just tell Mom. The two of them were worse than a couple of gossips in a hair salon when it came to family. Mom wanted to know if I'd found out anything about Burt yet and if I had any word about my job. I told her no on both, which was easy to slip past her because neither was a lie. Then she filled me in on the drama of the seniors' trip and signed off, saying she was heading to a hot bingo game.

I was barely off the phone when Zee showed up on my doorstep with a casserole dish of her incredible chicken and dumplings. "This is for your dinner tonight," she said, taking the dish to the kitchen and slipping it into my fridge. Wainwright, tail wagging, followed her. I wasn't going to argue with her generosity. Her chicken and dumplings was one of my favorite things.

"I called Greg this morning to see how you were doing," she said when she joined me. I had planted myself into one of our recliners, my feet up, a carafe of iced tea and the TV remote by my side. "I wanted to make sure you weren't still in bed," Zee continued as she took a seat on the sofa near me. Wainwright, realizing no chicken was in his immediate future, went to his bed. Muffin was MIA. "Although I should have thought about you having to get up and down to answer the door — I'm very sorry."

"Don't be, Zee," I told her. "As much as it hurts, I'm finding it helps my overall body aches to move about periodically. It lessens the stiffness, even if does hurt like hell when I first try to move. The shoulder just needs time." I laughed. "You should see the bruise on my left thigh. It's as big as a dinner plate. If I was wearing shorts, I could show it to you."

"Are you taking anything for the pain?" she asked. "Greg said they gave you pain pills."

"They did, but I don't like those things. They make me loopy. I took some ibuprofen a little while ago, and it's starting to kick in."

"Well, don't be a hero, Odelia," Zee admonished. "If you're in pain, take one of the painkillers and take a nap." She fussed with her pale yellow blouse. "I also wanted to speak with you about something — something you may or may not like."

Now I was really glad I hadn't taken those painkillers. I shifted in the recliner and held my breath when aches ricocheted up and down my body. "That sounds ominous."

"After you called and said you couldn't make the trip back to the mailbox place," she began, "I went anyway."

"What? Zee, no, you shouldn't have," I protested.

"Why not?" She stuck out her chin in defiance. "If I hadn't insisted on tagging along, you would have gone alone — at least if you hadn't taken that spill."

I couldn't argue with that. "So did you meet her?" I asked instead. Remembering my manners, I also asked, "Would you like some iced tea or something?"

"Don't worry about me, Odelia," she said with a smile. "I know your home almost as well as my own. I'll get something if I want it. You sit still."

"So," I prodded. "What happened with Holly?"

"She seems like a very nice young woman, but somewhat tragic," Zee reported. "Then again, her mother recently passed. Like the boy in the mailbox store said, she's quite pretty, petite with long black hair. I didn't see her eyes because she was wearing large sunglasses. Oh, and she drives one of those cute little Mini Coopers."

"Did you actually speak with her?"

Zee nodded. "I did. I was very nervous at first but realized she was going to get away if I didn't move on her. So I got out of my car and kind of ambushed her as she was leaving the store."

"Ambushed?" I asked in amazement. Zenobia Washington was not the ambushing type. I was, but not her. She was too polite.

Zee nodded. "Yes, I actually stood between her and her car so she couldn't leave until we had a word."

I nearly laughed out loud picturing the short, stocky Zee standing in the way of a lithe millennial. My money would have been on Zee. "I'll bet you played the mom card," I said with a chuckle.

Zee smiled. "Of course. It's the only weapon I have. I just looked that girl in the eye and pretended she was one of my own. I needed answers and wasn't going away without them."

"And?"

"I told her who I was and that you and Greg needed to speak with her. That it was very important and you meant her no harm."

"And did she say she'd get in touch with us?"

Zee fussed again with her blouse, plucking at an imaginary piece of lint from the front. "Not exactly. She threatened to call the police if I didn't get out of her way." Zee looked up, her eyes wide. "She even got out her cell phone and started counting down."

I was really laughing now. "But I thought you said she seemed like a nice but tragic young woman."

"She is," Zee said, sticking to her assessment. "I mean, she didn't swear at me or give me the finger. Some young people would have done that without a second thought. And she did give me time to move out of her way, which I did." She paused. "But not without insisting that she call you. Then, as she was getting into her car, I blurted out that we'd met Jordon West."

"You didn't?" I was sitting straight now and not caring about my aches and pains.

"I did," Zee said. "I don't know what came over me, Odelia. It just sort of popped out, like a last-ditch effort. She stopped and I thought she was going to talk to me after all, but instead it was just a long pause.

Then she got into her car, slammed the door, and drove off."

"Sounds like you're lucky she didn't run over you." I hesitated, then added, "By the way, can I ask a favor of you?"

Zee looked surprised. "You can ask me anything — you know that."

I screwed up my mouth, not in pain but embarrassment. "Would you help me put on a bra before you leave? Nothing hard-wired, just one of my soft sports bras. I think my girls would be happier with a little support."

"What are best friends for?" she said with a big grin.

Shortly after Zee left, I took her advice and took a nap. I still didn't take a painkiller. I crawled on top of our made bed with my Kindle, intending to read, but was out like a light before I'd gotten through one page.

I woke two hours later to find Muffin curled up next to me and Wainwright in his spot on the floor at the end of the bed. I went through the now-common ritual of moving slowly, willing myself to keep everything functioning in spite of the pain. After a trip to the bathroom, which was taking much longer now, I decided to get out of the house. The weather had cooled and I wanted to take advantage of it. Even if I had to shuffle down the street, I wanted to walk to the beach. I felt it might clear my head and be good for my battered soul.

Wainwright wanted to walk faster than I was capable, but after a few tugs on the leash, he understood that we were not moving beyond a snail's pace. As soon as we got there, I plopped down on a bench, thankful one was open. I was exhausted, and my legs and hips hurt. I was seriously thinking I might have to call Uber to take me the two blocks back home when I was ready to go.

Wainwright was thrilled to be at the beach. He loves his morning walks and had missed a couple this week. The bench was located on a grassy hill above the actual beach. I let him off his leash, which was a no-no, but everyone knows Wainwright and turns a blind eye to our rules transgression. The dog nosed around and marked his territory before settling down on the grass by my feet. I'd worn a visor and sunglasses against the brightness of the sun, and I had slathered on some sun block before leaving home. It was about four in the afternoon, but the sun was still strong. I'd brought a lightweight cross-body tote in which to stash one of Wainwright's portable water dishes, a few doggie treats, and two bottles of water, along with my Kindle. I'd settled the strap on my left side, close to my neck so it wouldn't rest on my injured shoulder joint. I needed my one useful hand to hold the leash.

Wainwright's low growl immediately snapped me to attention. I must have dozed off in the sun. Startled, I pushed the brim of my visor back and looked to see what had put the dog on alert. He was standing in front of me, his flank against my legs, looking to my right. I knew the low growl was meant as a warning to whoever was there not to approach. The faithful animal was guarding me against strangers.

A young woman was standing a few feet away from my bench. She had long black hair and large sunglasses that covered most of the top half of her face, making the bottom half look almost childlike. In spite of it being summer and warm, she wore black jeans and a black short-sleeved T-shirt and carried a messenger bag slung over her shoulder. I noticed a couple of small tattoos on her arms. She looked unsure of what to do — stay or flee. Her hands were palms out and up about waist high, ready to protect herself against the dog.

I quieted Wainwright. He stopped growling and sat down but remained in front of me with his eyes on the stranger. "Can I help you?" I asked her.

It took her a moment to find her voice. "Are you Odelia Grey?"

I nodded and laughed. "Are you here to serve me legal papers of some kind?" But it really wasn't a joke, considering all the snooping I'd been doing in the past few days.

"No, of course not," she said, surprised. "Why would you even think that?" She was obviously someone who didn't know me.

I patted the dog, letting him know he could relax, and thought about who this young woman might be and probably was. "Are you Holly West?" I asked.

"Why do you ask?" she countered. "Are you going to serve me with a subpoena or something?" A slow smile crossed her lips briefly. It was then I knew I might like Holly West once I got to know her. She was quick, had a sly sense of humor, and she didn't swear at my best friend when stalked by her.

"How did you find me?" I asked, patting the vacant section of the bench next to me.

"I think the question is, how did *you* find *me*?" She eyed Wainwright with caution, making no move to sit.

"Don't worry," I told her. "Wainwright won't hurt you unless you try to hurt me. Otherwise, he's a big teddy bear."

Taking me at my word, Holly sat down on the other half of the bench. As soon as she did, Wainwright made a slow move to sniff her. She edged back, then relaxed and let him get a snoot of her scent. He sniffed her arms and hands as they lay still in her lap. His tongue shot out and licked a hand, which startled her, then she laughed softly. "He really is sweet."

"You have been Wainwright approved," I told her. "Scratch him behind his ears and you'll have a friend for life." Slowly she moved her hand to the dog's head and started patting him, then scratched him behind his ears. The dog's tail wagged.

"If you've been following Greg," I said, opening the conversation to the important stuff, "then you've seen Wainwright before."

She didn't deny my comment, nor did she answer it. Instead, she said, "Your friend Zee is quite persuasive."

Tit for tat.

"Really?" I turned to face her. Holly kept her face forward, her eyes on the gorgeous ocean view in front of us. "According to her, you didn't say a word except to threaten to call the police. And I know she didn't give you my address, so how did you find me today? You tell me your methods, I'll tell you mine."

She turned to me and the small smile returned. "Last month I tailed Greg home from his shop. Today I was sitting outside your place, wondering if I should knock or leave a note, when you came out with the dog."

"How did you know I was home?"

"Your car is in the back," she said, her voice even and matter-of-fact. "You usually work Thursdays, don't you?"

"Yes, but as you can see, I'm a bit beaten up right now."

"What happened to you?" she asked.

"I fell down some stairs yesterday while visiting someone," I told her, leaving out anything about Jordon West and Doris Hoffman. "I'm kind of a klutz."

An awkward silence wedged between us. "Just how long have you been following us?" I asked, not a little impressed at her skills in spite of my annoyance at being followed and not realizing it.

She shrugged. "A couple of months, off and on."

I did some quick calculations. "Did your mother's recent death trigger that?"

She nodded. "I didn't know who Greg was until a few months ago. It was after she was diagnosed." She paused, then added after a deep breath, "My mother had pancreatic cancer. Advanced. She went quick."

"I'm very sorry, Holly. Truly sorry." I turned on the bench to fully face her, taking off my sunglasses so she could see my eyes. "It's not easy to lose a parent when you're so young. Did she tell you that Greg was your father?"

She shook her head, her long hair waving with the motion. "No, she said he wasn't, but wished he was." She paused. "I wish he was too." She turned to look at me. "He seems pretty cool."

I chuckled. "He has his faults, believe me, but overall he *is* pretty cool. Since we discovered your existence, he's been wondering if he was your dad, and he's not upset by the thought. Neither of us are," I quickly added. "At least as long as you're not some kind of serial killer." That comment induced another small smile. "Are you sure he's not your father? We know about Jordon West and know he's not."

"Yeah," Holly said. "My mother always told me that the man on my birth certificate was not my father. She was clear about that. She always told me that he was just a very nice man she knew once, so she put his name down so my real father wouldn't try to find me. As for Greg, Mom said she was absolutely sure he wasn't my father. She said if it had been Greg, she wouldn't have done the whole secret thing."

We both stared out at the sea, letting the words rest and breathe. Holly broke the silence. "My mother could have had gotten an abortion, but she didn't. She told me my real father would have pressured her to have one. It was just the two of us, but I always knew that I was wanted and loved."

I noticed Wainwright was panting. I pulled his water dish from the tote bag with my good arm.

"Here," Holly said, "let me help you." She took the dish and filled it with some water from one of the bottles I'd brought. As soon as the dish was on the ground, Wainwright attacked it. I offered Holly the other unopened bottle, but she declined, saying she'd use the bottle in her hand. I opened the new bottle for myself.

"This reminds me of the day you guys rescued that poor little dog," she said, watching Wainwright. "That was so awesome."

"So you followed us that day?" I asked before taking a drink of my own water.

She nodded. "I was thinking about talking to you on Saturday, but then the whole thing with the dog and Marla Kingston happened." She turned to me. "I was shocked to see her there, at least I was at first."

True to my word, I gave Holly a brief explanation of how we stumbled upon her information but left out Marigold specifically, just saying, as I usually do, that I had access to a lot of good search engines. "When we looked into you and your videos, we noticed that you had filmed the Kingstons a couple of times. After, we wondered if you were following Marla on Saturday."

"I've followed both her and Kingston several times. Not everything I video is on my YouTube channel." She made a sound of disgust. "Kingston is the real stain on humanity, isn't he?"

"That he is," I agreed. I wanted to tell her that Kingston was the reason I wasn't at work, but couldn't without linking him to our firm. "What about Burt Sandoval?" I asked instead. "Had you ever followed or seen him before Saturday and Monday?"

"Not intentionally," she answered, which raised my eyebrows. She hesitated. "Monday was a real surprise. I've . . . I've . . . ," she said, stuttering.

"You've never seen a man killed before," I said, finishing what I expected her to say.

She shook her head. "I was standing across the street just shooting random video, which I often do, sometimes just to calm my nerves. I was trying to get up the courage to go into Ocean Breeze. I'd decided over the weekend to finally go ahead and approach Greg. When I saw you drive up, I was glad because I thought it might be better to talk to both of you at once." She took a long drink of her water. "I kept filming and finally decided I was ready. I was about to cross the street when I saw Burt pull into the lot with his truck. I was surprised, so I hung back and started filming again. I did it more out of curiosity because I'd seen him before and thought it odd that he was a friend of yours."

"We weren't friends with Burt," I told her. "We had never met him before Saturday."

Holly turned toward the ocean again. "Well, anyway, he was halfway out of his truck when I heard the shot and saw he was hit. Then he stumbled into the shop." She looked back at me. "I didn't know what to do, so I kept filming."

"Holly," I began, after giving her words some thought, "you said you'd never *intentionally* filmed Burt before. So you'd videoed him before *un*intentionally?"

She nodded. "A couple of times when I'd followed Marla Kingston. They knew each other. I was surprised to see her at the grocery store that day until I saw Burt.

They'd met at Starbucks there before."

"You're sure about this?" I asked.

She nodded. "I have it all on my computer. I tracked you all down and started following you shortly before Mom died, after she told me some stuff. Burt and Marla had met a couple of times before Saturday."

"Were they lovers?" I asked, unable to picture the two of them together.

Holly shook her head. "I don't think so. The few times I saw them together they were always off by themselves talking, but it didn't look romantic, more adversarial."

So Marla could have been waiting for Burt Saturday when she was hiding in the clothing store. But why, if they weren't lovers? And *adversarial* was a specific and interesting word choice. Did Marla have anything to do with his death? Did Burt have something on Marla? In digging back through my brain, I came across the bit when Marla first arrived on the scene of Maurice's rescue. She'd pointed directly at Burt and asked if he'd done the damage. She didn't consider anyone else, just him, at the beginning. She hadn't been racially profiling him after all. What did poor Burt know that got him killed? And why was he interested in meeting with Greg?

"Have you gone to the police yet with

this?" I asked Holly.

"Just with the video I took that day," she said. "I got them a copy of that as soon as I posted some of it to my site."

"I've seen the video on your YouTube channel," I said. "You didn't post the actual shooting."

"No," she answered. "I felt it was too graphic. I often film human suffering as a statement, but watching a man die is something else." She shook her head again. "Sometimes I wish I'd never posted what I had of that day. It put too much of a spotlight on me. People asking too many questions."

I turned and stared at her, wishing she'd take off her sunglasses. Holly West was a very interesting character, full of tragedy, purpose, and good intentions. "What did you tell the police as to why you were there that day and the day of the dog rescue? I'm sure they looked at your videos, same as we did, and wondered why you were in both places."

"I don't think the Huntington Beach police have realized yet that I was in the parking lot Saturday," she said. "I didn't offer that video, just the one of Burt being shot. I told them I was in the neighborhood filming background for a video sequence I was putting together and just stumbled upon the shooting. They questioned me for hours and hours, then let me go."

"Did you speak with Detective Chapman and his partner?" I asked.

"Yes. I figure it's only a matter of time before they connect me to the dog thing, so I took that video down just to buy myself time to figure this out."

"Holly," I said, my voice gentle, "if your mother told you there was no way Greg was your father, why did you start following him?"

Again Holly got lost in the ocean view. A few people walked by, but she didn't notice them. "When Mom was dying, she started telling me a lot about her life, especially when she was young. My mother was a loner, like me. She told me about her friendship with Greg, saying how much she'd liked him and wished he'd been my father. She told me that she'd kept track of him over the years and often thought about reconnecting with him but never did. She told me that over the past several years, his name and yours had popped up connected with solving some crimes, and she said if I ever needed help, I should go to him. She said that even after all these years, he would help me."

I smiled. "Your mother was right. Greg would never turn away the child of an old friend."

Twenty-Two

My phone rang just as I was about to ask Holly if she knew who her father was. The call was from Greg. He was calling to see how I was doing and asked if I wanted anything special for dinner.

"Zee brought over chicken and dumplings, so we're good to go for dinner," I said into the phone. Holly got up to leave, but I signaled for her to stay put. "Will you be home soon?"

"Yeah," he said, "I'm leaving right now and just wanted to make sure you didn't need anything." There was a short pause. "I know I was an ass this morning. I'm sorry, sweetheart. I'm just worried about you and don't want you going back to the firm. I think it's time for you to move on to something else."

"I know, honey," I told him softly. "We'll work it all out, and we'll do it together."

"Are you sure you're okay? Are you still in

a lot of pain?"

"Yeah, I'm still pretty sore, but I managed to take Wainwright for a walk. We're at the beach now."

"Really?" he asked, his voice perking up. "Then you must be feeling a lot better."

"Not really," I said, "but I thought moving would help the stiffness in my legs. It did, but I'm going to feel it tonight. We're about to do the slow shuffle home." I glanced at Holly. She was kneeling on the ground making friends with Wainwright. "By the way, Greg, we may have a guest for dinner. Someone I bumped into at the beach. Do you mind?"

"No, not if you're up to it," he said. "I don't want you to get too worn out. Who's the guest?"

"It's a surprise," I told him. "See you soon."

"Well, if it's Dev," Greg said with a chuckle, "tell him not to drink all my beer before I get there."

Holly needed some convincing to stay for dinner. She'd left her car near our house, and on the slow walk back I wore her down until she accepted. I also learned during those two long blocks that she'd graduated from the UCLA film school. She lived in Belmont Shores, a nice section of Long

Beach, in the home she'd grown up in with her mother, and earned her living as a consultant, shooting and editing videos for web content, including for a couple of very popular YouTube channels. She liked working for herself, she told me. It gave her the freedom she needed to pursue her own art while still earning a living. If Greg had a daughter, I thought, this was probably the type of path she would have taken, and she would have been just as independent. I couldn't wait for them to meet.

When we got back to our house, she looked around with appreciation. "Wow, this living area is huge," she said. "You'd never know it from the outside."

"This used to be a duplex, two identical two-bedroom units attached in the middle by a common wall," I said. "Greg bought the building and combined them to make one large house to suit his needs. He designed it himself," I told her proudly. "To the left is the master suite and bath, which he totally redid. He left the two bedrooms and the bath on the right pretty much the same except for widening the doorways and adding a hidden laundry area behind those folding doors." I headed to the left. "I'll be right back. If you need to use the bathroom," I told her, "the guest bath is down the hall to the right. Just make sure to shut the door when you're done."

When I came back out, Holly was studying the sticky notes plastered to the dining table. In her arms Muffin was sucking up a lot of pets and strokes. Wainwright was in his bed, tired from the excursion. Holly glanced up. "There's a duck in your tub," she announced with curiosity.

"Just a temporary resident," I told her. "His name's Dumpster. He'll be going to a new home in a few days. And the scamp in your arms is Muffin."

"Cool," she said without emotion and went back to studying the notes. "Were you trying to figure out who I was or why Burt Sandoval was killed?" she asked without taking her eyes off the table.

I looked down at the notes. "Both." I tapped the sticker with Jordon's name. "Zee and I met him. He's a lovely man. A quadriplegic living in an assisted care place. Your mother never mentioned him?"

She slowly shook her head. "Just to say that he was not my father."

She'd taken off her sunglasses and I could finally see her full face. It was slender, with smooth, youthful skin, a small nose, and a delicate mouth. I knew she was twenty-six, but her petite build and clothing made her look much younger, almost high-school age. But her eyes were not the eyes of a teen. They were sharp and curious, absorbing and weighing the information she took in through them, much as her videos did. Her eyes also spoke to her Asian roots.

Holly put Muffin down and pointed at the note between Marla and Burt. "What does *home remodel* mean?"

"That's the connection between them," I explained as I went into the kitchen to turn on the oven. "They might have met when the company Burt worked for did a remodeling job at a home the Kingstons used to own. But that was a couple of years back. We honestly didn't think there were any other connections, but today you told me you've seen them together recently."

She nodded. "Yes, definitely." She turned to me. "What about Burt's wife? Have you talked to her yet?"

I spun around to look at Holly. The sudden movement sent shock waves of pain through my battered body, and I grabbed the counter for support. "Burt wasn't married. He was divorced."

"A girlfriend maybe?"

I had been trying to wrangle the heavy casserole dish from the fridge, which was difficult with one arm incapacitated. "Here,"

Holly said, coming into the kitchen. "Let me get that." She lifted the dish out of the fridge and set it on the counter by the stove. "What's this?" she asked, indicating the dish.

"Zee's wonderful chicken and dumplings. She brought it over this morning for our dinner tonight." I glanced at Holly. "I should have asked you, are you vegan or gluten-free or anything like that?"

She shook her head. "Nope. I eat most anything. Let me know when the oven's ready, and I'll stick it in for you."

She went back to the table and looked down again at the notes in Burt's column. "The last time I saw Burt meet with Marla Kingston there was a woman in his car. She stayed behind while he went into the coffee shop for the meeting."

I went back to the table and sat down, exhausted from doing not much of anything. "When was this?"

"About a week or so before he was killed. The meeting was at the Starbucks that's in that same strip mall." She closed her eyes and was silent for a bit. "In fact, I'm pretty sure she was there last Saturday, the day you rescued the dog."

"Are you sure?" I asked. "Burt slipped

away, but I never noticed where he went or when."

"Pretty sure," Holly answered. "He left right after the police arrived and started questioning you guys. He watched everything going on as he melted to the back of the crowd. I turned to watch him leave and saw his truck in the next row. The same woman I'd seen with him before was in it."

"Did you get that on video?" I asked.

She shook her head. "No, I had my camera still fixed on the commotion with Marla. But I definitely saw Burt go to his truck, and the woman was in the truck."

"Do you remember what the woman looked like?" I asked, leaning forward with expectation.

"Hard to say since I'd only seen her a few times and it was always in the vehicle, but I think she had blond hair, dark blond or very light brown. In her forties, maybe, or late thirties. I could only see her from the shoulders up, but I'd say she was on the thin side." Holly paused in her narrative. "Oh, and one more thing. She wore glasses, big ones, and they were red or maybe dark pink."

I reached toward the pad of yellow sticky notes. Holly picked them up and handed them to me, along with a pen. On the top one I wrote *Donna,* tore it off, and handed the note to Holly. "Would you please put that in Burt's column for me?" She did as I asked.

"You know her?" she asked after placing the note.

"I've met her," I said. "She works for the same company Burt did, and I think it's time I pay her a visit for a little one-on-one chat."

The same small smile I'd seen on Holly's face before made an appearance. "I'll drive." She pulled car keys from her jeans pocket and started for the door.

"Hold your horses," I said, amused at her eagerness. "It's too late today. The office is either closed or will be by the time we get there."

If Greg and I had a daughter, she'd be like this — smart and creative like him, nosy and impulsive like me.

Instead of tracking down Donna, I instructed Holly to pop the casserole dish into the oven. She'd just done that when Wainwright got to his feet and headed for the back door, his tail wagging with excitement. "Greg's home," I said.

"I didn't hear anything," Holly said, looking out the back slider.

"Give it a second," I said with a smile.

Sure enough, seconds later we heard the garage door open and Greg's van come up the alley. We couldn't see it because of the wall that separated our property from the car port and alley, but we could hear it as it slowed and made the turn into the garage.

TWENTY-THREE

"So you're Holly West," Greg said, holding out his right hand to our guest. His face was a blank, except for curiosity. She nodded and took his hand. As soon as he had come into the house, Greg planted a big kiss on me and greeted the animals. Holly had hung back, watching our nightly ritual. Finally, I'd urged her forward and introduced them.

"Sweetheart," Greg said, turning to me, still holding on to Holly's hand, "never in a million years would I have guessed that this was our mystery dinner guest." He gave her hand a little squeeze, then let it go, his face still noncommittal. On his lap was a six-pack of his favorite beer. "I was so sure it was Dev, I even bought more beer on the way home." He rolled over to the fridge and put the beer in. Before he closed the door, he asked Holly, "I'm going to have a beer; would you like one?"

She nodded but didn't say anything. He turned to me, but I declined. A pain pill was in my future, and I didn't need alcohol on top of it. Greg pulled two out and handed one to Holly. "I think we have a lot of talking to do tonight," he said.

"Honey," I said to Greg, "dinner won't be for about another thirty or forty minutes. Why don't you clean up first?"

He put one of the beers back. "You're right, Odelia. I'm just so anxious to talk to our guest."

Less than ten minutes later Greg was back in the dining area, washed up and wearing a clean T-shirt. Holly and I were both seated at the table. "So, girls," he said as he retrieved his beer from the fridge. "Fill me in."

By the time the casserole was heated through, we'd filled Greg in on everything we'd talked about at the beach and on the way home, and the fact that Holly had seen Donna with Burt and Burt with Marla.

"So there might be a link between Burt's murder and the Kingstons," Greg said. I knew he was eager to pin something on Kelton Kingston since we couldn't go public with the settlement with Jordon West. "We need to talk to Donna — see what she knows."

"I was thinking of doing that tomorrow," I told him.

Greg wasn't sure of that plan. "Are you sure you're up for that, Odelia?" he asked. "It seems just the walk to the beach did you in today."

"I'll be fine," I said, getting up to check on the casserole.

"Let me get that," Holly said. She got up from the table. Grabbing a couple of potholders from the counter, she pulled the dish out of the oven. I exchanged a glance with Greg while her head was down. He raised his brows at me, as impressed by her as I was. Holly also threw together a small salad to go with dinner and set the table, which made me want to adopt her.

"This is great," Holly said after a couple bites of Zee's dish. We had decided to eat at the picnic table on our patio since it had turned out to be such a nice evening, and we didn't want to disturb the sticky notes. Holly and I took seats opposite each other while Greg positioned his wheelchair at the end between us.

"It's Zee's signature dish," Greg said. "She's a wonderful cook."

"I have a couple of food vlogs as clients," Holly told us. "But I'm not much of a cook. I'm not a bad cook, just not fancy."

"That's kind of like me," I said. "Greg and I mostly grill, but I can throw together a mean pot roast or beef stew."

"Odelia's mother is the baker in the family," Greg said. "Her banana bread is magical. Not dense like most of them."

"Speaking of my mom," I said, "she's a big fan of yours, Holly."

Holly looked skeptical. "Your *mother* watches my vlog?"

I nodded and swallowed the bite I'd just taken. "She subscribes to it. She's the one who told us about the dog rescue being online and the one who caught that you had posted something about Burt's murder."

Greg chuckled. "Grace is a real piece of work. She's in her seventies but keeps up on all the trendy techie stuff. She even has her own blog, but she hasn't gone to videos yet." He took a swig of beer. "But I wouldn't be surprised if that's next."

Holly put down her fork and looked at us, her brows knitted. "Are you talking about Grace Littlejohn? The blogger on An Old Broad's Perspective?"

I nearly groaned. It never failed to surprise me how wide Mom's blog readership was. Next to me Greg was laughing. "That's our Grace," he said. He flashed me a wide grin.

"I know her!" Holly said with excitement.

"Not personally, but we've exchanged emails. She wrote me about my blog and told me about hers. I looked it up and found it fascinating. She talks about everything on her blog, even though a lot of it seems too fantastic to be real."

Another look flashed between Greg and me, but this time he wasn't amused. Holly caught that one.

"Is it all fiction," Holly asked, "or just the nutty parts, like the time she wrote about being shoved out a bathroom window while a gunman was after her?"

"The thing about my mother's blog," I said after taking a deep breath, "is that the nutty stuff is true. Maybe a bit embellished, but true."

"And Grace was pushed out of bathroom windows *twice* while running for her life, not once," Greg added.

"No, honey, you're wrong," I said. "The first time I pulled her through the window. The second time I pushed her."

For the first time since I'd met her, Holly was laughing. "I'd love to meet her."

"Right now she's on a trip with a bunch of senior friends," I said. "But she'll be home this weekend. I'm sure she'll be excited to meet you too."

Finished with dinner, we relaxed on the

patio. I had a bowl of washed strawberries in the fridge and brought them out for a light dessert. Wainwright was curled up on the grass. Muffin was in Holly's lap.

"Thanks for dinner," she said.

"It comes with a price," Greg told her, leaning forward. "We've talked about everything but the elephant in the room. You said your mother was sure I wasn't your father. Did she ever tell you who is?"

Holly lowered her head until it almost touched Muffin's. When she raised it, she said, "Yes, at the end she told me everything. It was her deathbed confession."

"And?" Greg pressed.

I put a hand on his shoulder, warning him not to be too aggressive. I was pretty sure what Holly was reluctant to say.

She still didn't raise her head, and the silence grew awkward. I gave her a little push, keeping my voice low, as if my normal one might be too harsh. "Your father is Kelton Kingston, isn't he?"

"What?" asked Greg, turning to me in surprise.

Still with her head down, Holly nodded. Slowly she raised her eyes to mine. "How did you know? Was it something you discovered in your research on me?"

"No, just piecing together a few things," I

told her. I pointed toward the back door to our house with my one working arm. "Not everything I know is stuck to that table in there." I lowered my arm and used it to pick up a glass of iced tea. I took a quick drink. "I can't see any reason for you to be following Marla Kingston unless it was something personal, and you started it about the same time you started following Greg — about the time your mother took sick. She told you then about Greg and how he wasn't your father. So I'm taking a guess that she told you Kingston was."

Greg was clearly lost. "But Jane wasn't seeing anyone during that time except for me on occasion. She was working that intern job. She didn't have time for a steady boyfriend."

"You don't know that for sure, Greg," I said to him. "She could have been seeing someone she worked with. Didn't you say she dropped the intern job unexpectedly and took the job in the assisted living place where Jordon West lives?"

"Yes," he said. Greg leaned back in his wheelchair and I could see the gears grinding, connecting the same dots I had. "But why that place?" he finally asked. "The only explanation was that she must have known about Kingston's connection to West —

about what he did."

"I don't know anything about Jordon West," Holly said, her attention totally on us, "or about any job in an assisted living place. She just said West was some nice guy whose name she put on my birth certificate to keep my real father away from me. She told me that she got pregnant by a married man she worked with and he wasn't a very nice person. Kingston certainly fits that bill." She paused.

I glanced at Greg. "See? It was someone she met at work."

Holly was fighting tears. "After she got sick, she finally told me my father was Kelton Kingston, but she said I must never contact him because he didn't know I existed." A tear ran down one of her cheeks. Greg handed her a napkin. "Mom said he paid her off. He gave her a huge amount of money to have an abortion and disappear." Her voice warbled from emotion. "She said while she worked at this company, she found out something very bad about him, something he'd done to another kid, so she knew he might try to hurt me, whether I was his or not."

"That's why she left his company," Greg put together, "and why she probably took that job where she could meet Jordon West.

She wanted to see if it was true."

"I don't understand," Holly said, her tears under control, "what Jordon West has to do with this."

Greg and I exchanged glances. He nodded at me, letting me know the decision was mine on what to tell Holly. "Jordon West," I began, "was the kid Kingston hurt. It was a car accident that Kingston caused, but he paid Jordon and his family off for Jordon shouldering the blame. Jordon West is a severe quadriplegic because of that accident. He can't even speak. He and your mother became friends when she worked there. She even visited him for several years after you were born. Obviously, I don't know why your mother decided to meet him in the first place, but I'm guessing that she wanted to see if whatever she'd learned about Kingston was true. Once she did, she put distance between herself and Kingston and you."

"Kind of a sweet twist," Greg said, "that Jane named Jordon as Holly's father, since Kingston took away all hope of Jordon ever having a family or normal life."

"Yes," I agreed. "Now that everything is falling into place, it makes sense why his name is on Holly's birth certificate. I'll bet Kingston doesn't even know about that."

Holly listened, her mouth hanging open as she tried to piece together what she knew with our theory.

"But why were you following Marla Kingston?" I asked. "I understand your curiosity about Kingston, but why Marla? She and Kingston didn't even know each other when you were born. He was married to someone else."

She shrugged. "Once I found out that Kingston was my father, I looked up everything I could about him. He really is nasty, and I could see why my mother wanted me to stay away from him. I followed him once in a while, but he's difficult to video. He always has lots of people around him. So I started following Marla, more out of curiosity." She stopped talking and looked sad again. "She's pretty miserable and unhappy, in spite of all that money. Then she started seeing that Burt guy, but, like I told Odelia, I don't think they were lovers, but something was going on."

"How did your mother support the two of you?" I asked as another thought came to me. "Did she have a job?"

"She worked off and on, mostly for non-profits," Holly told us. "She also had a trust. It was the money left her by her adoptive parents when they died. She came into that money after she turned twenty-one. She was very good at investing, which was how she spent most of her time. We lived off the interest. Not extravagantly, but comfortably." Her mouth turned down. "It's all mine now, but I'd rather have her back."

Greg reached over and took her hand. "I remember her talking about the trust. But I also recall her saying it wouldn't support her much beyond college. Are you sure, you lived off that trust?"

"I can't imagine how else we lived," Holly said, her words coming out slow. "She was very good at investing."

It was a very sad and now-familiar story: a bad situation with money thrown at it to go away. "I know you're hurting, Holly," I said to her, "but I need to know something. Do you get monthly checks from that trust?"

She shook her head. "No. Mom said that when I was born, she set up a new trust for us and funded it with the other trust's money. As we needed it, she withdrew money out of a checking account attached to the main investment account. Both of our names were on it. When she passed, I contacted a law firm to handle the probate for me and make sure everything with the investment companies got changed over to my name only."

I covered part of my face with my right hand. "What's the name of the law firm?" The question nearly came out as a groan.

"Gower, Werk and Reynolds," she answered. "Mom used them for years, so I went there. Was that okay?"

I breathed easy, happy with her response. "You did exactly what you were supposed to do," I told her, giving her an encouraging smile.

"I wasn't sure," Holly said. She went back to stroking Muffin. "I was wondering if I should go back to the firm that drew up the original trust. It was a firm called Templin and something, but I knew Mom liked this other firm and had used them for years, so I went there."

Under the table, Greg gently pounded my knee with his fist. I would have kicked him hard in return, but it would have been useless.

We started cleaning up dinner. Greg and Holly told me to relax and they would take care of everything. They shuttled our dirty dishes into the house, and Greg put them into the dishwasher. I followed them in and sat at the dining table, considering the sticky notes. If I hadn't been hurting, I would have been eating up this lazy lifestyle.

I could tell that Greg was itching to tell

Holly everything but was restraining himself. Instead, he rolled over to the table and looked at the columns. "Well, now we know who Holly West is." He grabbed a note, wrote *Kingston* on it, and stuck it under her column while she looked on. "I think the only mystery left on the table is who killed Burt Sandoval and why."

"But we'll question that Donna person tomorrow, right?" Holly asked.

"We?" Greg asked.

"Well, I know you have to go to work, Greg," she said, "but I can go with Odelia. She shouldn't be driving in her condition."

"You're right about that," Greg said.

"I'm right here," I protested. "And I'm not disabled. I can drive."

Greg fixed me with a stare that said *no way.* "You can hardly move, Odelia. You can talk to Donna next week, when you feel better."

"But you know the sooner I do it, the more likely she'll be to spill her guts," I protested. "We need to strike while she's grieving — or before she takes off, if she's scared."

"See," Holly argued, "you need me. If Grace were here, you'd let her tag along, wouldn't you? And she's old."

In spite of himself, Greg broke out into a

big belly laugh. "Don't let Grace hear you say that."

I wasn't sold on this idea, and Holly's logic wasn't helping. "My mother tags along because she's a pill. She's like a sticky booger you can't shake off your finger." Both of them were laughing now.

"The last time Odelia went to question someone," Greg said, "she was pushed down some stairs. That was just yesterday. You ready for that kind of reception?" he asked Holly.

Holly snapped her head in my direction. "You told me you fell."

"I did fall," I told her, "after I was pushed."

"If you don't take Holly with you," Greg said to me, "then ask Zee."

"No," Holly begged, "take me. I'm the one who told you about Donna in the first place."

I hung my head in defeat. I was hurting and overruled. "Okay. Okay," I said, caving. "But we're getting an early start."

Greg turned to Holly, his face lit like a bulb. "How about you stay here tonight?" he asked her. "We have a guest room, and I'm sure we can find you something to wear to bed and a toothbrush." He looked at me. "Don't we have a couple of new toothbrushes in the guest bathroom, sweetheart?"

I nodded. I felt run over by them and by my body aches. I just wanted to go to bed.

"No need," Holly said, excited about the sleepover idea. She went into the living room and grabbed her messenger bag. "I have my go bag."

"Go bag," I echoed. "What are you, some sort of spy? Do you have multiple passports in there too?"

"No," she insisted with a laugh. "It's just that sometimes when I'm following a video story, I end up far from home and have to crash somewhere for the night. But if you need multiple passports, I know a guy." She shot me a big grin that made me wonder if Jane was wrong about Greg not being Holly's father.

TWENTY-FOUR

I was quiet on the drive to Torrance, which Holly read as physical discomfort. "Are you feeling better today?" she asked, casting glances my way.

"I am, thanks," I told her. "I took a painkiller last night and it really helped." I glanced over at her. We were in her tiny car and she was at the wheel. From somewhere in her go bag she'd pulled out a white V-neck knit shirt to wear today. "You and Greg stayed up late," I noted.

"I hope you don't mind," she said. "We talked a lot about my mom and how she was back then."

"He liked her a lot," I assured her. "They weren't in love, but he liked her and thought highly of her."

"That's what he told me last night." She sighed. "I just wish she had stayed in touch with him, though. It would have been nice growing up with him in my life, even if just as a friend of the family." She shot me a smile. "Mom would have liked you, too."

I went back to my thoughts. While Greg and Holly made breakfast this morning, I had taken my laptop into the living room. Although I doubted it would be there, I wanted to see what I could find about Jane Newell on our firm's system. This time, though, I had been blocked from access. It made me wonder if they had noticed my snooping yesterday and cut me off or if our IT department had finally gotten around to deactivating my access now that I was on leave, which they should have done on Monday. I didn't think Steele would have gone back to the office and squealed on me. I didn't need the information from the firm's records, but it would have been interesting to see if Jane Newell had been a client for other things besides the initial trust. Holly had said Jane had used another firm for most of her legal needs, and that would make sense if she had any misgivings about T&T and their association with Kingston.

My cell phone rang. I hadn't stored it in the cross-body tote I was now carrying out of convenience. Instead, I held it in my hand like a lifeline. The display said it was Jill Bernelli, and it wasn't her T&T number but her personal cell phone number. It was 9:45 in the morning. Jill should be at work already.

"Hey, Jill," I answered as the thought struck me that she didn't want anyone to know she was calling me. A call from our office phones could be traced easily. I kept my voice upbeat, but my gut tightened as I held the phone to my ear.

"Odelia," Jill whispered, confirming my thought about this call being off the books. "Where are you?"

"In a car heading out to meet someone. Why?" I asked. Holly kept glancing over, curious about the call. "The question is, where are *you*?"

"In the ladies' room in the café in our building," she whispered. "I didn't want anyone to know I was calling you."

Chalk up another bingo for the fat lady in the arm sling.

"Big stuff is going down here this morning," Jill continued. "Steele has been on the phone this morning with the LA office, and there's been a lot of yelling and screaming. While that was going on, I got a call from HR telling me to pack up the personal stuff in your office." She paused. "Odelia, you're being fired!"

I sucked in air as if gut punched. It wasn't

totally unexpected, but it still felt like an assault. "Do you know why? It can't be because of the dog thing?" I asked her the question even though I knew the answer. I'd been caught snooping on a client, and that client was hitting T&T hard to be rid of me. Doris Hoffman might even have contacted Kingston herself, saying I was snooping around her son.

"Eddie took your computer out of your office," Jill reported. "He said you violated company confidentiality. Did you, Odelia?"

"No," I told her, "but I did access the firm's records yesterday, after they put me on leave. Hang on." I looked down at my cell and went to the home page. I had separate icons for my personal email and my firm email. I punched the icon for my T&T email and found my user name and password no longer worked. "They've already removed me from the firm's email," I told Jill. "Any idea when they're going to do the deed? Steele's the manager of the OC office, so it will fall to him to toss me out the door."

"Oh, Odelia, you know that's the last thing Steele would want," Jill said, her voice sad. "I'm telling you, Jolene and I thought he was going to have a stroke this morning. He was still yelling at Joe Templin when I slipped out to call you."

"Don't worry, Jill," I said, trying to reassure her. "I'll be fine. Greg doesn't want me to go back to the firm, and I'm beginning to see things his way. I'll call you tonight after you get home. Okay?"

"Okay," she said.

"And, Jill," I said to her, "stay out of this. There's a lot of shit coming down soon, and I don't want you to get hit by any of it. Do you understand?"

"But I want to help you," she said, her voice changing to strong and defiant.

"You can help by staying out of the way. Really, Jill, that will be a big help, knowing you're not in the way of Kingston's wrath. He's a very nasty man."

When I ended the call, I filled Holly in on what was going on. "Kingston wanted you fired because of that stupid little dog?" she asked.

"Originally, yes," I told her, "but now I think he wants me gone in order to stop me from snooping into his affairs." I snorted. "Like that's going to happen now!"

I called Greg and filled him in. He was both pleased and pissed off. "Any official contact from the office yet?" he asked me.

"Not yet, but when it happens, you'll be the first to know, honey."

"I'm going to call Seth," Greg said. "If the firm calls you in, I want Seth with you. Do you know if he's back from Sacramento yet?"

"I think it was just an overnight trip," I said, "but if he's not available, we can ask his partner, Doug Hemming. He's pretty cool."

I was barely off the phone with Greg when I received a call from Steele.

"You're not getting that?" Holly asked.

"Let him cool his heels." I let the call go to voice mail. The message was short and noncommittal, telling me to please call him back as soon as possible. We were about fifteen minutes from Torrance. I waited a full five minutes before returning Steele's call.

"Hey," I said in a forced cheerful voice. "You rang?"

"I need you to come into the office today, Grey," he told me, his voice crisp. "Around noon."

"I can't make it then, Steele," I said, working hard to keep the anger out of my voice. "I'm actually heading somewhere with a friend right now. How about three?"

"I need you here no later than one, Grey."

"And I'm telling you I can't make it until three." I wasn't about to tell Steele I was in the midst of lawyering up. "It's either three today or tomorrow — your choice. I'm a busy woman these days."

"So I hear," he quipped. Steele was quiet for a bit, then said, "See you at three."

"LA office or OC office?" I asked, letting him know I knew he wasn't calling me in to have coffee.

"OC," he said, his voice so weary and worn, I felt sorry for him. Steele was being caught in the middle, but it couldn't be helped.

I called Greg and gave him the skinny on the time of the meeting. He told me Seth was available and eager to help. Greg had filled him in. "Seth said he'd meet us at my shop around twelve thirty. Can you make that? I hope you don't mind, sweetheart, but I want to be in on this." I was glad of that.

"We're almost to Church Construction now," I told him. "If we're quick with Donna, then yes, I can make that."

Twenty-Five

When we entered the Church Construction office, it was as empty of people as it had been two days before. For a fleeting moment, I wondered if Donna had taken off, then a flat, familiar woman's voice came from the back. "Be right out."

I pointed at the photos of the former Kingston home. "This is the project where Burt met Marla Kingston. It was about two years ago."

Holly took off her sunglasses and studied the photos. "Nice digs."

"What are you doing back?"

I turned around to find Donna standing behind her desk. She was dressed similar to how she had been dressed when I last saw her, and she was just as unhappy to see me.

"Ben isn't in right now," she said, assuming I was there to see Ben Church.

"I'm not here to see him," I told her. "I want to speak to you."

"I've got nothing to say to you," she said. "The police have already talked to me, and I'm not as nice or as patient as Ben."

"That's obvious," I shot back. "But how nice were you to Burt Sandoval?" I took a step toward her. "Were you nice to Burt after business hours?"

"That's none of your business," she said. "Burt's gone and it's your fault."

"My fault?" I asked, using my good hand to point at myself. "How do you figure? I didn't shoot Burt. My husband and I tried to save his life."

Donna's eyes took in Holly. "Who's she?"

"My stepdaughter," I told Donna without any hesitation.

Donna was about to say something else, then decided against it. Instead, she returned to her accusation, her face as hard and set as a profile on Mount Rushmore. "Like I said, if not for you and your husband's heroics, Burt would be alive. The dog lived, but Burt was murdered. I told him not to go see your husband, but he wouldn't listen."

"Okay," I said, "let's talk about that." I placed a hand on the back of one of the visitor's chairs for balance. I wanted to sit, but I didn't think Donna would take kindly to that. "Greg and I had never met Burt until last Saturday, so we're rather stumped as to why he wanted to talk to Greg in the first place. He helped us with the dog, then took off before the police could question him. Next thing, he's calling Greg for a meeting. Before the meeting, he's gunned down." I squeezed the chair back as my still-sore hips cried for relief. "All I want to know is why did he need to talk to Greg?"

Donna's mouth twisted. "Burt was in over his head. He said the police seemed to know you guys, so when we got back to his place, we looked you up on the internet. Seems you and your husband are some kind of PIs, so he wanted some advice. It wasn't something he could go to the police about."

"We're not PIs," I told her, "but sometimes trouble seems to find us or people ask for our help. So what did Burt need our help on?"

Donna eyed Holly again, then turned back to me. "Sunday, the day after the thing with the dog, Burt received a death threat."

"Excuse me," I said, interrupting her, "but I need to sit down. I had a bad fall recently." I moved to the front of the chair I was using for support and sat in it. Holly remained standing, leaning against a file cabinet set against one wall.

"Okay," I said once settled, "let's start at

the beginning. What was your relationship with Burt? I know he wasn't married."

"Burt and I were seeing each other for about eight months," Donna told me with some reluctance. "But we kept it quiet because we worked together and . . . well, because I'm still married. I work with mostly men here, and you know how they can be about that kind of stuff."

It was a start, giving me hope that I might be able to pry other information out of her before I had to be in Huntington Beach at twelve thirty. "Donna, I'm very sorry for your loss." I paused a few heartbeats before continuing. "Do you know why Burt received the death threat?"

She nodded. "It was because of her," she said looking at Holly.

"Me?" Holly asked with great surprise. "I didn't know the guy."

"Not you, stupid," Donna said. She pointed at the photos of the grand house. "Her, the Kingston bitch."

Ah, there's the opening I needed.

"Burt and Marla met on that job and stayed in touch after, didn't they?" I asked, shifting my weight in the chair to find a comfortable spot.

Donna took a seat behind her desk. She took off her glasses and rubbed her eyes.

She looked even more tired than last time. Her shoulders slumped forward and I felt she might crack if pressed in the right place.

"That job," I prodded. "Something happened between them during the project, didn't it? Something that came back to haunt Burt into his grave."

"Yes and no," Donna admitted. "They met on that job. One day Burt found her sitting in her car out front crying. He comforted her and from time to time they talked. She told him about how unhappy she was and how brutal Kingston was to her."

"Did they have an affair?" Holly asked.

Donna nodded and replaced her glasses. "Yes. Burt told me it lasted during the remodel and for about a month after. During the remodel, the Kingstons were staying at their home in Orange County, so Burt and Marla would stay in the Beverly Hills house after the crew went home. Burt said she became paranoid about her husband finding out after the remodel was done and broke it off. That was long before he and I became close."

The phone on Donna's desk rang and she answered it, forcing her voice to sound professional. She told the caller that Ben Church wasn't in but she'd be happy to take a message for him. Quickly, she grabbed a pen and jotted down something on a message pad positioned by the phone.

I glanced over to Holly. She remained leaning against the cabinet, her arms crossed in front of her. We exchanged meaningful looks. There was a gleam in her eye, like the one Muffin gets when she's about to trap a bird.

"We've learned that Burt had been meeting Marla recently," I said, turning my attention back to Donna when she was done with the call. "And that you were at those meetings but stayed in the truck."

Donna's mouth dropped. "How could you possibly know that?"

"Let's just say we do," Holly replied.

"Obviously, those meetings between Burt and Marla Kingston weren't lovers' trysts if you were there," I added. "And witnesses have said that the meetings weren't always friendly. What were those about?" I asked. "Could that have a bearing on why Burt was shot?"

"It had everything to do with why Burt was shot," Donna admitted. "You see, during their brief affair, Marla told Burt a lot of crazy stuff about her husband — stuff he'd done that was crooked and just plain horrible. Stuff that could ruin Kingston if it ever got out."

I leaned forward. "Did she ever mention the name Jordon West to Burt?"

Donna's eyes widened. "You know about Jordon West?"

"Yes," I said. "I even met him recently."

"But he's some kind of vegetable," Donna said.

"He's quite incapacitated physically," I told her, "but he's hardly a vegetable."

"Marla told Burt that the West guy was a vegetable and that it was because of Kingston," Donna said. "It was an accident and a coverup that had happened years ago. Kingston paid off the family."

"Were the recent meetings with Marla about that?" I asked.

"Yes, and other stuff," Donna said. "Burt was blackmailing her. He told her that unless she gave him a half million in cash, he would go to the press with the thing about the West kid and about their affair. One would sink Kingston and the other would sink Marla. If she's ever found unfaithful, Kingston can kick her out with nothing."

"Something's not right here," Holly said, leaving her post and moving toward the desk. "Marla Kingston told all this to Burt Sandoval two years ago, but he waited until *now* to try and put the screws to her?"

That's my girl! It was something I was wondering myself.

"He needed the money," Donna said. "*We* needed the money. My husband's crazy. Burt wanted me to leave my husband, but the only way I could is if we left the area. To do that, we needed money."

My gut was telling me the blackmail plan had been Donna's idea.

"Burt had been negotiating with Marla, but she said she needed time to get that kind of money together. The Saturday you rescued the dog was payday for us." Donna twisted up her face again in my direction. "If you had let the damn dog die, Burt wouldn't have offered to help and he and I would be out of the country by now, starting new lives." She plucked a tissue from a nearby box and blew her nose.

"So what did Burt expect from Greg?" I asked.

"Help, I think. After he got the death threat, he had no idea where to go for help. He couldn't go to the police because he'd been blackmailing Marla. In one of the articles he found on you, there was a suggestion that you had connections with some unusual people in the underground. He wanted to see if Greg could hook him up with a way to get us safely out of town,

342

money or no money."

So Burt had stuck around long enough to hear the officers talk about our identities, particularly mine, and had been curious enough to check us out. Then he drifted away while the attention was elsewhere.

I really need to Google us and see what's out there about our past activities.

"Burt knew some other people who might be able to help," Donna continued, "but he said he didn't trust them not to sell us out to Kingston for cash. He said there was something he trusted about you and your husband, so he wanted to start there."

"So whoever was after Burt followed him to Greg's business and took him out," Holly said. "What exactly did the death threat say?"

"I have it here," Donna said. She opened a lower drawer in her desk and pulled out a large crumpled piece of paper. She put it on the desk and pushed it across in my direction.

There was no way I was going to put my fingerprints on that thing. I looked around for something to use to open it without touching it when Holly pulled a pair of latex gloves from her go bag and handed them to me. "Here, use these."

That girl had to be an undercover something

343

— or maybe she was a serial killer.

I took the gloves and slipped them on. They were for smaller hands than mine and barely fit, like a pair of too-small condoms. I reached for the note and smoothed it out. It was handwritten, using printed words, not cursive: *Back the fuck off or die.*

"How did Burt get this?" I asked.

"It was stuck on his windshield on Sunday morning," Donna told us. "We met later that day and discussed what to do about it."

"But none of those plans included the police?" I asked. "Not even after Burt died and they came here asking questions?"

Donna shook her head and started to cry. "I didn't want to be part of it — you know, the blackmailing. If I gave that to the police, they'd assume I was part of it."

"But you were, Donna," I told her firmly, barely hiding the disgust in my voice. "My husband and I didn't cause Burt's death. You did, and so did Burt himself when you went after Marla Kingston. Do you realize how easy it is for people like Marla and her husband to destroy other people? Look what happened to Jordon West, and he was just an innocent seventeen-year-old in the wrong place at the wrong time. The Kingstons think they are above the law. Kingston probably has people on retainer to take care of

344

gnats like you and Burt." I tapped the note. "This was not a death threat. This was a death sentence. They didn't even wait to see if Burt would heed the warning. They went after him the very next day, as they probably planned to do all along. The only person this is a warning to is you."

Donna blew her nose again. Her tears were real but not sloppy and emotional. This was a woman out to save her own skin. "So what should I do?" she asked. "Go to the police and hope I don't wind up in jail for blackmail?"

I stood up and peeled off the gloves. My hands and fingers were happy to be released from the casings. "Would you rather end up dead?"

Twenty-Six

"What's with the gloves?" I asked Holly once we were back in her car.

She flashed me a smile. "I sometimes Dumpster dive."

"What? Why would you do that? I thought you were comfortable financially."

"I am," she answered. "Another of my interests is art made from junk. If I see something interesting, I pull it from wherever I find it and use it in my pieces. Often the stuff I drag home is quite dirty, so the gloves come in handy."

"You're a woman of many interests," I noted.

"That's what life is about, isn't it? If something catches my interest, I learn about it. Sometimes it turns into something I enjoy doing, like the art, and sometimes not." She glanced at me. "Besides, the gloves are also great for not leaving fingerprints when I pull a heist."

"That last part was a joke, wasn't it?" I asked, staring right at her.

"Maybe."

Oh, dear Gawd, this girl was Greg, me, and my mother all rolled into one. How could she not be a blood relative?

"We still don't know who killed Burt," Holly pointed out once we were back on the 405 Freeway and heading toward Huntington Beach. "We kind of know why he *might* have been killed, but it also could have been Donna's husband who bumped him off."

"Yeah, I wondered that too," I said. I glanced at the time displayed on my cell phone. If traffic remained good, we'd be on time for the meeting with Seth Washington.

"It doesn't make sense," she said, her eyes fixed on the road. "In order to make that threat or hire someone to do it, Kingston would have had to know about Marla's indiscretions. Do you really think she went home to Kingston on Saturday and said, 'Oh, by the way, dear, I was slumming at the strip mall because I was paying off a blackmailer who I told about all your criminal activities during pillow talk.' " I laughed. Holly had changed her voice to that of a bored socialite for the last part.

"No, I don't," I said. "Especially if Marla

347

has an iron-clad prenup that leaves her with nothing in the event of infidelity. Donna's husband may go to the head of the suspects list."

"Or," Holly said, "Burt's murder may have had nothing to do with the Kingstons. If he was looking for ways to come up with quick cash and lots of it, he might have crossed the wrong people."

It was another great possibility.

My cell phone rang. I looked at it. It wasn't a number I knew. I answered with a cautious hello.

"Is this Odelia Grey?" a woman's voice asked in a whisper.

"Yes." The voice was vaguely familiar, but I couldn't quite place it.

"This is Celeste Jackson at Bayview Assisted Living." Before I could greet her properly, she rushed on with her purpose, still whispering. "No one can know I called you, Odelia, but something fishy is going on and I wanted to give you a heads-up. The law firm for Jordon West's trust got or are getting a restraining order against you."

"What?" I nearly shouted.

"Yes," she said. "I got a call from them earlier. I'm not to let you anywhere near Jordon or even through the front door. They said you mean him great harm. Now, I don't know you very well, but I clearly saw that you would never hurt that man. What's going on?"

"It's a long story, Celeste," I told her as my blood began to boil, "and if I have my way, it's all going to come out very soon. In the meantime, protect yourself and your job and don't contact me again, but I sure appreciate this call."

When the call ended, I said to Holly, "Well, I'll be. My law firm just put a restraining order against me so I can't see Jordon West again. I'll bet that mother of his called Kingston and Kingston called Templin."

"Maybe that's why they're firing you," Holly suggested.

"They're firing me because I'm on to something and they're trying to block me from learning anything new." I was fuming. "The thing is, I already know everything I need to know about Kingston's dirty hands; the trouble is going to be providing proof. Jordon's mother certainly isn't going to speak to me again — not unless it's to push me down another flight of steps."

When we reached Ocean Breeze Graphics, Seth was already in Greg's office sipping coffee. I introduced him to Holly and told Seth and Greg about what we'd learned from Donna, and about Celeste Jackson's call. Greg had told him everything else before we got there. When I was done, Seth asked Holly to excuse us. He needed to speak with me in private since it involved a client of T&T. She understood and went to sit out front and talk with Chris and Aziz. Greg didn't want to leave me, but Seth insisted. It reminded me of the times Seth had counseled me at police stations.

Seth offered to go to the meeting with Steele in my place. "You don't have to go, Odelia," he said. "I can go with you or as your representative."

"No," I said with a shake of my head. "I want to look Steele in the eye when he lowers the axe."

"Don't be too hard on Mike Steele," Seth advised. "Both you and Greg need to understand that he's only doing what he's been ordered to do. Same with the firm. They were only carrying out the directives of their client when they set up that trust. You don't know if they knew the whole story or only what Kingston told them. Same with Holly's mother. If T&T set up a settlement between her and Kingston, they were doing their job. But you did go snooping around in the firm's file system after you were put on leave. You know better than that, Odelia.

You know that was wrong."

I nodded. "Yes, I do. But on the moral sliding scale, it's a molecule of dust compared to covering up an accident that put a kid in a wheelchair for the rest of his life."

Seth nodded. "I totally agree with you on that, but you did break the rules." Seth is a handsome man, big and powerfully built, with a deep mahogany voice that matched his skin color. He's like a brother to me, and I trust him with my life.

"So, when we get to T&T," he said, "you'll let me do the talking, right? They are probably going to offer you an exit package. We will negotiate for more. After all, you didn't learn about Kingston's involvement with Jordon West from your snooping in the firm's system. You were only confirming what you'd learned elsewhere."

"Okay," I reluctantly agreed. "Just don't mention anything about Bayview. Celeste could lose her job. One lost job is enough."

"Don't worry, I won't mention that. Just remember, Odelia, your job is gone; we're just going to make it hurt on their side a little more. Steele's not your enemy, but for today he's not your friend. You can kiss and make up after the smoke clears."

"Guess I'll go home and change," I told him, "unless you think my capris and shirt give off a certain air of disrespect, which I definitely feel right now."

Seth laughed and shook his head. "Actually, I think the sling is a nice touch." He paused. "Funny, I was thinking on the way down here that this isn't the first time you've negotiated an exit package from a firm after your snooping uncovered something nasty. Didn't Steele negotiate that last one for you?"

"That he did," I confirmed. "And I'm sure he's remembering that today too."

"Maybe, Odelia, you should think about staying away from law firms and think about finding something where you can work for yourself."

"That's what Greg's campaigning for," I told him, "and he's campaigning hard."

"By the way," Seth said, "Greg and I talked about you guys going to the police with the stuff you know. I think it's time."

"Me too," I agreed, "especially the stuff about Burt's murder."

"And the stuff about Kingston might be okay, too, at least the stuff you learned on your own and not through the firm. I'll double-check on that and let you know when I see you later. And I'll go with you and Greg to the police if you like." He gave me a hug. "With you and Greg on the loose, maybe I should become a criminal attorney."

"We're not criminals," I reminded him.

"You spend as much time in police stations as they do."

There was a knock on Greg's office door. It was Greg. "Sorry to interrupt, but I think you need to see this, Odelia." In his hands was an iPad. On his heels was Holly.

"No worries, Greg," Seth said. "We're done, and I need to leave. I have to run by my office before the T&T meeting." He turned to me. "Do you think, Odelia, that you can stay out of trouble until at least three?"

As soon as Seth left, Greg thrust the iPad at me. "This is Holly's. This is the uncut footage from the day Burt was shot." He started the video, which was shot from across the street from the strip mall where we were currently located. Vehicles of all kinds, including busses and delivery trucks, drove past in both directions, with the occasional gap in traffic where the camera caught a full view of the front of Ocean Breeze, the parking lot, and the small businesses around it. Once in a while people walked past on the sidewalk or a bike or two went by or someone on skates or a skateboard. Then my car was viewed pulling into the parking lot. A while later, Burt's truck pulled into the lot and Burt got out. There was a shot, and Burt was hit.

"We've seen this before," I said.

"Not this clip," Holly pointed out. "This is the entire video, not the edited one I posted."

"Look again," Greg said. "But don't watch the building, watch the people on the street."

I watched it again. Then again, trying to concentrate on the pedestrians. Nothing jumped out at me until the third viewing. I stopped the video. "Can we enlarge this?" I asked. "Just this section here."

Greg turned to Holly. "She finally saw it."

Holly stepped up and enlarged the video. I studied it. "What's he doing down here?" I finally asked no one in particular.

"Interesting, isn't it?" asked Greg. "And now that you know what you're looking for, go back to the beginning to view it again."

I did as he said. One person made a couple of passes in front of the camera. He was on the same side as the shop, not the side where Holly stood. It was Charlie Cowart on a skateboard.

"Charlie told me he lived up near the grocery store in Long Beach. He couldn't have skateboarded all the way down to

Huntington Beach, could he?"

"It's about ten to twelve miles," Greg estimated. "It's not impossible. More likely he drove down, then hopped on the skateboard when he got here. The real question is why he's going back and forth in front of the shop. Did he know Burt was coming and was waiting for him? Or was he watching me? He started doing this before you even showed up."

I didn't like the thought of that at all. I moved the video forward to see the last time Charlie showed up on the screen, then moved it forward slowly to see how soon it was before Burt showed up after that. "Look at this," I said. "Charlie's last pass was right before Burt showed up. It's almost as if he was waiting for him." I played more of the video to see if Charlie, who seemed to be a natural voyeur, stuck around to video the hullabaloo with the police and ambulance. "And as soon as Burt was shot, he disappeared," I noted. "Saturday he stuck around to film the dog rescue, but on Monday he took off as soon as Burt was shot."

"But how did Charlie know Burt would be here and when?" Greg asked. "If he's the shooter, someone would have had to tell him."

"Donna told us that she and Burt discussed it on Sunday after Burt got that death threat," Holly said. "I got the feeling only she knew Burt was coming here."

"Me too," I said. "And even if Charlie had followed him here in a car, he wouldn't have had time to roll back and forth before Burt pulled into the parking lot." I shook my head. "No, someone set up Burt, and that someone knew Burt was heading here."

"Unless," Holly said, pacing the office, "there was a bug planted somewhere." She stopped. "Think about it: it would be easy for someone to plant a bug in Burt's place when he was out. Maybe Kingston was having his wife followed and that led to Burt. Donna did say they went back to Burt's to discuss stuff."

Greg and I looked at each other, agreeing that Holly could be right. "Did anyone notice you filming?" Greg asked. "I'd hate to think Charlie saw you taking this."

"It's not like I stick out like a sore thumb," she said with sarcasm. "I blend in with the background. Everyone is looking at their phone or tablet these days. No one even considers that they might be on camera, even though there are cameras everywhere."

"Cameras everywhere," I repeated. "I'll bet the police got footage from the security cameras from each of the businesses around here to see if the shooter was caught on one of them."

"I know they asked for my camera feed," Greg said. "Do you think they noticed Charlie going back and forth like a duck in a carnival shooting gallery?"

"That was the Huntington Beach police," I noted. "They might not realize Charlie was the same one who took the footage of the dog rescue. They might not have linked him to both places yet." I tapped the screen. "Holly, is this what you gave the police or was it the shortened version you posted on the web?"

"I gave them this full video," she said, "just in case there was something on it I didn't see."

Greg brought up what was on my mind. "We need to contact Detectives Chapman and Suarez about this. Charlie might not be the killer, but they need to know he's a common thread. I have their cards here."

Greg rolled to his desk and retrieved two business cards that had been clipped under his desk phone for safekeeping. He picked up the phone and dialed the number for one of them. While he did that, I went to Greg's computer and called up Marigold. Once there, I input the name Charles Cowart with birthdate parameters that would put him anywhere from seventeen to twenty-nine in age.

"I got voice mail on both their numbers," Greg reported. "I told them to call us because we may have something new on the murder."

"I think you should talk to them," I said to Holly. "You're the video queen and can also tell them about Burt since you were with me at the construction company. I need to get to that meeting at T&T."

"But I drove you here," Holly noted.

"No problem," Greg said. "I can take Odelia there. I want to go anyway."

"Okay," she agreed. "Although I'd rather be anywhere but at a police station."

"Why?" Greg teased. "You have a secret past you don't want catching up to you?"

"Don't ask, Greg," I said, "unless you really want to know."

Holly laughed. "You guys are so weird and funny."

Detective Suarez called Greg back first. Greg quickly explained to the detective what we had stumbled upon. Detective Suarez asked if Holly could come down to the station immediately. They'd be waiting for her.

After Holly left, I used the bathroom. The Marigold report hadn't come in yet when I returned. "I guess we'd better get going," I said to Greg.

"You want to go home and change first?" he asked. "I was thinking I should drop off Wainwright before heading into your office. We have just enough time if we hurry."

I looked down at my casual clothes and well-worn sneakers and shook my head. "Nah," I said. "Home is in the other direction, and it's not like I'm going to a job interview. Let's bring Wainwright. He can stay with Jill during the meeting."

We were crossing through the main part of the shop toward the front door when we noticed everyone gathered around, staring up at the TV, including two customers. We stopped too and looked up, like a crowd watching an air show.

I grabbed Greg's shoulder as the breaking news sunk into my skull. On the screen an anchor was reporting on the death of Marla Kingston, wife of tycoon Kelton Kingston. According to the report, Marla had died of a drug overdose. We stood rooted to our spots. Onscreen now was a makeshift press conference in front of the Kingston mansion in Newport Coast. In front of the microphones was a spokesperson for the Kingston family. I recognized him as one of the junior partners from the LA office of

T&T but couldn't remember his name. He said it had happened less than two hours earlier. A maid had found Mrs. Kingston in the bathtub, but she was already dead. The spokesperson went on to say that Mrs. Kingston had been battling severe depression for quite some time, and the recent public criticism over leaving her dog in a hot car had been too much for her to bear. He asked the public to respect the family's privacy.

As soon as Greg, Wainwright, and I were in the van, I said, "Overdose, my ass! I say Kingston found out about Marla and Burt and is just tidying up loose ends. I'll bet Holly was right about there being a bug."

Greg's face was dark as he patted my knee. "Let's just be glad all he wants to do to you is kick you out of your job."

TWENTY-SEVEN

We weren't very far from Ocean Breeze when my phone rang. It was the number that had called me earlier — the number belonging to Celeste Jackson.

"Hi, Celeste," I said after putting the phone on speaker. "I'm surprised to hear from you so soon."

"Am I on speaker?" she asked.

"Yes," I told her. "I'm in the car with my husband. Don't worry, he knows all about this."

"I told you something was fishy," Celeste said in a deep whisper. Greg turned down the AC so we could hear her better.

"Now what's happened?" I asked with worry as my mind went to the death of Marla Kingston. "Is Jordon okay?"

"He's fine, but his mother is not. I just got another call from the law firm advising us that Jordon's mother passed away last night unexpectedly. All this time I thought she was living out of state and she was in Aliso Viejo. Can you imagine that?"

I had stopped breathing and only noticed when I couldn't hold my breath any longer. I had just seen the woman. Our last encounter had been her sending me down a short flight of steps.

"Odelia, are you there?"

"Yes, Celeste, I am. How did Doris die?"

"How did you know her name was Doris?"

"It's a long story," I told her. "I actually met her a couple of days ago when I was following up on some other information."

"Fishy, I tell ya," Celeste said, still whispering, "and now I'm thinking you're fishy, too."

"Celeste, I know this looks bad, but you have to do me a favor." Before she could say *hell no,* I added, "Stay close to Jordon. Make sure no one gets anywhere near him but you. His life may be in danger."

"What?" The question wasn't a whisper.

"Please, Celeste. I've uncovered some really nasty stuff, and it might cause people to want to hurt him."

There was a long pause from the other end of the line. "Heart attack," she said. "Jordon's mother passed from a heart attack in her home. I heard she was alone so there was no one there to help."

"Will you take care of Jordon?" I asked.

"I will sleep in his room if I have to."

After the call, I turned to Greg. "Okay, so Marla Kingston, Doris Hoffman, and Burt Sandoval are all dead. All of them knew about Kingston's coverup of Jordon's accident."

"Anyone else except for you, me, and Holly?" he asked. "How about that Donna?"

"Yes, and Steele," I added.

"How about Zee?"

"I don't think so," I answered. "She and I thought it might be possible, but I never confirmed that with her, ever."

"Good." He looked over at me. "Call Holly. Tell her she's not to leave the police station and go home or even go to our house. We can't assume she's not on their hit list by now."

Holly didn't answer her phone, so I left her a voice mail and a text. I told her to call one of us when she was done with the police. In the text I told her about Marla and Doris Hoffman, and how we didn't think their deaths were accidental. She was to tell the cops that. My poor thumbs had never typed anything so fast or furious. And who knows what auto-correct did to my message? I didn't take the time to check.

Next, I looked up the number for Church

Construction and called it, leaving the phone on speaker. Donna answered. "I don't want to talk to you," she said as soon as she heard my voice. "Haven't you done enough?"

"Donna, did you see the news that Marla Kingston is dead?" I asked.

"Yeah, I heard about it just a few minutes ago," she told me. "Ding, dong, the bitch is dead. So what?"

"So, someone else died too: Jordon West's mother. She died last night. And Burt was killed on Monday. See any connection between them?" I asked. While I waited for her to process the information, I heard the theme from *Jeopardy* in my head. Greg rolled his eyes at the phone to indicate her denseness.

"Let me help you," I finally told her. "What all three of them had in common was knowledge of what really happened to Jordon West, and you're in that small club too. Think about it."

"Oh my God, what am I gonna do?" she wailed as the possibility of her demise sunk in.

"Get yourself to the police station," Greg yelled into the phone.

"Who is that?" Donna asked.

"That's Greg, my husband," I told her. "I

know you're worried about being implicated in the blackmail, but the alternative may be death."

After that call, I noticed my phone was low on juice. Greg always keeps a car charger in the middle storage bin between the seats. I plucked it out and plugged my phone into the power in the dash. Then I leaned back in my seat, thoroughly exhausted. "I really don't want to face Steele right now."

"We can always postpone the meeting until Monday," Greg suggested. "In fact, why don't we? Who cares when they fire you."

"You have a point." I picked up my phone and called Seth. When he answered, I said, "Greg and I want to postpone the three o'clock meeting with Steele. Tell him I'll come in on Monday, as early as he'd like, no dragging butt, no complaints."

"Actually," Seth said, "I called Steele to let him know I'd be joining you. I wanted to make sure he knew you were represented and not going to roll over on this."

"Did he argue with you?" I asked.

"No, and he was about to call you and postpone the meeting himself. Seems Joe Templin wanted to be in the meeting too, but an emergency cropped up."

Greg and I exchanged wide-eyed looks. "Did he say why Templin couldn't make it?" I asked.

"Of course not, Odelia," Seth said. "Steele just said he would email the settlement agreement over to my office. Officially, as of today, you are no longer an employee of Templin & Tobin. On that Steele and I agreed. Hell, you might not ever have to step foot in that place again. We can handle the settlement over the phone and email, and your things can be messengered to your home."

I honestly couldn't believe that Mike Steele was tossing me out on my ass, in spite of what Seth had said about Steele just doing what he was told. Steele wasn't the type to do everything by the book. I was so disappointed in him that my heart nearly broke.

"Well," I said, shoving my personal feelings aside, "I can tell you some of what that emergency entailed. Did you see the news that Marla Kingston died?"

"No," Seth said with surprise, "but I've been tied up ever since I left you guys. What happened?"

"They're saying it was an overdose," I reported. "She was found in her tub this morning by a maid. But that's not all.

Seems that Jordon West's mother died last night of an unexpected heart attack while alone in her home."

Greg and I heard a slight swear word come from the phone. It was several seconds before Seth found his voice. "Isn't it Dev Frye who always says there ain't no such thing as a coinkydink?"

"Yep," I said. I went on to tell him what we discovered about Charlie Cowart and how Holly was with the Huntington Beach police at the moment, filling them in.

"Now that you guys don't have to go to this meeting," Seth said when we were finished, "I suggest you get out of Dodge for the weekend and lay low. Let the police deal with this. Tell Holly to do the same. You broke the story, now let someone else run with it."

It was sound advice.

When the call ended, Greg said, "Hey, earlier today I got a text from Tip Willis. They returned from their trip today, so they can take Dumpster anytime we want to bring him down. How about tomorrow? Or we can leave tonight, drop Dumpster off, and spend the weekend somewhere. We'll take both Wainwright and Muffin." He winked at me. "Maybe we won't even come home until Monday."

"But I thought Tip's family was going to be gone at least a week," I said.

"They were," Greg explained, "but one of the kids got sick with some kind of bug and it ran through the whole family, so they decided to come home early to recover."

"Sounds like a plan to me," I agreed.

"In fact," added Greg, "why don't we take Holly with us? That way we could get to know her and also know she's safe. There's that cabin Willie owns in Big Bear. He said we could use it anytime we wanted. Call Clark and see if it's available." We weren't far from the T&T office when Greg made a U-turn and started us back toward home.

"Yeah," I agreed with a smile, "we can all grab our go bags and go." Greg laughed.

During the call with Seth a notice had popped up that I had new email. I checked it. The sender was Marigold. Opening it, I found that Marigold had delivered the report on Charles Cowart. I tapped on the attached document, wishing I had a bigger screen, like an iPad or other tablet, on which to view it. But I need not have worried. I didn't need a bigger screen because there was nothing in the report except that Charles Cowart had a driver's license issued by the State of California. Nothing else. I noted the address on the driver's license and looked it up on Google Maps. It was a vacant lot near the oil fields in Long Beach. Chills ran up and down my spine like scales played on a piano. Charles Cowart wasn't a kid bound for college. He was a ghost — a deadly ghost.

I told Greg about the report. "I wonder," I said, "if he's the one who's responsible for Marla and Doris's deaths?"

I called Holly again. This time I got her. "Are you still at the police station?" I asked her.

"Yes, we're done though," she said. "I was just about to call you and let you know that the cops are seriously all over this."

I told her about Charlie Cowart having no background information and Seth's recommendation that we get out of town for a few days. I extended the invitation for her to come with us.

"Sure," she said with enthusiasm. "Should I meet you at your place?"

We set a time to meet back at our house. It would give her time to replenish her go bag and us time to pack up the animals and ourselves. We'd be leaving town in the middle of rush hour, but at least we'd be leaving it and all the danger and drama behind.

Rush hour always started early on a Friday, and traffic on the 405 Freeway was already heavy. Instead of getting on the freeway, Greg made his way to Pacific Coast Highway. It was the route he'd taken from his shop to here; now we were taking it back. Even though it was summer, PCH wasn't nearly as busy as the freeway, and it was a much prettier drive. On Saturday it would be bumper to bumper and the freeway would be the best choice for travel.

We were driving north on PCH. Between Newport Beach and Huntington Beach is a long stretch of the highway that runs right along the beach. To our right were businesses and condos. To our left was the gorgeous Pacific Ocean and beach, separated from the highway by public parking lots. Traffic was moving along nicely. Greg had turned off the AC and opened the windows. It was a glorious end to a horrible week.

I was on the phone with Clark, asking him about Willie's Big Bear cabin. "Sure it's available, sis," Clark told me. I had him on speaker phone.

"Great," Greg called over toward the phone in my hand. "If it's okay with Willie, we'd like to show up there tonight and stay through either Sunday or Monday. Key still in the same place?"

"Yeah, it is," Clark confirmed. "Does this

sudden need to flee the city have anything to do with Marla Kingston's death?" Except for the dog rescue last Saturday, Clark knew nothing yet about our insane week.

"Yes and no," I said. "We just need to leave it all behind for a little bit. Once we're at the cabin tonight, we'll call and fill you in on everything that has happened, including me losing my job."

"You lost your job?" Clark asked. From his voice, I could tell he was getting slightly agitated.

"Long story; I'll tell you later," I said. "Right now we just want to grab our bags and animals and head to the mountains."

"Look at that idiot!" Greg yelled as a black, low-slung muscle car came up fast behind us, then passed us, barely clearing the oncoming traffic.

"What's going on?" asked Clark, his voice coming out of the phone loud and clear.

"Just some fool driving crazy," I told him. "He almost caused an accident on PCH."

Clark and I gabbed about Mom and her trip. She hadn't called either of us for a few days, which probably meant she was having a great time or was dead in a ditch. With Mom, you never knew. "We met one of Mom's internet heroes this week," I told Clark. "She lives near us. It'll be a nice surprise when Mom gets home."

"God, here comes that idiot again," Greg said with a shake of his head.

Sure enough, the black car was now heading south, but instead of speeding past us, it started to slow down as it approached. When it got close, I saw something sticking out the window.

My heart stopped. It was a gun, and holding the gun was a grinning Charlie Cowart. I screamed.

Greg saw him too and, making a quick decision, he turned the wheel of our van into the other vehicle, smashing into it just in front of the driver's seat. If he'd turned the van the other way, it might have hit innocent people. A bullet shattered the windshield, and I felt horrible pain in my injured shoulder.

The van spun as it hit the other car and my side of the van came around to smash into Charlie's car. Our airbags deployed. Then — nothing.

TWENTY-EIGHT

I was reading aloud from *Treasure Island,* one of Greg's favorite childhood books. In the background, the sounds of medical equipment provided backup vocals. I looked up from my reading and studied Greg's face. His eyes were closed, his skin pale. Every morning I groomed his beard and hair. Ronald and Renee Stevens come to the hospital every day to visit Greg. They sit next to him for hours, solemn and stoic. I watch them sometimes and know they're remembering a time decades before when they did the very same thing after the accident that had landed Greg in a wheelchair for the rest of his life.

It had been just over a week since the accident, and my beloved, my life, was in a coma. The bullet that shattered the windshield had lodged in my bad shoulder. It didn't penetrate far thanks to the windshield and the sling I had been wearing, and a

373

simple surgery had fixed me up. The bumps and bruises were almost gone. The second bullet, the one we didn't hear, had penetrated the left side of Greg's temple. The surgeons said the bullet didn't appear to do any permanent damage, but it might take weeks or months to know for sure. The coma had been induced to help the swelling and healing, but when they tried to bring him out of it the day before, Greg didn't respond.

Charlie Cowart was injured in the accident too, but after a few days in the hospital he was released to the county jail, where he's awaiting charges for, at the very least, attempted murder. This time there were witnesses, lots of them.

Our dear Wainwright did not make it. He'd suffered minor injuries in the crash, but while recovering at the animal hospital his old, faithful heart gave out. Greg doesn't know yet. It's going to break his heart, as it had mine and everyone who knew the wonderful old dog.

The Stevenses were coming back later. They'd left with the rest of their family for a quiet lunch. I'd been invited, but I declined. I never wanted Greg to be alone. Many nights I slept in his room, hunched over in a chair, my head on his bed while I slept fitfully. Many times that's how my mother and Zee and Seth found me. Zee often kept vigil with me, spending entire days quietly praying while I silently cursed God. When Mom sat with me, she seldom took her eyes off Greg, as if willing him to survive.

Greg's hospital room was filled with flowers. Getting up from the chair, I went around the room and touched each bouquet and plant as if touching the loving people who'd sent them. Even more than a week later, flowers kept arriving. Templin & Tobin had sent a huge arrangement several days ago. I'd quietly handed that arrangement off to a nurse and asked that it be given to the children's ward. Greg also had a lot of visitors. Clark had come from Arizona; Willie and his wife, too. Dev often spent time with us, as did Andrea Fehring. Greg's business partner and employees were beside themselves, but they were making sure the business ran smoothly in Greg's absence.

"Odelia," I heard. I turned to see Holly West standing in the doorway. She visited off and on. Today my mother was with her. They had become fast friends, bonded together by common interests and their concern for us.

"Come on in," I told them. "I just finished

our reading for the day."

My mother held out a foil-wrapped package to me. "It's banana bread," she told me.

"Mom, Greg can't eat right now."

"It's not for him, silly," she said, "it's for you. You're becoming skin and bones. Eat something, please," she pleaded. "I even sliced it up for you."

Skin and bones. Now there was a description I never thought I'd hear in regard to myself. I had lost weight since the accident. I wasn't sure how much, nor did I care, but my clothes were beginning to hang on me. I took the bread and placed it on the counter by an arrangement of yellow roses. "I'll eat some a bit later," I told her. "I promise."

"Good," Mom said, "because I'm gonna check." She put her purse down. "Oh, by the way," she said as she lowered herself into one of the visitor's chairs, "on the way in we bumped into Mike Steele. He's with some other guy, and he said they need to see you. I told them I'd fetch you."

I glanced at Greg, and Holly noticed. "Don't worry, Odelia," Holly said. "We'll keep an eye on Greg for you."

Mike Steele and his wife, who is a doctor, had been to see Greg several times since the accident, so I was surprised he hadn't come straight to the room. It was still strained between us, but I knew how much he loved Greg so I put our differences aside. But when I came into the waiting area and saw who was with Steele, I knew why he'd hung back. With him, portly and self-important, was Joe Templin. They were in the far corner of the waiting area, away from the other visitors.

Templin held out his hand to me when I approached. "Hello, Odelia. How is Greg doing?"

I looked down at the offered hand as if it were a coiled rattlesnake. "Why are you here? I have nothing to say to you."

"We come in peace, Odelia," Templin said, giving me a meaty smile. "In fact, we come with an offer."

"Seth Washington has already negotiated my severance package. There's nothing more to discuss." I turned to leave.

"Odelia, please hear us out," Templin said.

I looked him up and down in disgust. "*Us* as in you and Steele, or just you?" I glanced at Steele, who was standing a step or two behind Joe Templin. I could have sworn he gave me a small wink.

"Me," Templin admitted. "I knew you wouldn't see me unless Mike was with me."

"You got that right, and now I'm going back to my husband."

"Wait, Odelia," Templin said. "It's in your best interest to hear what I have to say."

In silence I stood before him, waiting. My jaw was so locked, it hurt.

Templin cleared his throat. "After careful consideration, we want you to come back to Templin & Tobin."

"Are you out of your mind?" I said, my voice raised. The other people in the room turned to stare at us. "You threw me out of there," I continued, my voice lower out of consideration to the others. "You paid me to leave."

"You can keep the severance," Templin told me. "Think of it as a bonus."

"What in the hell are you smoking, Templin?" I asked. Behind him a tiny smile crept across Steele's face and disappeared. "You fired me because of Kelton Kingston, the very man who is behind my husband being in a coma."

"You have no proof of that, Odelia, and you'd better be careful about making such accusations," Templin warned. "Mr. Kingston feels bad about what he did over that dog. He's had his own tragic loss, you know."

"Bullshit," I hissed. "I have no doubt he was behind the deaths of his wife, Burt Sandoval, Doris Hoffman, and the attempt on my life and Greg's. It's just a matter of time before that hitman spills his guts. He doesn't look like the type to survive jail for too long. You're trying to hire me back to keep me quiet." I put my hands on my hips in defiance. "You're throwing money at me like you did those other people Kingston hurt. Well, I'm not for sale, and neither is my husband."

"You have to understand, Odelia," Templin said, his voice low and calm, as if talking to a crazy person who might explode. "The firm's first duty is to its clients. Kelton Kingston is one of our longest and most active clients. I am merely his agent."

I stared at Templin. "But I thought T&T was offering me my old job back. You make it sound as if Kingston is offering me a job."

"Let's just say Mr. Kingston no longer has a problem with you being employed by us," Templin said, smugness tattooed on his face.

"Oh, he doesn't, does he?" I said, mocking Templin's imperious tone. "How magnanimous of him, especially considering that he's currently under all kinds of investigations for murder and fraud, as well as the civil suits probably coming his way, including one from us. I hear people he's injured in the past are coming out of the woodwork."

"Odelia," Templin said, "I've really run out of patience with you. You can take this very generous offer of gainful employment at a higher salary, something a soon-to-be widow should seriously consider, or you can go off and let your anger send you on a fool's journey."

Soon-to-be widow.

Without a second thought, I pulled back my good right arm and let my fist fly forward and up, catching Joe Templin on his jaw with a solid punch. It knocked him to the ground, less from impact and more from surprise.

I stood over him. "Now you really have something to fire me for."

Steele approached. I thought he was going to help Templin to his feet, but instead he pulled an envelope out of his inside jacket pocket. He tossed it down on top of Templin. "That's my resignation, Joe. Effective immediately."

"Odelia, come quick!" It was Holly. "It's Greg!"

Steele and I ran to Greg's room. Inside, several doctors and nurses surrounded Greg's bed. One doctor was examining Greg. Mom shuffled over and wrapped her arms around me. She was sobbing. I expected the worst.

"No!" I cried out. "Please, no!" I clung to my mother.

"No, Odelia, it's good," Holly said. "Really."

I disentangled myself from Mom and slowly approached the bed, truly scared for the first time in my life. The doctor hovering over Greg stepped back and gave me a weak smile. I looked down at Greg. His eyes were fluttering. One of his hands on the bed moved. I grabbed the hand and hung on to it, my sobs turning joyful. I looked over at the door and saw Steele supporting both my mother and Holly, the three of them willing Greg back from the brink.

Soon Greg's eyes stopped fluttering and opened. He looked around, confused and dazed. Then his gaze fell on me and his lips turned up into a small smile.

"He's finally come out of the coma, Mrs. Stevens," the doctor told me. "It's still too early to speak to the damage caused by the bullet, but it looks promising."

"Hi, sweetheart," Greg said, the words coming slow and barely audible.

I pressed his hand to my lips and didn't let go.

I was going to hold the universe to those promises.

ABOUT THE AUTHOR

Like the character Odelia Grey, **Sue Ann Jaffarian** is a middle-aged, plus-size paralegal. In addition to the Odelia Grey mystery series, she is the author of the paranormal Ghost of Granny Apples mystery series and the Madison Rose Vampire mystery series. Sue Ann is also nationally sought after as a motivational and humorous speaker. She lives and works in Los Angeles, California.

Visit Sue Ann on the internet at

WWW.SUEANNJAFFARIAN.COM

and

WWW.SUEANNJAFFARIAN.BLOGSPOT.COM